8-31-64

THINGS AS THEY ARE

BY PAUL HORGAN

NOVELS

The Fault of Angels

No Quarter Given

Main Line West

A Lamp on the Plains

Far From Cibola

The Habit of Empire

The Common Heart

Give Me Possession

A Distant Trumpet

Mountain Standard Time (*a collected volume
containing* MAIN LINE WEST, FAR FROM CIBOLA, *and* THE
COMMON HEART)

OTHER FICTION

The Return of the Weed

Figures in a Landscape

The Devil in the Desert

One Red Rose For Christmas

The Saintmaker's Christmas Eve

Humble Powers

Toby and the Nighttime (*juvenile*)

Things As They Are

HISTORY AND BELLES-LETTRES

Men of Arms (*juvenile*)

From the Royal City

New Mexico's Own Chronicle (*with Maurice Garland Fulton*)

Biographical Introductions to Volumes I and II of

Diary and Letters of Josiah Gregg (*edited by Maurice Garland Fulton*)

Great River: The Rio Grande in North American History

The Centuries of Santa Fe

Rome Eternal

Citizen of New Salem

Conquistadors in North American History

THINGS AS THEY ARE

by Paul Horgan

NEW YORK ❧ FARRAR, STRAUS AND COMPANY

Copyright © 1951, 1963, 1964 by Paul Horgan
Library of Congress catalog card number 64-1279
Second Printing, 1964

Published simultaneously in Canada by
Ambassador Books, Ltd., Toronto

Manufactured in the United States of America
by American Book–Stratford Press

for D.

AUTHOR'S NOTE

Using the devices of autobiography in order to invite the reader's belief, this book, though not a conventional novel, is a work of fiction. Of its ten chapters only one reflects in its central event a direct experience of my own life. The other nine are fabricated after observation, surmise and memory of other lives, young and old. This means that—even if backgrounds and places suggest the real—more of this book belongs to the imagined life than to the strictly factual; and that these pages are not to be taken as fragments of an autobiography of my early self.

Contents

CHAPTER I ❧ *Original Sin*   page 1

CHAPTER II ❧ *The Dawn of Hate*   21

CHAPTER III ❧ *Muzza*   35

CHAPTER IV ❧ *Far Kingdoms*   66

CHAPTER V ❧ *Magic*   97

CHAPTER VI ❧ *Black Snowflakes*   120

CHAPTER VII ❧ *Center of Interest*   145

CHAPTER VIII ❧ *The Spoiled Priest*   161

CHAPTER IX ❧ *A Discharge of Electricity*   194

CHAPTER X ❧ *Parma Violets*   220

Praise we the just—
Who are not come to judge, but bless
Immortal things in their poor mortal dress.
                    —*Edith Sitwell,* THE OUTCASTS

. . . Hugo said that to grow old was to possess all ages and the
essence of each one, particularly that of childhood; that which
the child represents to adults, something he himself does not
understand or experience: newness, and the sense of existence
in the process of both, the idea of a new world about to be
born. . . .
            —*Jean Guitton,* JOURNALS, 1952–1955
            Translated by Frances Forrest

During all this time there were two worlds of which one
gradually became conscious: the inside world and the outside
world. . . .
                —*Maurice Baring,* THE PUPPET
                SHOW OF MEMORY

THINGS AS THEY ARE

CHAPTER I

✻

Original Sin

"RICHARD, RICHARD," they said to me in my childhood, "when will you begin to see things as they are?"

But they forgot that children are artists who see and enact through simplicity what their elders have lost through experience. The loss of innocence is a lifelong process—the wages of original sin. Guilt is the first knowledge.

"Richard," they said, "are you terribly sorry?"

"Oh, yes."

✻

Coming home from the country, I remembered everything, though I did not want to.

My grandfather was interested in a farm about fifty miles from home in up-state New York. He knew the farmer well and used to go out for a week or two in the hot summer weather to stay at the farmhouse. I heard long afterward that he owned a mortgage on the farm. In that particular summer—it must have been in 1908 or 1909—he took me along.

[1]

I did not particularly want to go, for my grandfather—my mother's father—was sometimes formidable when his mood changed. I did not care for anything to be different from one time to another, and I could never be sure when he would be stern or remote, lost in some lofty inner criticism of life—his life in particular, with its circumstances of old age, loneliness since the death of my grandmother, and the loss of his many children to their many worlds. I was a very small boy in that summer—four or five years old—and young enough to be homesick, especially at night, when it was time for me to be put to bed.

They put me in a narrow wooden bed in a small room under the eaves, where the ceiling leaned over me at a sharp angle. The farmer's wife, Mrs Klopstock, was a kind woman, all the color of dough, hair and skin, and made as lumpishly. But she declared that she knew all about children through her own, who were now gone away, and she always gave me a few extra moments at night, when the only sounds in the humid dark outside came from crickets and nightbirds, and the only ones from inside came from the rumbling talk downstairs between my grandfather and Mr Klopstock.

On the first night I was muted with longing for home and the touch of my mother, and when Mrs Klopstock tried to have me speak, I could think of nothing to say but that I wanted to go home, which I could not bring myself to say.

On the second night I asked her,

"Do you know how to hug?"

Her eyes grew larger with ready tears and she threw herself down to her wide knees by my bed and took me in her arms and hugged me till my ribs ached.

"There!" she said, "was that a hug?"

"Oh, yes. Thank you."

"Now will you be able to sleep?"

"Yes."

"Good night, Richard."

"Good night, Mrs Klopstock."

She went downstairs. Falling asleep I had a vision of the meadowy world in which I had spent the day and which would await me in the morning.

꙲

I was there a giant among grasses that rose to my waist. Long wide slopes lay up behind the white farmhouse and showed waves of white stars and snowflakes bent into shadow by the breezes—daisies, milkweed, Queen Anne's lace, poppies, with here and there goldenrod and wild cosmos in every color. When I slashed my way through this meadow with important strides, the soft stems of the wild flowers gave up a tickling fragrance, and the long grasses stung my bare legs with their wiry whips. I had to watch out for bees, and if I fell down I had to look along the tiny forest aisles of the plants and grasses at my very eyes to see if a garter snake might be watching me there on the damp brown earth which smelled like a cellar. Getting up, I went on to a real woods. It stood where the meadow became a low hill which dipped down to meet another hill making a wandering cleft where flowed a steep and narrow little creek.

They told me at the house not to go out of sight, but I did not know whether they could see me at the creek, and I did not think about it. It was the best place to play. I could walk up into the little copse, and though I wished hard for someone to be there to play along the creek with me, I still managed to have a splendid time. I took off my shoes and stockings and walked in the creek bed, knowing how the chill of the water and the sharp stones and the slipperiness would hurt and feel full of chance. The sunlight broke in little darts and coins and pools through the woods. The creek was swift, full of miniature rapids along the small stones yielded to it by the slopes. It took several turns, winding against the cheeks of the low hills, until it came free in the meadow, when it ran deep and open across the farm, and then under the road in front, and then out of sight in distant green country which I never explored.

When they wanted me at the farmhouse they would ring a heavy dinner bell out on the back stoop, and I would dry off my feet and go to dinner, which they had at midday, or supper, which they had at five o'clock.

On some days my grandfather took me all through the barns and pens to see the cattle, the horses, the pigs and the chickens. He touched them with his cane and when the cows turned slowly to look at him, he gave his wheezy, low laugh. The rank smells of the animals, as strong as ammonia, and their frank beings, with their wettings and their droppings, their dripping mouths, the heavy hang and sway of their sex or their udders, made me thoughtful and dimly self-aware. Sometimes my grandfather had me walk in the meadow with him, saying nothing much, but pleased to have someone for whom he was responsible. Now and then,

"Be careful, my boy," he would say, pointing to a great flat animal dropping which lay buzzing with jewelled flies in the grass, "don't step in the cow pie."

A meadow was for boys. He looked sad to me in the pathless grasses, among bees that set blossoms to nodding on their long stems. He wore a wide-brimmed panama hat which according to word in my family cost him one hundred dollars, and a gray alpaca suit with cutaway frock, and shiny black leather boots with elastic inserts at the sides. They said I looked like him, but how could I, when I had no white beard and mustache, or tiny, gold-rimmed eyeglasses, or heavy pink cheeks, or such a wide front that extended far out and looked as hard as wood? At that age I valued him chiefly because he was familiar. He served in no way to relieve my lonesomeness in the country. I finally found relief otherwise, but in the end, when it was time for me to be taken home to Dorchester again, I tried to forget how my lonesomeness was lifted for a while and then restored worse than ever. But in spite of myself, I remembered.

※

We went home on the train. I was allowed to sit next to the window, which was open. The fields we ran through were like the ones we had just left, and I was glad to know what "the country" was, after hearing about it for so long. Engine smoke spangled with hot cinders flew in the train windows, and several times my grandfather had to use the corner of his handkerchief to take a cinder out of my eye, which he did with much suppressed wheezing, and with joy at having something to do for someone other than to shout orders when he was furious in his own house, which at best was a lonely pleasure, and which left him with a dyspeptic upset. I was not certain of how to manage it, but I said to myself that I would never be an old man. I did not mean that I would not live a long life—I intended to live forever, but certainly not as an old man.

Glad as I was to leave the country, I wished, the nearer we came to Dorchester, that I was back with Mrs Klopstock and the creek and the meadow, even in spite of what happened there. What if my mother and my father should see in my face the secret I must never tell?

[5]

I went silent in the train and my grandfather said, in his grand German accent (he was born in Bavaria),

"Richard? You do not feel well?"

"Yes, Grosspa."

"Your stomach?"

"No, Grosspa."

"Come. We must have smiles for Mother."

"Will she be at the station?"

"No. We will go in a cab to your house. Then I will go to my house."

A weight of love and guilt lay about my heart at the prospect of seeing my mother again.

Over an exciting triangular system of switches and tracks the train backed into the station at Dorchester so it would be headed right for its return trip. The station was built of brick long begrimed with engine smoke. It had high round vaults overhead in the waiting room which gave me the feeling I had in church—lost and small in familiar surroundings.

We went rapidly through the station to the cab rank where my grandfather summoned a cab with an imperious lift of his gold-headed cane. The cab-horse was a bony creature who seemed to be asleep. The driver had to cluck him up several times before he moved. My grandfather put me into the dark blue padded interior which smelled of wet straw, and then stepped in himself, making the lightly-sprung brougham tip under his weight. Pushing back against the cushions I tried to have the cab go more slowly; but now that he was stirring, the old horse went off at a bright trot, while we rocked and jogged gallantly along over cobblestones and streetcar tracks, and came at last to our street, where my mother would be waiting for me.

Under elms meeting overhead, it was a shady street. The houses were set back fairly deep. Our house had a wooden-railed porch with a round bay at one end, tracing the shape of a round alcove in our living room. A little shingled turret rose above this at the top of the house three stories up. It was all of wood, painted brown, with white trimwork. With all my heart I wished we had lightning rods; I would pray at night that before lightning could strike us and burn us to the ground, as a house up the street had burned recently after midnight amidst shouts and gongs and falls of fire and spark, God would send us lightning rods. Watching the fire, and listening to it, and recalling the lightning, my heart beat until it hurt.

It did this now as we drew up at our house, yet I knew I must show nothing of the trouble which inhabited me as if my very body were designed to be its shape.

My grandfather stepped to our cement carriage block and then with comic ceremony turned and held the door for me. I hopped forth and immediately saw that loved and dreaded face in the window of the round sitting room upstairs, at the turret end of the house. My mother was holding the curtains aside, smiling and waving; and then the curtains fell together and I knew she was hurrying down to meet me.

On any other return I would have run to her as fast as my legs would carry me, like a very small boy in a story, but now I made a great affair of lingering to watch my grandfather pay the cab driver, who lifted his scuffed and dented top hat as he received his tip and then drove off above the humping old bones of his horse. There was nothing more to detain me. We went up to the porch. The front door opened and I was in my mother's embrace.

"Oh, Richard, Richard, my darling, how good to have you home again. How we have missed you. Every day I unrolled your napkin and then rolled it up again and put it back in its ring. Let me look at you."

It was the moment I sorrowed for.

Holding me away she looked dearly into my eyes and touched

a cinder smudge on my cheek and then pulled me close again, and said,

"Did you miss us? The country agreed with you, darling, you look so sunburned and well-fed and sweet."

I buried my face in her breast and my heart went whirring on. How astounding that I could look just as usual, with nothing to notice in my appearance of what lay buried in my soul.

"Was he a good boy?" asked my mother of her father and he replied,

"He was a very good boy, ate everything on his plate, said his prayers every night, so Mrs Klopstock told me, and played alone all day, quite happily. If we did not hold long philosophical conversations the fault must be more with me than with him."

"Oh, Papa," she said, "you mustn't tease him in front of me. Come. I will ask Anna to bring us some tea."

She held her arm about my shoulder and took us to the round bay in the living room and disposed us for tea and cakes, which our lifelong friend and servant brought. When Anna came in, lumbering heavily with the tray, I thought perhaps I could run away with her to the kitchen and escape my trouble; but she gave me a little nod of mock elegance, set the tray down, and retreated with an air which indicated that she knew when to leave the family alone to theirself. The effect was a reproach to me, as though Anna, with her pale, deep-set eyes in her wide, gray face, could see through me, and must hold herself above what she saw.

"Now tell me what you did in the country," commanded my mother playfully, and I was face to face with my dreadful test. In my fear of revelation, I thought she must already know what I would never tell, and was asking me to do so explicitly. But her smile was so lovely, her love so calm, that in another breath I knew she knew nothing, and my guilt turned to guile, and I made a cheeky face, quite as though I were acting the role of a small boy, which small boys deliberately do at times, in order to discover what they themselves are really like, and I said,

"Why, Mother, you never saw such a wonderful place. We had a creek out in the meadow, and I played there all day long. I made some tiny boats with little sticks and leaves and things—you know how—and I had them do all kinds of things."

"Did you swim?"

"Oh, no, it wasn't deep enough for a boy to swim."

"Oh? How deep was it?"—idle inquiry, dangerously close to my hidden subject.

"Oh, about so"—holding my hands apart to show. "But I went wading all the time."

"I went too, you know," announced my grandfather.

I stared at him. When?

"Yes," he said, "one afternoon while you were having your nap, I took off my shoes and stockings and went wading."

"Why Papa!" exclaimed my mother.

What was it? There seemed a curious shame in the fact that my old grandfather should have bared his feet and rolled up his gray alpaca city trousers and gone wading like a child. A part of him was naked which otherwise was always clothed—this was shocking in one I knew so well.

"Yes," he added, "it cooled me off."

"Did you have anyone to play with?" asked my mother, brushing my hair lightly down across my brow with her exquisite hand which was so clever at so many charming skills.

"No," I said.

"Ah, but yes," said my grandfather. "He had a cat."

"A cat? Darling, did you have a cat?"

"A kitty," I said, nodding brightly over a sense of doom.

"How sweet. What color?"

"Black and white."

[9]

"How sweet. Did it have little white boots?"

"Yes." I felt hollow with apprehension. How did my mother know so well that particular cat?

"Where did you find it?"

"It came to the farm one day. Mrs Klopstock gave it some milk on the back stoop. She said I could have it if I would take care of it."

"And did you?"

It was a frightful question to answer. I said,

"I fed it."

"Did it sleep on your bed?"

My mother, through half-closed eyes, and with her head a little on one side, studied how I looked with my hair brushed forward over my brow, and changed her mind. She brushed it back off my forehead and said,

"I love to see your whole forehead. Like your Daddy's. So wide. Those little shadows you can hardly see. So young."

"It did sometimes," I replied.

"Ach, Papa," she cried, turning to her father, "do you remember the *times* we used to have at home with cats? Oh! how furious you used to be when"—speaking of her sisters and brothers—"we would smuggle a new kitten upstairs and keep it for days without letting anyone know. And then the time the Right Reverend Bishop came to dinner, and the cat got away, and ran downstairs, and Fritz chased him, trying to catch him, and chased him right through the living room before dinner, and almost knocked the Bishop over without even seeing him! Oh! What a licking he got for that! But Mama told us afterward the Bishop laughed so hard she thought he was going to choke to death. —What was your kitty's name?" she asked, turning to me again.

"I just called him Kitty."

"What a perfect name for a cat. Tell me, what did you do with him when you left?"

My grandfather spared me an answer.

"The cat disappeared one day," he said.

"Disappeared?"

"Simply vanished. Richard went calling, 'Here, kitty, kitty, kitty,' and Mrs Klopstock put out some chicken wings for it, and we looked everywhere, a cat just doesn't disappear like that on a farm with only one house for a mile or two, but no, there was no answer, and we never saw it again. Richard was miserable."

"Of course, darling," said my mother. "It is awful to lose a pet." She looked at me. "But no, my darling, it is over, and you must not cry for it any more. Here. Have another little cake. Chocolate, that one, with the little silver pill on top."

For there were tears in my eyes, and she thought she knew why. I took the cake and ate it with my jaws moving ruefully, while fear and guilt tasted of chocolate crumbs and crushed silver sugar, and I wished I were alone.

"Well," said my grandfather, standing up, "I think I must be going along now."

"Did you send your cab away?"

"Yes. I will take the street car."

"But you will have far to walk to get it, and then when you get off."

"Very well, I will have far to walk," he said testily, rejecting her concern for his age, weight and dignity. But she was no longer his child, she belonged to my father, who would soon be home from his office, and with a little lift of her head, she let my grandfather know that his days of tyranny over her were no more. It was my mother's gift that she could show independence and love to the same person. My grandfather now gave a heavy sigh at the betrayals which any man knew if he lived long enough, and went heavily to the door, and took his way home.

[11]

"Oh, Richard, how glad Daddy will be to see you. We have missed you frantically. Come here."

She hugged me and gave me a kiss. Something in my rigid body was so unfamiliar that she set me off to look at me and asked,

"What a strange boy you are. Aren't you glad to be home again?"

"Oh, yes, yes."

"Do you feel all right?"

"Yes, Mother."

"Is something wrong?"

"No."

"Did anything happen in the country that upset you? Weren't they kind to you, those Klopstocks, I never could see what Grosspa saw in them, they are so common, he is quite fond of them, they weren't mean to you?"

"Oh, no."

With a little tremor of exasperation which threaded through her whole body, she suddenly grew formal with me.

"Well, perhaps after you've been home a little while you may find that you like it after all."

I wanted to throw myself into her arms in a passion of longing to be forgiven for everything in the world, but this would have led to loving questions, and then to revelations. She took up the tea tray instead of ringing for Anna, and went to the pantry. I went upstairs to the nursery, which was what they still called my room, and wondered what I could do until my father got home, and what would happen about everything then.

※

Leafing through some of my favorite books, I read little, for my senses were all attuned to the latening of the day. The later the hour, the sooner would my father return. Daylight began to show gradual but ominous change out in the treetops above the street. Autumn was pressing against the trees. Twilight fell below them sooner than it did above. I was sorry that night was not already here, with all in darkness, and myself in bed, asleep, safe from the calm and loving gaze of my father.

His eyes were blue, like all of ours in the family, and they were as clear as water, and his open, wide brow showed the frontal bone of his skull without wrinkles to hide it. His forehead seemed like the abode of honor. How could I face it? His smile was complete, using all his features and even changing the sound of his voice when he spoke. He had several voices—one for my mother, which often made her catch her breath a trifle and expel it in a little gust of pleasure, as if to say, "What am I going to do—I love him so." Another voice was for the world, a half-mocking but friendly sound. And one was for me, which sounded confidential, a little husky, as if to put secrets between us even in the presence of other people. He had a trick of grinding his jaws together gently and sticking out his chin when he talked to me or when he worked with me on some project, and now and then he adopted some of my early mispronunciations to give our exchanges a more intimate feeling—*insteresting* for *interesting, vomick* for *vomit, sippise* for *surprise.* When he uttered my variations, they seemed to mean far more than the originals. It was a private language and it bound us together. When he came home every night and I heard the welcome signal of the heavy front door closing after him, I always went flying down the stairs into his hug. We made a great commotion, which moved my mother to pretended crossness—"Oh, you two!" she would exclaim—but she usually joined our embrace, after which she took his hat and coat and put them neatly in the hall closet, and with him home again, I fell into the richest contentment, for all was in order, and my evening was the happiest time of the day, even if all too soon I had to go to bed and leave the components of my joy for another long night.

The sky was turning yellow as the sun declined, and on that evening I listened without joy for the front door to rumble shut after my father. Hearing it at last, I pretended that I had not. I stayed in my room, resembling a boy lost in a book. It was so that he found me when, with my mother right after him, he came into the nursery bearing a large package. Ordinarily my expert guess what a present might be, judging by its size, shape and wrapping, would have combined with my greed to hurl me upon it.

But now I looked up, as if startled, and when he called out in his "my" voice, "Hello, Doc!" I merely replied, "Hello, Daddy."

My mother gave him a glance as if to say, *You see how he is acting, I told you.* He shook his head slightly to put her off, set the package on the floor, and came to me and took me in his arms. He chinned my cheek once or twice with a rough rub, and said, with happy excitement,

"Guess what."

"What."

"I'm glad to see you."

I longed to say the same to him, and I tried, but could not. He set me down and indicating the package said,

"See that?"

"Yes."

"It's a sippise."

"For me?"

Being funny, he looked around and said,

"I don't see anybody else here. Yes. It's for you, Richard. Don't you want to see what it is?"

"Yes."

My mother said in a cold, unfamiliar voice,

"He may not touch it until he thanks his Daddy for thinking of him and bringing it to him."

"Let Richard open it first," said my father, "then he can thank me. —That is, if he likes it—," and he grinned with perfect confidence that I would be overcome with happiness at what he had brought.

I knelt down by the package and tore at the wrappings so wastefully that my mother exclaimed at the loss of so much good parcel paper. There on my floor I exposed a toy fire engine—the kind they used to call a steamer—with three horses in harness, and all its nickel brightly polished, and all its red paint glaring in splendor. A toy fireman made of cast iron sat on the box and drove the forever plunging horses, and another stood behind the boiler on the rear step of the steamer. Both wore firemen's hats with white front plates bearing the legend "Engine Company Number 9" and both wore firemen's water-coats. I was appalled at the sacrifice I faced—for of course in my unworthiness I could not receive the present. I said nothing.

"How about it, Doc?" said my father, coming down to the floor next to me. "It's your homecoming present. Do you like it?"

The love and the trust of my father and mother were all mixed up with the glorious toy they had brought to welcome me home, and I did not deserve them or their fire engine. I broke into a sob and hid my face in my arm.

"Why Doc!" exclaimed my father. My mother had another response. She leaned down to feel my forehead to discover if I had a temperature.

"Come on, Doc, what's the matter?"—and my father took me up and put his knuckle under my chin to raise my face and make me look at him.

I shook my head.

[15]

"I'll call Doctor Grauer," said my mother.

"No," said my father. "He's not sick. It's something else. —Come on, Doc. Come on up here and tell me about it."

He went to a chair and took me with him and hauled me on to his knees. His gentleness anguished me. I was eaten within by my first knowledge of evil and I longed to confess it. Like all men, I was the victim of original sin, whose forms in daily life are as many as there are beings. The fact that the evil I mourned was my own was the most dreadful part of my trouble.

"Poor old Doc. It's all right. It's all right."

"Something happened in the country," said my mother. "I told you."

"Let him wait. It's all right, Doc."

Finding a thread of voice, I said,

"It was the kitty."

"The what?"

"Yes," said my mother, "he had a kitten at the farm. Grosspa told me."

"What about the kitty, Richard?" asked my father. "Is there something about the kitty you are worried about?"

"I hurt it," I said.

"You did? How."

"I put it in the creek."

"You mean you drowned it?"

"The water went by some stones and there was a deep little place and I grabbed the kitty and threw him in the rough part of the water. He tried to get out."

"What did you do then?"

"I grabbed him again."

"Didn't you feel it try to get away?"

"Yes."

"Did it scratch you?"

[16]

"Yes."

I pulled up my sleeve and showed the long scaly tracks of the claws.

"Oh, Richard," murmured my mother, "it didn't want to be hurt!"

"I know it. I know it. I hurt it."

※

I could remember the hot thin supple body of the kitten under its wet fur, and the pitifully small tube of its neck, and the large clever space between its ears at the back, where all its thoughts seemed to come from, and the perfectly blank look on its wide-eyed face as it strove to escape me and the hurt I was possessed of, the hurt I must do the little animal who had been my cunning companion for days, and whom I loved. Even as I clutched it with strength I did not know I had in my fingers and forearms, I felt sorry for the kitten. My belly was knotted with excitement, sorrow, and zest. The fever of a game arose in me and as the kitten fought me I was determined to win my victory over it. I fell down beside the creek and threw myself half into it, holding the kitten in my arms with the embrace of dear love, and the smaller and feebler it began to feel in my grasp, the more I loved it, and sorrowed for it, and the more expertly I pressed its doom. The current rushed down to us from between the rocks, making a roar next to my ear, but even so I could hear the kitten's tiny gasps mixed with water.

※

My father looked at me for a long quiet moment. His wide brow was lumpy with an inquiring frown, as though he were trying to look past me to the creek where I had become a criminal. Finally he said softly,

"What else, Doc? What finally happened?"

"I don't know. I let the kitty go and the water took him away to the deep part."

"Did he climb out and run away?"

"I don't know."

"Did you ever see him again?"

"No."

Without using the word, he was trying to discover if the kitten was dead.

"It didn't come back to the farmhouse?"

"No."

"What did you do afterward?"

"I played in the meadow till my shirt was dry. Then they rang the dinner bell and I went back to the house."

"How did you feel?"

I burst into tears again.

My mother felt the contagion of my remorse and also began to cry.

"To think that my boy Richard—" she said, but my father said her name once, strongly and mildly, and she halted her expression of adopted shame. He then shook me by the shoulders, and said,

"Doc, what you did was horribly wrong. Do you know that?"

"Yes."

"And are you terribly sorry for doing it?"

"Oh, yes."

"Then you must ask God to forgive you and help you to be kind all the rest of your life to poor little things whom you can hurt if you want to. Do you understand?"

"Yes, Father."

"Now stop your blubbering and think of this. Perhaps the kitty got away. How many lives has a cat?"—this playfully said, to restore a livable world.

"Nine."

"Well, you had a young kitty, and he probably had eight to go. He's probably hiding right now in the meadow, wondering if you are coming back to play with him."

"Do you think so?"

"It could be."

"But I'm not there."

"But if you were, would you be good to the kitty?"

"Oh, yes, yes, I would."

"I think you would. Oh, my little boy"; he said solemnly, talking past my ear, as though counting the sum of his own life, "I hope you can be good even when it is hard to be, the rest of your life.—Now do you feel better?" he asked, setting me off. He searched my eyes to see if there was anything more I must expel before I could be his son again, but finding nothing, he energetically went down to the floor and the fire engine, and hauled me down beside him, and cried, "But you have not seen what goes on in here!" indicating the shiny toy boiler of the steamer of Engine Company Number 9. I knelt down beside him and watched him create a marvel.

He took a little brown paper envelope, tore open its corner, and poured a half spoonful of some brown powder into the fire door of the steamer, and then struck a match and lighted the powder. At once, white and black smoke began to pour out of the chimney of the boiler. And then he drew the horses ahead on the rug, and as he did so, a toy gong hidden under the carriage rang out with every revolution of the high red rear wheels, and he called out in an assumed voice full of urgency and magic,

"Look out, look out, here comes Engine Company Number 9, where's the fire, where's the fire!"

And in my imagination I rode the rear step of the steamer, and I became the master of fire, even fire that may once have frightened me, and we played intently until it was time for my supper. This, as a concession, I was allowed to have downstairs while my parents sat with me and watched my meal. The fire engine was on the floor beside me at the table.

"He must promise," said my mother, "never to light the powder when he is alone."

"Yes. Do you promise?" asked my father.

"I promise."

It was an evening of promises. The final ones were made to God in my night prayers. I promised not to sin again, and I meant it, but the burden of self-knowledge was upon me now, and as I fell asleep, I felt again the kitten's tiny, striving will to live, and I knew yet another hidden thrill at the memory of the struggle by the creek, and since all I knew about anything was only what had happened to me in my life so far, I wondered and wondered over the sinner's eternal question about his resolve to be good, which was—how could I be sure?

CHAPTER II

❦

The Dawn of Hate

But if I had made promises to God, He let me go to sleep in His promise to me. Even then I knew it was a stronger promise than mine. In this knowledge there was the beginning of the end of innocence. Another stage of this loss presently came along.

One day I built a boat out of a board with twigs for masts and string for railings. I took it to show Anna in the kitchen.

"Can't we go and sail it?" I asked.

"I'm busy," she said in her sing-song, dreamy voice. Anna, our old cook and laundress, lived a visionary life which she pursued above the task in hand. Dreaming awake, she would sing monotonously to herself of love (her husband had disappeared years ago), or of God (she went to Mass every morning), or of nothing at all; and when she had time she tended me as nurse. A friend to us all, she could bridle with privilege and mourn her estate in the same instant. Now and then she would seize me in her large, lumbering grasp in which she hugged fugitively the graces of a time when she was young and venturesome long ago, before living in other people's kitchens, or spending long mornings in their basement laundries whiling away the acrid steamy hours with hooted song and muffled memory. Her ardent nature expressed itself in one way through her pores, which exuded a fume of oniony sweat that for a reason I cannot quite capture always gave me the feeling of, "Poor Anna!"

"Well," I said, blurring my eyes to see my boat as great and real, "I will go and sail it by myself, then."

"You-will-not."

"Why not?"

"You know you're too young to go out alone."

"I'm five."

"And I'm a hundred and five, and I'm busy, and I'm tired."

She leaned aside, looking upward, a martyr, with her lonely life, her sense of sin, and this boy nagging at her.

"Please, Anna, don't you love my boat?"

"Oh, Lord, it's glorious!" she shouted, but she began to take off her apron and joyfully I knew we were going to Yates Circle, at the end of our street, where in the center an immense round bowl of polished granite enclosed a pool from which rose a forest of water spouts. It was the finest fountain in Dorchester, and it made music in air and sunshine all day long. All the children of the neighborhood, and some from across town, came there to sail their boats.

"Come on, Richard," sighed Anna, "bring your old boat."

"It's my new boat."

"Your new boat, then, God give me strength."

This was on a golden afternoon in October. My mother was upstairs sewing in the bay window of her bedroom, where thin white curtains blurred the sunlight all about her, until she seemed to me a creature of light herself.

Anna called up from the foot of the stairs that she was taking me to the Circle.

"Put on his light overcoat," replied my mother in a lifted, happy voice. "It's chilly even in the sun. Come straight home. Do you want me to watch anything in the kitchen?"

"No," said Anna, "we'll be back to start things for dinner."

While I held my boat first with one hand and then the other, she roughly hauled my overcoat on to my arms and buttoned me up.

"That boat," she said scornfully. But her voice and acts were full of love, and I was content, for I loved her as she loved me. I never thought of her grey, pock-marked, wide face, and her loose, colorless hair, and her dark tight clothes that strained across the full shapes of her old womanly arms and bosom and belly. She was to me neither young nor old, beautiful nor ugly. She belonged to me, and was therefore worthy. All persons seemed to commit their acts for my benefit, and all events were interesting only as they pleased me or met my needs.

"Come on," she said rudely, and we went out the front door.

※

Leaves were whispering down through the yellow air. The street was empty, or so we thought. Far ahead I could see the white crests of the water at the fountain.

"Come on, Anna, you are so slow."

"Wait till your feet kill you some day."

"Well, I know, but come *on.*"

She began to sing gently one of her hooting tunes. She was holding one of my hands while with the other I cradled my ship. It was meant to be an ocean greyhound. I could not wait to learn whether it would float on an even keel.

We were not even half-way to the Circle when Anna stopped and halted me.

"What's the matter?" I asked.

"Never mind."

She was peering up the street at a figure which came idling into view along the sidewalk on our side of the street. It was a man. He moved slowly, with little steps that hardly advanced his progress. His body was oddly in motion, almost as if he were dancing in his shoes with tiny movements. From a distance I could see that he was dressed in old grey clothes, very shabby, which were too large for him.

"Is it a tramp?" I asked, with a leap of interest and fright—for the word tramp was one to strike terror in the women of our household, who took great precautions against tramps when my father was not at home.

"I think so. Come," said Anna, "we will cross the street and go on the other walk."

She led me abruptly across and quickened her pace. Looking proud and unafraid in case the man really was a tramp, she lifted her head and began to exhibit her idea of what a grand lady was like, striding daintily yet hugely, and making angry little tosses of her head. She picked up with thumb and one finger a fold of her dress and held it athwart her hip. She seemed to say, I'll show him, that tramp, I'll dare him to ask me for a nickel for a glass of beer, he wouldn't dare try anything, me with my boy along here with me, going to sail a boat in Yates Circle, where there's often *a policeman* around to see that the children don't fall in the water and drownd theirself!

I lagged, staring at the tramp with fascination as we approached to pass each other on opposite sides of the street. Anna refused even to see him, but kept up her lofty plan to pass him by as if he did not exist.

Now I could see him clearly and intimately. He had a wide grin on his unshaven grey face with red cheeks and nose and bleached-looking places about the eyes. He blinked at us and bowed in a friendly way. Shabby, drifting, uncertain, he seemed to be reaching for us—for me, I was sure, since all life was directed toward me. There was an ingratiating gaiety about him, and when he left his sidewalk to come toward us, in his shambling little dance, I saw something else which puzzled me.

He nodded and smiled, and I thought he nodded and smiled at me. When he was halfway across the street toward us, keeping pace now with Anna's angry, ladylike advance—her eyes forward and her head up—I tugged at her and asked,

"Anna, what's he doing?"

At the sound of my voice the tramp laughed weakly in a beery little cough, and ducked his head, and smiled and smiled, hungry for response. I then saw how his clothes were disarrayed in what was later called indecent exposure.

"Anna!" I insisted.

"Never mind, come along," she said with a toss of her head as though she wore plumes.

"But he wants to show me something," I protested.

At this, she glanced aside at the tramp, who presented himself and his antic lewdness hilariously at her.

It took her only that glance to understand.

"Holy God in heaven!" she cried, and turned and in a single sweep of her heavy arm swung me all but through the air toward home, causing me to drop my boat. At a half-run she dragged me along the walk toward our house.

"My boat! My boat!" I kept crying, but she paid no heed, only muttering and groaning the names of saints, giving forth holy ejaculations. We came breathless to the house, where she slammed and locked the front door behind us, and ran through to the kitchen door and locked that too. Hearing this, and the sound of my angry sobs at the loss of my new ship, my mother came downstairs laughing, and saying,

"Slam, slam, cry, cry—what on earth is happening? Why are you home so soon?"

"My boat!" I stormed, running against her and angrily hugging her hips and butting my head against her waist. "She made me lose it! We didn't even sail it once!"

"Anna?" called my mother through the hall.

Anna loomed in the pantry door and beckoned to my mother.

"Don't bring him," Anna said, raising her chin at me. "I must tell you."

The manly voice which Anna now used as she caught her breath conveyed to my mother an air of something ominous.

"Then, Richard," said my mother, "take your coat off and put it away, and go upstairs and wash your face. You are a fright. Wait for me in your room."

Unwillingly I took the stairs one step at a time, and as the pantry door closed after my mother, I heard in Anna's voice the words "tramp" and "crazy drunk," and then a grand, long, running line of narrative blurred away from detail by the shut door, punctuated by little screams of shock and horror from my mother.

※

My room was at the front of the house next to the bedroom of my father and mother. I sat in the window seat looking out, mourning for my ship, which lay broken and worthless up the street, and then I saw the tramp, of whom I still thought as my funny new friend, come idling into view along the sidewalk. Now restored to modesty, he was eating with a sad air a crust-end of a sandwich. He leaned against a tree and rubbed his back against the bark like an old dog. He nodded right and left at the afternoon in general. He was a small man, I now saw, and he seemed sleepy and lonesome. In another moment, he slid gently against the tree trunk to the ground, and fastidiously searched in his loose pockets for something, and brought it forth—it was a pint bottle, empty. He raised it to his mouth. Nothing to drink ran forth, and with a little heave, he threw the empty bottle up on the lawn of the house next door, and then he fell sideways into a deep sleep on the ground, resembling a bundle of old clothes ready for the poor.

The voices downstairs went on, now heavy and baleful, now light and firm. I heard my mother use the telephone—she was calling my father at his office. Then a long silence fell in the house, while I wondered. In a quarter of an hour I heard a thrilling sound of clanging gongs come down the street, mixed with the rattle of hooves on the pavement. I leaned to see, and sure enough, it was a police patrol wagon, all shiny black with big gold lettering on the sides of the van.

The driver slowed down before our house to let two policemen, in their long-coated blue uniforms and domed grey helmets, and carrying their gleaming clubs, jump down from the rear door. I greatly admired the police for their uniforms, their horses, and their power. Anna had threatened me with their authority many times when I misbehaved. I watched now with abstracted excitement as they went to the tree where the tramp lay asleep. They took him up and shook him awake.

With an air of courtesy, he awoke and smiled his dusty, weak-necked smile at the two policemen.

For being smiled at by a degenerate, one of the policemen struck him in the face with his immense open hand.

A look of bewilderment came into the tramp's face.

The other policeman gave an order to hold the tramp, and then ran up to our front door and jabbed at the bell. In a moment Anna was taken forth to confront the man whom she had reported as a committer of public outrage. I saw her nod when the police pointed at the tramp. She identified him, though in her agitated modesty she could only look at him over her crooked elbow.

But this was enough for the police. They told her to go, she returned to the porch, and I heard her heavy steps running for the door and then the door slam behind her.

At the street curbing, while I knelt up on the window seat to see, one policeman knocked the tramp to the ground with his club and the other kicked him in the belly to make him stand up again. He tried to become a ball like a bear asleep in the zoo against the cold of winter, but they pulled his arms away from his head and between their hands they punched his head back and forth. They knocked his knees down from protecting his loins and kicked him there until he screamed silently. Suddenly he went to the ground of his own weight. The policemen looked at each other and in silent, expert accord took him up between them and carried him to the patrol wagon, threw him in the door, climbed in after him, and the wagon got up and away from a starting trot. I watched until they were all gone. My thoughts were slow, separate, and innocent.

Why did they beat him so?

Did they arrest him just because he was a tramp?

Or because he didn't look like everybody else?

Or because he was a "crazy-drunk?"

Or for sleeping under somebody else's tree?

Or for how he had presented himself to me and Anna?

Why didn't they want him to do what he had done up the street?

Didn't they know it hurt when they kicked and beat someone else?

In any case, it was an immense event, full of excitement and mystery, and I fell asleep on the window seat from the sheer emotion of it. When I awoke it was to find the barricade of our house lifted, and my mother, pretending that nothing whatever had happened, standing by me to say that it was time for me to get ready for supper.

"Daddy will be home soon, and he will come and see you when you have your tray."

※

But he did not.

I heard him come in, and then I heard the famous sounds of private, grown-up discussion in the living room, with the sliding doors closed. Anna was summoned to give all over again her account of what had happened, while my father listened in silence, and my mother made little supplementary exclamations.

The mystery grew for me as all such attention was paid to it, and it became complete when my father ran upstairs at last to put me to bed. There was something stern and righteous in his air. I understood that we had all survived a dreadful danger, though of what nature I was not sure.

"Well, Doc," he said, "it was quite a day. Sit down here on my knee and listen to me for a minute."

He pretended to knock me out with a fisted blow to my chin, and he smiled and scowled at the same moment. In his dark blue eyes there was a light like that of retained tears, as he mourned for the presence of evil in the world and the tender vulnerability of innocence. Trying his best to resolve for us all the event of the afternoon, he said,

"Doc?"

"Yes, Daddy."

"Promise me something."

"Yes, Daddy."

"Promise me to forget absolutely everything that happened this afternoon, with that tramp. Will you?"

[29]

"Yes."

"We must never keep thoughts about those things"—(what things?)—"in our heads. God does not want us to. When we see something terrible that happens near us we must get away and forget it as fast as we can. Do you understand?"

"Yes."

"Good."

"You mean," I asked, "what the policeman did to the man?"

"No, no, I mean what the man did. He was crazy and he was drunk and nobody else acts that way. Don't think other men are like that. They don't go around in public that way."

"Was he a bad man?"

"Oh, yes. A very bad man. But forget him. Promise?"

"Yes."

"He can't scare you again if you forget him, you see."

"He didn't scare me. He scared Anna."

"Well, then, Doc, it is because you didn't understand." He set me down and stood up. "All right, now? We won't have a thing to do again about it?"

"No."

"Good. Then up comes the young giant and the old giant will take him to his castle for the night!"

And he swung me to his shoulders and walking hunchily and with great heavy spread steps the way giants walked he took me to my bed across the room and undressed me and put my pajamas on me and laid me down and kissed my forehead and said, "We'll leave just a crack," and went to the door and left it open just a crack so the upstairs hall light would stand like a golden lance of safety all night long between me and the dark, and went downstairs to dine with my mother. Their voices grew easier as the minutes passed and faded into sleep.

But the very first thing I thought of when I awoke was the tramp, and the more I said to myself that I had promised to forget him and all of it, the more I remembered. During the morning, when Anna was in the basement laundry, I went down to see her.

"Anna, why was the tramp a bad man?"

"You are not to talk about it."

"But he didn't do anything!"

"Oh, God," she said, reviving her sense of shock with hushed pleasure.

"He was trying to make friends with me. He was doing something funny, but—".

"Don't you know," she asked in a hoarse whisper, "what he was doing?"

"No, I don't."

She pointed to my groin.

"There, and all like that," she moaned, "and it was a terrible sin he committed, doing that, and doing it to a lady and a little boy, and Hell don't have fires enough to punish him for what he did!"

"It doesn't?"

"Not fires enough!"

I stared at her. Her tired, sad, grey bulk was alive with some glory of rage, some fullness of life, and suddenly I knew for the first time in my years what it was she and all the others in the house had been talking about. From I could not know where, the knowledge of new sins, and their power, dawned within me, and they seemed to reside just there where Anna had pointed.

I began to jig up and down.

"Anna!" I cried, "He was a bad man, my father said he was! He was bad!"

"Well," she said with the massive placidity of vested virtue, "why do you suppose I dragged you away from seeing such a thing, and why do you suppose your Máma called your Pápa, and he called the police station, and they sent a patrol wagon for the man? Well, I know, and you know, now."

"The police beat him!" I cried exultantly.

"I saw," she said. "Nothing they could do to him would be too much."

How could I ever have liked the tramp, or have felt sorry for him?

"Bash!" I exclaimed, imitating the blows of the police, "Blong!"

"Run along now, and don't think any more about it, it is all over."

But my interest was at a high pitch since I knew how to think about the affair, and I ran next door to see my friend Tom Deterson, who was my age, and with whom I exchanged secrets.

❀

"Did you hear about the tramp?" I asked out of breath.

"No," said Tom. "What tramp?"

I had the rich opportunity, then, to tell him everything—all that I had seen and heard and was supposed to forget. Tom and I were in the old carriage house at the foot of his yard. Nothing was kept there but the discards of the Deterson household. It made a fine playhouse, for it was removed, musty, dim, and private. As I told him what I knew, we sat on an old ruined sofa whose springs sagged into view below. Its cushions were awry and stained.

Tom's eyes were huge in his flushed, thin little face. He had curly hair and jangling nerves. He was never at rest. He was like a hot-nosed, insistent puppy climbing against all objects and persons and mysteries with an assumption of universal good will. At that time he was my best friend.

When I reached the most dreadful part of my story, I showed in pantomime what the tramp kept doing. Tom stared and jiggled as if he saw the actuality instead of a mockery of the scandal.

"What for?" he asked.

"I don't know. But he was crazy-drunk. They all do it. You know what?"

"No. What."

"He was a bad man."

"He was?"

"Yes, he was. My father said so, and Anna said so, and the police took him away."

"What did they do?"

"I'll show you what they did."

I seized an old split cushion from the sofa and threw it on the floor of the carriage house and I began to kick it.

"This is what they did!" I cried in heightening excitement. I picked up the cushion and punched it and threw it to Tom. He caught it and punched it and his eyes fired with power and purpose, and he threw the cushion down and he kicked it, and I kicked it again, and then we found some old thin brass curtain rods on the floor and we took these up and with them whipped the cushion.

"I'll tell you what I would do to that tramp!" I shouted. "I would beat him and push him until all his stuffing came out, and I would hit him"—and I did—"and I would kick him"—and I did—"and I would burn him in hell with all the fire that all the fire engines can't put out!"

"I have some matches!" cried Tom.

"Get them!"

[33]

He dug them from under the upholstery at the arm of the sofa and he lit a match and touched it to the split cushion where its dismal cotton stuffing showed through. It took on a feeble flame, making heavy white smoke. Exalted, we danced about the victim, telling each other to kick him, to whip him, to burn him. Suddenly the cushion made a spurt of fire and scared us. We had more fire than we expected.

"Say!" shouted Tom in a changed voice.

"Yes, yes, put it out!" I called.

He began to stamp with his flat sandalled feet at the burning corner of the cushion, but without much effect.

"Danged old tramp!" he said, "doing that!"

The cotton stuffing made little explosions with flying sparks.

"I know what," I said, "we can put out the fire—let's both of us—" and seeing what I did, Tom did the same, and with a sense of high glee, triumph, and even carnal fulfillment, we made our water together over the cushion and quelled the flame. The fire in the cushion guttered down into little worms of crinkling coal which finally expired yielding up a few last threads of noisome smoke.

"There!" said Tom.

"Yes!" I said.

We made ourselves proper again as passion gave way to shame. We kicked the cushion against the brick wall behind the sofa and went out into the unknowing, cool, golden October morning.

This loss of innocence was not in seeing what I saw, but in hearing what I was told about it—for we are subject to what we are taught to hate.

꙼

Muzza

How do we manage to love at all when there is so much hatred masquerading in love's name? I saw, if I did not understand, how this could be when I lost forever a friend whom I tried to rescue from peril. But a larger peril claimed him.

His name was John Burley. Nobody ever loved him enough to give him a natural nickname. Instead, he was the subject of a mocking refrain.

"John, John, the dog-faced one," sang the other boys our age when they saw John and me playing together in our neighborhood. He was my next-door neighbor, and I didn't know there was anything really different about him until I saw him abused by other children.

Before we were old enough to go to school we owned the whole world all day long except for nap time after lunch. We played in the open grassy yards behind and between our houses, and when John was busy and dreaming with play, he was a good friend to have, and never made trouble. But when people noticed him, he became someone else, and now I know that his parents, and mine, too, out of sympathy, wondered and wondered how things would be for him when the time came for him to go off to school like any other

[35]

boy and make a place for himself among small strangers who might find his oddness a source of fun and power for themselves.

In the last summer before schooltime, 1909, everyone heard the cry of "John, John, the dog-faced one," and even I, his friend, saw him newly. I would look at him with a blank face, until he would notice this, and then he would say crossly, with one of his impulsive, self-clutching movements,

"What's the matter, Richard, what's the matter, why are you looking crazy?"

"I'm not looking crazy. You are the one that's crazy."

For children pointed at him and sang, "Crazy, lazy, John's a daisy," and ran away.

Under their abuse, and my increasing wonderment, John showed a kind of daft good manners which should have induced pity and grace in his tormentors, but did not. He would pretend to be intensely preoccupied by delights and secrets from which the rest of us were excluded. He would count his fingers, nodding at the wrong total, and then put his thumbs against his thick lips and buzz against them with his furry voice, and look up at the sky, smacking his tongue, while other boys hooted and danced at him.

They were pitiably accurate when they called him the dog-faced one. He did look more like a dog than a boy. His pale hair was shaggy and could not be combed. His forehead was low, with a bony scowl that could not be changed. His nose was blunt, with its nostrils showing frontward. Hardly contained by his thick, shapeless lips, his teeth were long, white, and jumbled together. Of stocky build, he seemed always to be wearing a clever made-up costume to put on a monkey or a dog, instead of clothes like anybody else's. His parents bought him the best things to wear, but in a few minutes they were either torn or rubbed with dirt or scattered about somewhere.

[36]

"The poor dears," I heard my mother murmur over the Burley family.

"Yes," said my father, not thinking I might hear beyond what they were saying, "we are lucky. I can imagine no greater cross to bear."

"How do you suppose—" began my mother, but suddenly feeling my intent stare, he interrupted, with a glance my way, saying,

"Nobody ever knows how these cases happen. Watching them grow must be the hardest part."

What he meant was that it was sorrowful to see an abnormal child grow physically older but no older mentally.

※

But Mr and Mrs Burley—Gail and Howard, as my parents called them—refused to admit to anyone else that their son John was in any way different from other boys. As the summer was spent, and the time to start school for the first time came around, their problem grew deeply troubling. Their friends wished they could help with advice, mostly in terms of advising that John be spared the ordeal of entering the rigid convention of a school where he would immediately be seen by all as a changeling, like some poor swineherd in a fairy story who once may have been a prince, but who would never be released from his spell.

The school—a private school run by an order of Catholic ladies founded in France—stood a few blocks away from our street. The principal, who like each of her sisters wore a white shirt-waist with a high collar and starched cuffs and a long dark blue skirt, requested particularly that new pupils should come the first day without their parents. Everyone would be well-looked-after. The pupils would be put to tasks which would drive diffidence and homesickness out the window. My mother said to me as she made me lift my chin so that she could tie my windsor tie properly over the stiff slopes of my Buster Brown collar, while I looked into her deep, clear, blue eyes, and wondered how to say that I would not go to school that day or any other,

"Richard, John's mother thinks it would be so nice if you and he walked to school together."

"I don't want to."

I did not mean that I did not want to walk with John, I meant that I did not want to go to school.

"That's not very kind. He's your friend."

"I know it."

"I have told his mother you would go with him."

Childhood was a prison whose bars were decisions made by others. Numbed into submission, I took my mother's goodbye kiss staring at nothing, eaten within by fears of the unknown which awaited us all that day.

"Now skip," said my mother, winking both her eyes rapidly, to disguise the start of tears at losing me to another stage of life. She wore a small gold fleur-de-lys pin on her breast from which depended a tiny enamelled watch. I gazed at this and nodded solemnly but did not move. With wonderful executive tact she felt that I was about to make a fatally rebellious declaration, and so she touched the watch, turning its face around, and said, as though I must be concerned only with promptness,

"Yes, yes, Richard, you are right, we must think of the time, you mustn't be late your first day."

I was propelled then to the Burleys' house next door, where John and his mother were waiting for me in their front hall, which was always filled with magic light from the cut glass panes in bright colors flanking their front door.

Mrs Burley held me by the shoulders for a moment, trying to tell me something without saying it.

"Richard," she said, and then paused.

She looked deep into my eyes until I dropped my gaze. I looked at the rest of her face, and then at her bosom, wondering what was down there in that shadow where two rounded places of flesh rolled frankly together. Something about her personality led people to use her full name when they referred to her even idly—"Gail Burley"—and even I felt power within her.

Her husband had nothing like her strength. He was a small grey man with thin hair combed flat across his almost bald skull. The way his pince-nez pulled at the skin between his eyes gave him a look of permanent headache. Always hurried and impatient, he seemed to have no notice for children like me, or his own son, and all I ever heard about him was that he "gave Gail Burley anything she asked for," and "worked his fingers to the bone" doing so, as president of a marine engine company with a factory on the lake-front of our city of Dorchester in up-state New York.

Gail Burley—and I cannot say how much of her attitude rose from her sense of disaster in the kind of child she had borne—seemed to exist in a state of general exasperation. A reddish blonde, with skin so pale that it glowed like pearl, she was referred to as a great beauty. Across the bridge of her nose and about her eyelids and just under her eyes there were scatterings of little gold freckles which oddly yet powerfully reinforced her air of being irked by everything.

She often exhaled slowly and with compression, and said "Gosh," a slang word which was just coming in in her circle, which she pronounced "Garsh." Depending on her mood, she could make it into the expression of ultimate disgust or mild amusement. The white skin under her eyes went whiter when she was cross or angry, and then a dry hot light came into her hazel eyes. She

seemed a large woman to me, but I don't suppose she was—merely
slow, challenging and annoyed in the way she moved, with a flowing
governed grace which was like a comment on all that was intoler-
able. At any moment she would exhale in audible distaste for the
circumstances of her world. Compressing her lips, which she never
rouged, she would ray her pale glance upward, across, aside, to express her search for the smallest mitigation, the simplest endurable
fact or object, of life. The result of these airs and tones of her habit
was that in those rare moments when she was pleased, her expression of happiness came through like one of pain.

"Richard," she said, holding me by the shoulders, and looking
into my face to discover what her son John was about to confront
in the world of small school children.

"Yes, Mrs Burley."

She looked at John who was waiting to go.

He had his red and black plaid japanned collapsible tin lunch
box all nicely secured with a web strap and he made his buzzing
noise of pleasure at the idea of doing something so new as going to
school. Because he showed no apprehension over what would seem
like an ordeal to another boy, she let forth one of her breaths of disgust. She had dressed him in a starched collar like mine which extended over the smart lapels of his beautiful blue suit, with its
Norfolk jacket. His socks were well pulled up and his shoes were
shined. She looked at me again, trying to say what she could not.
Her white face with its flecks of fixed displeasure slowly took on a
pleading smile. She squeezed my shoulders a little, hoping I would
understand, even at my age, how John would need someone to look
out for him, protect him, suffer him, since he was a child of such
condition as she could not bring herself to admit. Her plea was
resolved into a miniature of the principle of bribery by which her
life was governed—even, I now think, to the terms on which
Howard Burley obtained even her smallest favors.

[40]

"Richard," she said, "when you and John come home after school"—and she pressed those words to show that I must bring him home— "I will have a nice surprise waiting for you both."

John became agitated at this, jumping about, and demanding, "What is it, Muzza, what is it?"

She gave one of her breaths.

"John, John, be quiet. Garsh. I can't even say anything without getting you all excited."

For my benefit she smiled, but the gold flecks under her eyes showed as angry dark spots, and the restrained power of her dislike of John was so great that he was cowed. He put his hands to his groin to comfort himself, and said, using his word for what he always found there, "Peanut."

At this his mother became openly furious at him.

"John! Stop that! How many times have I told you that isn't nice. Richard doesn't do it. Doctor Grauer has told you what will happen if you keep doing it. Stop it!"

She bent over to slap at his hands and he lunged back. Losing his balance, he fell, and I heard his head go crack on the hardwood floor of the hall where the morning light made pools of jewel colors through the glass panels. He began to cry in a long, burry, high wail. His mother picked him up and he hung like a rag doll in her outraged grasp. The day was already in ruins, and he had not even gone off to school. The scene was one of hundreds like it which made up the life of that mother and that son. I was swept by shame at seeing it.

"Now stop that ridiculous caterwauling," she said. "Richard is waiting to take you to school. Do you want him to think you are a cry baby?"

John occasionally made startling remarks, which brought a leap of hope that his understanding might not be so deficient as everyone believed.

[41]

"I *am* a cry baby," he said, burying his misery-mottled face in the crook of his arm.

A sudden lift of pity in his mother made her kneel down and gently enfold him in her arms. With her eyes shut, she gave her love to the imaginary son, handsome and healthy, whom she longed for, even as she held the real John. It was enough to console him. He flung his arms around her and hugged her like a bear cub, all fur and clumsiness and creature longing.

"Muzza, Muzza," he said against her cheek.

She set him off.

"*Now* can you go to school?" she asked in a playfully reasonable voice.

John's states of feeling were swift in their changes. He began to smack his lips, softly indicating that he was in a state of pleasure.

"Then go along, both of you," said his mother.

She saw us out the door and down the walk. Curiously enough, the self-sorrowing lump in my throat went away as I watched the scene between John and his mother. Things seemed so much worse with the Burleys than with me and my start in school.

※

I led John off at a smart pace, running sometimes, and sometimes walking importantly with short busy steps. We paused only once, and that was to look in the window at a little candy and news shop a block from the school, where with warm, damp pennies it was possible to buy sticky rolls of chocolate candy, or—even better—stamp-sized films which when exposed to light darkened in shades of red to reveal such subjects as the battleship *New York,* or the Woolworth Building, or the Washington Monument.

John always had more money than I.

"Let's get some," he proposed.

"No. After school," I replied. "We will be late if we stop and we will catch the dickens."

"Catch the dickens," he said, and began to run away ahead of me. I overtook him and we entered the main door of the school—it was a red brick building with a portico of white pillars veiled in vines—and once in the dark corridors with their wood-ribbed walls, we seemed to lose ourselves to become small pieces of drifting material that were carried along to our classrooms by a tide of children. Boys went separate from girls. John and I were finally directed to a room containing twenty boys in the first grade, presided over by Miss Mendtzy.

She met us at the door and without speaking but sustaining a kindly smile, sent us with a strong thin finger on our shoulders along the aisles where we would find our desks. We gave her wary glances to see what she was like. She had a narrow little face above a bird's body. Her hair was like short grey feathers. Before her large, steady, pale eyes she wore a pair of nose glasses that trembled in response to her quivering nerves and sent a rippling line of light along the gold chain that attached her glasses to a small gold spring spool pinned to her shirtwaist.

John and I were at desks side by side. When all the room was filled, Miss Mendtzy closed the door, and our hearts sank. There we were, in jail. She moved trimly to her platform. Her slim feet in black, high-buttoned shoes, looked like feet in a newspaper advertisement, because she stood them at such polite angles to each other. On her desk she had placed a vase of flowers with a great silk bow to give a festive air to the opening day. Touching the blossoms with a flourish of artistic delicacy, she launched into a pleasant little speech. Everyone sat quietly out of strangeness while she said,

"Now I want all of my new first-graders to come up here one by one, beginning with this aisle on my left"—she showed where in a gesture of bloodless grace—"and shake hands with me, and tell me their names, for we are going to be working together for months and years, as I will be your home room teacher until the sixth grade. Think of it! Quite like a family! And so we are going to become great friends, and we must know each other well. Miss Mendtzy is ready to love each and every one of you, and she hopes each and every one of you will learn to love her. We are going to get along splendidly together, if everybody is polite, and works hard, and remembers that he is not the only boy in this world, or in this school, or in this room, but that he is a boy among other boys, to whom he must show respect, even while playing. Now, shall we start here, with this boy, at the front of the first row?"

One by one we went to her platform, stepped up on it, shook hands, spoke our names, received a bright, lens-quivered smile and a deep look into our eyes, and then were sent on across her little stage and down the other side and back to our seats. Some among us swaggered, others went rapidly and shyly, hiding from such a public world, one or two winked on the final trip up the aisles, and all felt some thumping at the heart of dread followed by pride as we went and returned.

❀

There was no incident until John's turn came. When it did, he would not rise and go forward.

"Come?" said Miss Mendtzy, beckoning over her desk and twinkling with her chained glasses. "We are waiting for the next boy?"

I leaned over to John and whispered,

"It's your turn, John. Go on. Go on."

He went lower in his seat and began to buzz his lips against his thumbs, terrified of rising before a crowd of small strangers, who were now beginning to nudge each other and whisper excitedly at the diversion. I heard someone whisper "John, John, the dog-faced one," and I could not tell whether John heard it. But, a professional, Miss Mendtzy heard it. She smartly whacked her ruler on the flat of her desk. It was like a nice pistol shot. Silence fell.

She put on her face a look which we all knew well at home—that look of aloof, pained regret at unseemly behavior.

"I must say I am surprised," she said quietly and deadlily, "that some of us are not polite enough to sit silently when we see someone in a fit of shyness. Some of the finest people I know are shy at times. I have been told that our Bishop, that humble, great man, is shy himself when he has to meet people personally. Now I am going down from my platform and down the aisle and"—she glanced at her seating plan of the classroom—"I am going to bring John Burley up here myself as my guest, and help him over his shyness, and the only way to do that is by helping him to do the same things everybody else has done. So."

She went to John and took his hand and led him to the platform and stood him where each of us had stood, facing her, in profile to the rest of the room. Speaking as though he had just come there by his own will, she said,

"Good morning, John. I am Miss Mendtzy. We are pleased that you are with us," first giving us a sidelong glare to command our agreement, and then like a lady holding forth her hand to John, with a slightly arched wrist and drooping fingers.

John put his hands behind him and buzzed his lips and looked out the window.

"John?"

"John, John, the dog-faced one," again said an unplaceable voice in the rear of the classroom, softly but distinctly.

[45]

"Who said that!" demanded Miss Mendtzy, going pink, and trembling until her lenses shimmered. The very first day of school, she seemed to say, and already there was an unfortunate incident. "I simply will not have bad manners in my room, and I simply will not have one of my boys treated like this. Whoever said that is to stand up and apologize instantly. I think I know who it was"— but clearly she did not—"and if he apologizes now, and promises never, never to do such a rude thing again, we shall all be friends again as we want to be. Well? I am waiting?"

The silence and the tension grew and grew.

John stood with head hanging. I saw his hands twitching behind his back. He was trying not to clasp them over himself in front.

"One more minute?" declared Miss Mendtzy, "and then I will do something you will all be very sorry for?"

Silence, but for a clock ticking on the wall above her blackboard.

John could not bear it. Moving as fast as a cat, he threw himself forward to Miss Mendtzy's desk and swept her vase of flowers to the floor where it shattered and spilled.

All the boys broke into hoots and pounded their hinged desk tops upon their desks, making such a clamor that in a moment the door was majestically opened and the Principal, always called Madame de St. Étienne, who came from nobility in France, heavily entered the room. Even as she arrived, someone in the rear of the room, carried on by the momentum of events, called out, "Crazy, lazy, John's a daisy."

The Principal was a monument of authority. Above her heavy pink face with its ice-blue eyes rose a silvery pompadour like a wave breaking back from a headland. Her bosom was immense in her starched shirtwaist. Over it she wore a long gold chain which fell like a maiden waterfall into space below her bust and ended in a loop at her waist where she tucked a large gold watch. Her dark skirt went straight down in front, for she had to lean continuously forward, we thought, if the vast weight and size behind her were not to topple her over backward.

She now glared at Miss Mendtzy with frigid reproach at the breach of discipline in her classroom loud enough to be heard down the hall, and then faced us all, saying in a voice like pieces of broken glass scraped together at the edges,

"Children, you will rise when the Principal enters the classroom."

She clapped her hands once and we rose, scared and ashamed.

"Now who is this?" she demanded, turning to the tableau at the teacher's platform.

"This is John Burley, Madame," replied Miss Mendtzy, and got no further, for John, seeing the open door, bolted for the hall and freedom.

Madame de St. Étienne gave another queenly, destructive look at Miss Mendtzy, and said,

"Pray continue with the exercises, Miss Mendtzy."

She then left the room, moving as though on silent casters, for her skirt swept the floor all about her short, light steps, amazing in a woman so heavy and so enraged.

Burning with mortification, Miss Mendtzy began our first lesson, which was an exercise in neatness—the care of our pencil boxes and schoolbooks. There was a happy material interest in this, for the pencils were all new, and smelled of cedar, and we went in turn to sharpen them at the teacher's desk. Our erasers—promises of foreordained smudges of error—showed a tiny diamondlike glisten if we held them in a certain way to the light of the window. If we chewed upon them, little gritty particles deliciously repelled our teeth. Our schoolbooks cracked sweetly when we opened them, and the large, clear, black type on the pages held mystery and invitation. We became absorbed in toys which were suddenly now something more than toys, and our cheeks grew hot, and we were happy, and we forgot to want to go to the bathroom, and I was hardly aware of it when the door opened again before Madame de St. Étienne. Late, but earnestly, we scrambled to our feet, as she said,

"Which is Richard—?" giving my full name.

I put my hand up.

"Pray come with me, Richard," she ordered, ignoring Miss Mendtzy entirely. "Bring your boxes and books."

A stutter of conjecture went along the aisles at this, which Madame de St. Étienne, gliding on her way to the door, suppressed by pausing and staring above the heads of everyone as though she could not believe her ears. Quiet fell, and in quiet, with my heart beating, I followed her out to the hallway. She shut the door and turned me with a finger to walk ahead of her to her office at the entrance way inside the pillared portico. I wanted to ask what I had done to be singled out for her notice which could only, I thought, lead to punishment.

But it appeared that she had enlisted me as an assistant. In her office, John was waiting, under guard of the Principal's secretary. He was sitting on a cane chair holding a glass of water, half full.

"Finish it, John," commanded Madame.

"I don't like it," he said.

"Hot water to drink is the best thing for anyone who is upset," she answered. "It is the remedy we always give. Finish it."

Raising a humble wail, he drank the rest of the hot water, spilling much of it down on his chin, his windsor tie, his starched collar.

"You are John's friend?" she asked me.

"Yes."

"Who are his other friends?"

"I don't know."

"Has he none, then?"

"I don't think so."

[48]

John watched my face, then the Principal's, turning his head with jerky interest and rubbing his furry hair with his knuckles in pleasure at being the subject of interest.

"You brought him to school?"

"Yes."

"Yes, *Madame.*"

"Yes, Madame."

"And you will take him home?"

"Yes, Madame. After school."

"I have spoken on the telephone with his mother, to arrange for him to go home. She prefers not to have him come home until the end of school after lunch. Until then, I will ask you to stay here in my office with him. You will both eat your lunches here and I will see that you are not disturbed. Tomorrow you will be able to return to your classroom."

"With John?"

"No. John will not be with us after today."

John nodded brightly at this. Evidently the Principal had given an ultimatum to Mrs Burley over the telephone. I can imagine the terms of it—careful avoidance of the words abnormal, special case, impossible to measure up to the progress of others boys his age, and such. With arctic, polite finality, Madame de St. Étienne would have read John out of the human society where his years put him but where his retarded mind and disordered nerves, so clearly announced by his rough, doglike appearance, must exclude him. Gail Burley's despair can be felt. How could she ever again pretend even to herself that her child, if only thrown into life, would make his way like anyone else? How could she love anything in the world if she could not love the son who was mismade in her womb? What a bitter affront it was to her famous good looks of face and body, her hard brightness of mind, her firm ability to govern everything else that made up her life, if she must be responsible for such a creature as John. How to face a lifetime of exasperated pity for him? How to disguise forever the humiliation which she must feel? The daily effort of disguising it would cost her all her confident beauty in the end.

"Why don't we go home now?" I asked.

"John's mother thinks it would look better if he simply came home like the other children when school is dismissed this afternoon."

Yes, for if they saw him come earlier, people would say once again what she knew they were always saying about John. I knew well enough the kind of thing, from hearing my own father and mother talk kindly and sadly about my playmate.

Let him come home after school, like everyone else, and tomorrow, why, then, tomorrow, Gail Burley could simply say with a shrug and a speckled smile, that she and Howard didn't think it was really just the school for John. There was something about those teachers, neither quite nuns, nor quite ordinary women, which was unsettling. The Burleys would look around, and meantime, John could be tutored at home, as Gail herself had been one winter when she had gone as a little girl with her parents to White Sulphur Springs. Leaving the school could be made, with a little languid ingenuity, to seem like a repudiation by her, for reasons she would be too polite to elaborate upon for parents of other children still attending it.

※

The day passed slowly in the Principal's office. At eleven o'clock there was a fire drill, set off by a great alarm gong which banged slowly and loudly in the hall just above the office door. The door was kept closed upon us, but we could hear the rumble and slide of the classes as they took their appointed ways out of the building to the shaded playgrounds outside.

"I want to go, I want to go!" cried John at the window. "Everybody is there!"

"No," said Madame de St. Étienne, turning like an engine in her swivel chair, "we will remain here. They will presently return."

John began to cry.

The Principal looked to me to manage him and calmly turned back to the work on her desk, placing a pince-nez upon the high bridge of her thin nose with a sweep of her arm which was forced to travel a grand arc to bypass her bosom.

＊

But at last, when the clock in the office showed twenty-five minutes past two, she said,

"Now, John, and now, Richard, you may take your things and go home. School is dismissed at half-past two. Perhaps it would be prudent for you to leave a little before the other boys. You will go straight home."

"Yes, Madame."

She gave us each her hand. To John she said,

"May God bless you, my poor little one."

Her words and her manner sent a chill down my belly.

But in a moment we were in the open air of the autumn day, where a cold wind off the lake was spinning leaves from the trees along the street. John capered happily along and when we reached the candy store, he remembered how we would stop there. I wondered if stopping there would violate our orders to go "straight home," but the store was on the way, and we went in.

John enjoyed shopping. He put his stubby finger with its quick-bitten nail on the glass of the candy counter, pointing to first one then another confection, and every time he made up his mind he changed it, until the proprietor, an old man with a bent back in a dirty grey cardigan, sighed and looked over his shoulder at his wife, who sat in the doorway to their back room. His glance and her return of it plainly spoke of John's idiocy.

"There!" said John finally, aiming his finger and his hunger at a candy slice of banana, cut the long way, and tasting, I knew, of cotton mixed with gun oil. The candy banana was white in the center with edges stained orange and yellow.

I moved on to the counter where you could buy the magic photographic plates which showed nothing until you exposed them to the light. I wanted to buy one but I had no money. John came beside me and said,

"Richard, I'll get you one."

"Oh, no."

"Oh, yes. I'll get you two."

He put down four pennies to pay for two prints and the storekeeper gave me the box to choose my prints. On the edge of each little plate was the name of its subject. I chose the liner *Mauretania* and Buckingham Palace.

"Here," I said to John, offering him one of them. "You keep one."

He put his hands behind his back and blew his tongue at me between his thick lips.

"All right, then, thanks, we have to go home now. Come on, John," I said.

Eating his banana John was compliant. We came out of the store and went on to the corner where we turned into our street. Our houses were a block and a half away. We could just see them. Under the billowing trees and the cool autumn light they looked asleep. They called to me. I wanted suddenly to be home.

"Let's run, John," I said.

We began to run, but we got no further than a large hedge which ran up the driveway of the second house from the corner.

※

It was a great house, with a large garage in back, and a deep lawn. I knew the brothers who lived there. Their name was Grandville. They were a year or two older and very self-important because of their family automobiles, and their electric train system which occupied the whole top floor of their house.

They now jumped out from behind the hedge. With them were three other boys. They had all just come home from school. While we had idled in the candy store, they had gone by to wait for us.

"John, John, the dog-faced one!" they called, and took John, and dragged him up the driveway toward the garage in the windy, empty neighborhood. "Crazy, lazy, John's a daisy," they chanted, and I ran along yelling,

"Let us go, let us go!"

"Shut up, or we'll get you too," cried one of the brothers.

"Richie!" moaned John, "Richie!"

The terror in his blurry voice was like that in a nightmare when you must scream and cannot make a sound. His face was belly-white and his eyes were staring at me. I was his protector. I would save him.

"Richie! Richie!"

But I could do nothing against the mob of five, but only run along calling to them to "let go of us"—for I felt just as much captive as

[53]

John whom they dragged by arms and legs. He went heavy and limp. They hauled him through the chauffeur's door—a narrow one beside the big car doors, which were closed—and shut the door after us all. The center of the garage was empty for the big Pierce-Arrow limousine was out, bearing Mrs Grandville somewhere on a chauffeur-driven errand.

"Put him there!" yelled one of the brothers.

Four boys held John on the cement floor by the drain grille while the other brother went to the wall, uncoiled a hose and turned the spigot. The hose leaped alive with a thrust of water.

"Now let go and get back or you'll all get wet," called the Grandville boy. As the others scampered back he turned the powerful blow of the hose water on John. It knocked him down. He shut his eyes and turned his blind face to the roof. His shapeless mouth fell open in a silent cry. Still clutching his candy banana he brought it to his mouth in delayed memory of what it was for, and what had been a delight was now a sorrowful and profitless hunger for comfort in misery.

"Get up, dogface," yelled one of the boys.

Obediently John got up, keeping his eyes closed, suffering all that must come to him. The hose column toppled him over again. Striking his face, blows of water knocked his head about until it seemed it must fly apart.

"I know!" cried an excited and joyful young voice, "let's get his clo'es off!"

There was general glee at this idea. The hose was put away for the moment, and everyone seized John and tore at his clothes. He made his soundless wail with open mouth and I thought he shaped my name again.

When he was naked they ordered him to stand again, and he did so, trying to protect his modesty with his thick hands. They hit him with the hose again and buffeted him like a puppet. The hose water made him spin and slide on the oily floor. The noise was doubled by echoes from the peaked high roof of the garage.

爻

Nobody thought of me.

I backed to the door and opened it and ran away. On the concrete driveway was a tricycle belonging to the younger Grandville. I mounted it and rode off as fast as I could. My chest was ready to break open under my hard breathing. My knees rose and fell like pistons. My face was streaming with tears of rage at John's ordeal and the disgrace of my helplessness before it. I rode to John's house and threw myself up the front steps but before I could attack the door it was opened to me. Gail Burley was watching for us and when she saw me alone in gasping disorder, she cried,

"Why, Richard! What's the matter! Where's John!"

At first I could only point, so I took her hand and tugged at her to come with me. It was proof of the passion and power I felt at the moment that without more questioning she came. I remounted the tricycle and led her up the street to the Grandvilles'. In a little while as I went I was able to tell her what was happening.

When she understood, she increased her stride. She became magnificent in outrage. Her hazel eyes darkened to deep topaz and her reddish golden hair seemed to spring forward into the wind. She was like a famous ship, dividing the elements as she went.

"Oh! Those horrid, cruel, little beasts!" she exclaimed. "Oh! What I would do to them—and Richard, you are an absolute *darrling* to get away and come for me. Oh! That poor John!"

We hurried up the driveway. The game was still going on. We could hear cries and the hiss of the hose. Gail Burley strode to the door and threw it open. She saw her son pinned against the far brick wall by the long pole of the spray. He tried to turn his face from side to side to avoid its impact. It swept down his white soft body and he continually tried to cover himself with his hands. Nonresistant, he accepted all that came to him. His eyes were still closed and his mouth was still open.

Stepping with baleful elegance across the puddles of the floor, Gail Burley threw aside the boys who were dancing at the spectacle, and came to the Grandville brother with the hose. She astounded him. In his ecstatic possession, he had heard no one arrive. She seized the hose and with a gesture commanded him to turn off the water, which he did. She dropped the hose and went to John and took him dripping and blue with cold into her arms. He fell inert against her letting his hands dangle as she hugged him. But he made a word at last.

"Muzza," he said thickly, "Oh, Muzza, Muzza."

"John-John," she said, holding his wet head against the hollow of her lovely neck and shoulder, "It's all right. It's all right. Muzza is here. Poor John-John."

The boys were now frightened. The oldest said,

"We were only trying to have some fun, Mrs Burley."

"Go to the house," she commanded in the flattest tone which held promises of punishment for all as soon as she could inform their parents, "and bring a big towel and a blanket.—Richard, you might throw together John's things and bring them along."

She was obeyed soberly and quickly. In a few minutes she and I were taking John home. He was huddled inside a doubled blanket. He was shivering. His teeth chattered.

"Where's my banana?" he managed to say.

[56]

"Oh, never mind," said his mother. "We can get you another banana. What were you doing with a banana anyway?"

"It was a candy one," I explained.

"I see."

Her thoughts were falling into order after the disturbance of her feelings by the cruelty she had come to halt.

※

My perceptions of what followed were at the time necessarily shallow, but they were, I am sure, essentially correct.

"Those wretches!" exclaimed Gail Burley, leading John by the hand while I trotted alongside. "What would we ever have done without Richard? You are a true friend, Richard!—Oh!" she said, at the memory of what she had seen. And then, as John stumbled because she was walking so fast and his blanket folds were so awkward to hold about himself, she jerked his hand and said, "Stop dragging your feet, John! Why can't you walk like anybody else! Here! Pull up and keep up with me!"

At her suddenly cold voice, he went limp and would have fallen softly, like a dropped teddy bear, to the sidewalk. But she dragged him up, and said with her teeth almost closed,

"John Burley, do you hear me? Get up and come with me. If you do not, your father will give you the whaling of your life when he comes home tonight!"

"No, Muzza, no, Muzza," muttered John at the memories which this threat called alive. He got to his feet and began half-running along beside her, dragging his borrowed blanket which looked like the robe of a pygmy king in flight.

I was chilled by the change in Mrs Burley. Her loving rage was gone and in its place was a fury of exasperation. She blinked away angry tears. With no thought of how fast John could run along with her, she pulled and jerked at him all the way home, while her face told us after all that she was bitterly ashamed of him.

For at last she took the world's view of her son. Represented by his own kind, other children, the world had repudiated him. Much as she hated the cruelty of the Grandvilles and their friends, sore as her heart was at what her son had suffered through them, she knew they were society, even if it was shown at its most savage. It was the determining attitude of the others which mattered. She had seen it clearly. Her heart broke in half. One half was charged with love and pity as it defied the mocking world which allowed no published lapse from its notion of a finally unrealizable norm. The other half was pierced by fragments of her pride. How could it happen to *her* that *her* child could be made sport of as a little animal monster? Gail Burley was to be treated better than that.

"John?" she sang out in warning as John stumbled again, "you heard what I said?"

Her cheeks usually pale were now flushed darkly. I was afraid of her. She seemed ready to treat John just as the boys had treated him. Was she on the side of his tormentors? Their judgements persuaded her even as she rescued her child. She longed for him both to live—and to die. Cold desire rose up in her. If only she knew some way to save this poor child in the future from the abuse and the uselessness which were all that life seemed to offer him. How could she spare John and herself long lifetimes of baffled sorrow? She made him dance along faster than he could, for being such a creature that others mocked and tortured him, at the expense of her pride.

When we reached her house, she said,

"Richard, you are an angel. Please drop John's wet things in the butler's pantry. I am going to take him upstairs to bed. He is having a chill. I'll never be able to thank you enough. Your after-school surprise is on the hall table, an almond chocolate bar. Come over and see John later."

※

But that evening just before my nursery supper when I went to show John the developed prints of the *Mauretania* and Buckingham Palace, his father met me in the living room and said that John was ill—his chill had gone worse. His mother was upstairs with him, and I must not go up.

"Well, Richard," said Howard Burley, "God only knows what they would have done to John if you hadn't come to get his mother. They will catch it, never fear. I have talked to their fathers."

I had been feeling all afternoon a mixture of guilt and fright for having snitched on the boys. Now I was sure they would avenge themselves on me. Something of this must have shown in my face.

"Never fear," said Mr Burley. "Their fathers will see to it that nothing happens to you. Come over and see John tomorrow."

But the next day they said that John was really ill with grippe.

"Did they send for Doctor Grauer?" asked my mother.

"I don't know," I said.

He was our doctor, too, and we would have known his car if he had come to attend to John. But all day nobody came, and the next day, John was worse, and my mother said to my father, with glances that recalled my presence to him which must require elliptical conversation,

"Grippe sometimes goes into pneumonia, you know."

"Yes, I know," replied my father. "But they know how to treat these things."

"Yes, I know, but sometimes something is needed beyond just home remedies."

"Then Grauer has not yet—?"

"No, not today, either."

"That is odd. Perhaps he isn't so sick as we think."

"Oh, I think so. I talked to Gail today. She is frantic."

"Well."

"But she says she knows what to do. They are doing everything, she says. Everything possible."

"I am sure they are.—Sometimes I can't help thinking that it might be better all around if—"

"Yes, I have too," said my mother hastily, indicating me again. "But of course it must only be God's will."

My father sighed.

I knew exactly what they were talking about, though they thought I didn't.

※

On the third day, John Burley died. My mother told me the news when I reached home after school. She winked both eyes at me as she always did in extremes of feeling. She knelt down and enfolded me. Her lovely heart-shaped face was an image of pity. She knew I knew nothing of death, but some feeling of death came through to me from the intensity of color in her blue eyes. The power of her feeling upset me, and I swallowed as if I were sick when she said,

"Richard, my darling, our dear, poor, little John died this morning. His chill grew worse and worse and finally turned into pneumonia.

They have already taken him away. His mother wanted me to tell you. She loves you for what you tried to do for him."

"Then he's gone?"

"Yes, my dearie, you will never be able to see him again. That is what death means."

I was sobered by these remarks, but I did not weep. I was consumed with wonder, though I was not sure what I wondered about.

There was no funeral. Burial, as they said, was private. I missed John, but I was busy at school, where I was cautious with the Grandvilles and the others until enough days passed after the punishments they had received to assure me that I was safe from their reprisals. Perhaps they wanted to forget that they had given away death in heedless play. Howard Burley went to the office quite as usual. His wife stayed home and saw no one for a while.

"I cannot help wondering," said my mother, "why she never called Doctor Grauer."

"Hush," said my father. "Don't dwell on such things."

But I dwelled on them now and then. They were part of my knowledge on the day when Gail Burley asked my mother to send me to see her after school.

"Mrs Burley has some things of John's that she wants to give you. You were his best friend."

I knew all his toys. Some of them were glorious. I saw them all in mind again. I went gladly to see his mother.

The housemaid let me in and sent me upstairs to Mrs Burley's sitting room. She was reclining against many lacy pillows on a *chaise longue* in the bay window. She was paler than ever, and perhaps thinner, and there was a new note in her voice which made her seem like a stranger—a huskiness which reflected lowered vitality. She embraced me and said,

"Do you miss John?"

"Yes."

"Poor little John."

Her hazel eyes were blurred for a moment and she looked away out the window into the rustling treetops of autumn, as though to conceal both emotion and knowledge from me. "Oh, my God," I heard her say softly. Then she let forth one of her controlled breaths, annoyed at her own weakness as it lay embedded in the general condition of the world, and said with revived strength,

"Well, Richard, let's be sensible. Come and pick out the toys you want in John's nursery. What you don't take I am going to send to Father Raker's Orphanage."

She led me along the upstairs hall to John's room. His toys were laid out in rows, some on the window seat, the rest on the floor.

"I suppose I could say that you should just take them all," she said with one of her unwilling smiles, "but I think that would be selfish of us both. Go ahead and pick."

With the swift judgement of the expert, I chose a beautiful set of Pullman cars for my electric train which had the same track as John's, and a power boat with mahogany cabin and real glass portholes draped in green velvet curtains, and a battalion of lead soldiers with red coats and black busbys and white cross belts tumbled together in their box who could be set smartly on parade, and a set of water color paints, and a blackboard on its own easel with a box of colored chalks. These, and so much else in the room, spoke of attempts to reward John for what he was not—and, for what they were not, the parents, too. I looked up at his mother. She was watching me as if never to let me go.

"Your cheeks are so flushed," she said, "and it is adorable the way the light makes a gold ring on your hair when you bend down. Richard, come here."

She took me in her hungry arms. I felt how she trembled. There was much to make her tremble.

[62]

"Do you want anything else?" she asked, again becoming sensible, as she would have said. Her concealed intensity made me lose mine.

"No, thank you, Mrs Burley."

"Well, you can take your new toys home whenever you like. You can't carry them all at once."

"I'll take the boat now," I said.

"All right. Garsh, it's big, isn't it. John loved to sail it when we went to Narragansett."

She took me downstairs to the door. There she lingered. She wanted to say something. She could have said it to an adult. How could she say it to me? Yet most grown people spoke to me as if I were far older than my years. Leaning her back against the door, with her hands behind her on the doorknob, and with her face turned upward, so that I saw her classical white throat and the curve of her cheek until it was lost in the golden shadows of her eye, she said,

"Richard, I wonder if you would ever understand—you knew, didn't you, surely, that our poor little John was not like other children?"

"Sometimes, yes."

"His father and I suffered for him, seeing how hard it was for him with other children; and then we thought of how it would have to be when he grew up—do you know?"

I nodded, though I did not know, really.

"We are heartbroken to lose him, you must know that. He was all we had. But do you know, we sometimes wonder if it is better that God took him, even if we had to lose him. Do you know?"

She looked down at me as if to complete her thought through her golden piercing gaze. When she saw the look of horror on my face, she caught her breath. Conventional, like all children, I was amazed that anyone should be glad of death, if that meant not seeing someone ever again.

"Oh, Richard, don't judge us yet for feeling that way. When you grow up and see more of what life does to those who cannot meet it, you will understand." She was obsessed. Without naming it, she must speak of the weight on her heart, even if only to me, a first-grader in school. In my ignorance, perhaps I might be the only safe one in whom to confide. "Garsh, when you see cripples trying to get along, and sick people who can never get well, you wonder why they can't be spared, and just die."

The appalling truth was gathering in me. I stared at her, while she continued,

"John was always frail, and when those horrid boys turned on him, and he caught that chill, and it went into pneumonia, his father and I did everything to save him, but it was not enough. We had to see him go."

Clutching John's beautiful power boat in both arms, I cowered a little away from her and said,

"You never sent for a doctor, though."

A sharp silence cut its way between us. She put one hand on her breast and held herself. At last she said in a dry, bitter voice,

"Is that what is being said, then?"

"Doctor Grauer always comes when I am sick."

She put her hand to her mouth. Her eyes were afire like those of a trapped cat.

"Richard?" she whispered against her fingers, "what are you thinking? Don't you believe we loved John?"

I said, inevitably,

"Did you have him die?"

At this she flew into a golden, speckled fury. She reached for me to chastise me, but I eluded her. I was excited by her and also frightened. Her eyes blazed with shafted light. I managed to dance away beyond her reach, but I was encumbered by the beautiful power cruiser in my arms. I let it crash to the floor. I heard its glass break.

Escape and safety meant more to me just then than possession of the wonderful boat. I knew the house. I ran down the hall to the kitchen and out the back door to my own yard, and home, out of breath, frightened by what I had exposed.

※

The Burleys never again spoke to my parents or to me. My parents wondered why, and even asked, but received no explanation. All of John's toys went to Father Raker's. In a few weeks the Burleys put up their house for sale, in a few months Howard retired from business, and they went to live in Florida for the rest of their lives.

CHAPTER IV

Far Kingdoms

I did not then recognize what I had so heedlessly exposed—the power of truth, which if it can create can also destroy.

But all growth is discovery of power—or powers. Language is one of these. The first time I ever heard anyone use the expression, "How dare you!" I thought I had never heard anything so splendid. Language became an instrument of power; style entered into character; and I learned how I might be someone else just by sounding different or special. From creating someone else for who I was, it was not much of a step to creating all sorts of other beings who could be believed in, if someone might only know of them. The artist must first create, and then communicate. But who would listen? Who would see?

One day my mother and I were on a streetcar coming home from the Catholic Union Library where we went for books every week or two—children's books for me at seven years old; Mrs Humphrey Ward, Edith Wharton, H. G. Wells, Monsignor Robert Hugh Benson for my parents.

It was a winter afternoon with brown slush on the streets and wan daylight failing into gaslight in the streetlamps with their mantles. People were hurrying home for the night.

The car was crowded. My mother held me on her lap to make room for someone else who came to sit next to us—a small, grey man with meek-looking eyeglasses and grey cloth gloves. His eyes watered from the cold—it was a heavy winter in Dorchester that year—and he kept making apologetic little sounds deep in his head behind his nose as he tried to clear congested air passages. He stared straight ahead and held himself stiffly. Just in front of us sat two small children who were taking care of each other as they were riding the car alone. Holding on to each other like waifs in a fairy tale, they occupied the space for one adult.

After one of its clanging stops, the car admitted a stout woman who came down the aisle like a blind force of nature, perhaps like a flow of congealing lava, making bulbous entries with her round hard shapes through apertures of the passenger crowd, to their murmured discomfort.

She came toiling toward us and when she saw the two children seated in front of us, she leaned down and with her huge red naked hand, which was packed with hard fat under shining, cracked skin, she pushed the children off the seat and squeezed past them to take their place, giving forth a loud, tired sigh. The children began to cry, standing together in an embrace. The small proper man next to us instantly stood up and leaned over the fat woman and said,

"Madam, how dare you do a thing like that!"

His eyeglasses now blazed with strong light which must have come from his little eyes, and his grey silk hands, now made into claws, trembled in the air beside his suddenly pink face. Transformed, he was a champion. He created opinion. People stirred in approval of his rebuke. I stared at him with awe.

The woman, now swollen further with added ill temper which

seemed to roil within her to find a way to emerge, as through a pustule which had not yet been formed, began to mutter, scowling straight ahead,

"I'll slap him to bits; see if I don't, the nasty little dandy!"

"Come, Richard," said my mother, who hated to witness any loss of grace, "we must start for the door. We must get off next. Hold tight to your books."

It would mean walking an extra block or two. Keeping over my shoulder with my gaze as much of the drama as I could until we left the car, I never knew what happened next. But enough had been discovered for me to know that I, like the mouse-grey man on the streetcar, could be anybody I wanted to be. Some of the consequences came to pass later in the winter when my Uncle Frederick appeared in Dorchester for a week.

❦

His work—his need—in life was to create transports of excitement for others. It was a dangerous magic, as at moments he seemed to know, yet he exercised it fully, with charm.

In evening, in winter, when the lamps were turned on, and the newel post in the downstairs hall upheld a lighted moon below me, just before bedtime I stood on the upper landing, gazing down, but not gazing, really—pouring myself, rather, through my eyes which must have looked huge and dark blue, and not standing, really, but almost dancing in eagerness and excitement within my dark red velours bathrobe and white flannel pajamas, while the joy of waiting was equalled by its anxiety.

For who was it who was arriving outside, in a carriage with horses, and who came in from the snow, was received and divested while snowflakes fell like little stars to the floor, and who then turned slowly, looked up, saw me, extended both hands upward and exclaimed, in a rich voice trained to convey loving expectation, among other emotions, including fulfilled joy,

"Ri-chard!"

How he said it gave my very name a new value which I would never forget. In that instant I became more Richard than ever, and to be Richard in just that way, called alive by that persuasive, grown-up voice, was to be the most desirable being in the world, and thus the most fortunate.

My Uncle Frederick came laughing up to me taking the stairs two at a time, and embraced my hot, striving person which was now suffused with a sense of its own dearness and worth. Then letting me go,

"Ha! my king!" he cried in his crackling, dark voice, falling to one knee and sweeping his right arm awide as he made a fast, courtly bow, "I have high and glorious matters for your ear. Full many a day have I hasted hither to give you news of your far kingdom, and it now me rejoices to pay Your Majesty my homage and my love."

"Fritz?" called my mother from the real world downstairs in a laughing irritation at his nonsense, for she knew its every possibility as his older sister, "do let him go to bed and come down and wash your hands and have your cocktail. Dan will be home any minute."

Uncle Fritz closed his eyes in comic patience, and then looked at me again, with a wink, to make us conspirators, and said,

"Let them run their world, Richard, my lord, and we will make our own.—I'll come upstairs again to tuck you in after I have been polite below."

I doubt if he ever left anybody without a promise of some sort, and it is known only in heaven—or hell—how many he ever kept. He was an actor, and his play was on tour, and he would be in Dorchester for two weeks, playing at the Shubert Theatre. I had been promised a matinee performance so that I could see him on the stage. My mother was more interested in seeing the once-great, and still famous, actress who had chosen him as her leading man in her present play, which was a period piece laid in Tudor England.

Uncle Fritz was like my mother in many ways, but the ways were exaggerated. His charm was like hers, darting and impulsive, but raised at times to invite rather than bestow admiration. His ruddy face had the same heart-shape as my mother's, though wider and longer. Under the heavy, dark eyebrows of the family, his eyes were blue, and could blaze like prisms with diamond-blue fire in the spotlight. Trimly made, he was very vain of his fine shoulders and legs. He moved swiftly, unless for dazzling effect he made long, grave gestures intended to be sombrely meaningful—though what about, did not always seem clear. His lips were full and his jaw was somewhat heavy, with chin thrust forward habitually. When he looked solemn, the world darkened for those with him, and when he smiled, his smile was repeated—sometimes reluctantly—on every face that saw him. Like all actors he was everybody and he was nobody. Who he was the first time I saw him I remember still. It was at the house of my grandmother—his mother.

She was still living, though she could not leave her bed, or speak, or move any part of her person except her eyelids. For twelve years she had lain in her bed in the front drawing room of my grandfather's house. One day long before I was born her carriage horse had run away, she had been thrown out and dragged, and paralysis resulted. Her patience was saintly—so much that it sometimes irritated those of her children who took care of her, for their inability to equal it. I was taken to see her once a week, and when I was four, I played on the flowered carpeting of her room, making public buildings out of a set of dusty red, blue and yellow stone blocks which included turret shapes, and pinnacles, and arches, as well as ordinary squares and oblongs.

From the front drawing room you could look down the whole depth of the house through a series of doors to other rooms—a sitting room, a parlor, a little library—until you saw the dining room at the far end. It was a perspective in miniature of the Kaiser's palace in Berlin, which my grandfather had visited one time to receive an imperial decoration for being a proper specimen of German culture in the United States. He brought home postcard views of the palace and used to show them to me as I sat on his slippery alpaca lap. If I held the cards close to my face until they blurred slightly, I could imagine that the receding doors in perspective were those of my grandfather's house in Dorchester. The farthest room seemed immeasurably far to me at four, and what might show there, if it was at all unusual, could be startling, and perhaps terrifying.

※

One Sunday morning I was building a railroad station on my grandmother's rug when I looked up idly and glanced along the long view through the tunnel of doors. What I saw made the blocks fall from my fingers.

In the dining room, infinitely far away, loomed an irregular pillar of black which soon took the aspect of a giant. It was robed all in black and it wore a black hat with odd flaring planes that stood upright on top. Smoke clouded its head and face. It posed for a moment in the farthest doorway and then began to move in gliding elegant strides down the rooms toward me. As it came by windows in the third room, then the second, it passed through zones of light, and then after each doorway it entered relative darkness, with changing effect and aspect. I fell back and my throat closed in dry terror so that I could not free the scream that filled me. Still the black column wreathed in smoke moved toward me, making long human steps. As it reached the door of the front room, I was thrown into action at last.

"Grossma, Grossma," I cried so forcefully that my voice split into two notes, "save me, save me, it is the Devil!"

I threw myself upon my grandmother's immense bed and burrowed into her vast, pitiably inert shape, sobbing. She made the only sound she could make—a dove-like mourning note that fell and fell each time, by which she meant to comfort me. My shrieks continued and I dared not look up or around until my mother, in answer to my fright, came and took me up. She was laughing till the tears ran down her cheeks as she soothed me, while I kept up my cry of,

"It is the Devil, the Devil!"

"Nonsense, Richard, my darling, it is your Uncle Fritz, home from the seminary for the weekend. Now come and see him and give him a kiss and be friends.—Fritz, now do be sweet to him. He is really frightened."

"It is a new experience," said my Uncle Fritz, "to be mistaken for the Devil himself while studying for the priesthood and wearing its habit."

For his career had started with a determination to become a priest, a great philosopher, and eventually a bishop. His father told him he must absolutely become a bishop, and this was a command to be obeyed. I had never seen him before. Other priests who had come to our house were dressed in black suits, never in black cassocks and birettas like my uncle. I looked at him now with subsiding grief. But if resentment was mixed with the drying salt of my tears, wonder grew as I was exposed to his comic charm.

"Yet I suppose," he said, "with my black skirts and the cigar smoke around my head, he might be excused for his conclusion. And what if he were right, after all? Out of the mouths of babes." He seemed to look inward for a moment, escaping us all, while he murmured, *Ora pro nobis, nunc et in hora.* When his features lost their animation, they sagged. But he brightened resolutely, and cried, "Come on, my cherub," taking me from my mother, "let us get acquainted. Did you ever see smoke come out of anyone's eyes? Then I will show you."

He sat down and put me facing him on his knees and took a mouthful of cigar smoke and held it behind shut lips, and then brought his face slowly to mine and when we were eyelash to lash he released a wisp of smoke which drifted upward and truly seemed to come right out of his eyes.

"Did you see?" he asked.

"Yes."

"Now watch my ear—this one, the right one."

And he made me see smoke come out of his right ear, just because he said it would.

"Now watch me build a cathedral," he said, and began to twine his fingers so that the two middle ones remained upright together making a spire.

"Now see the front doors," he said, and showed how he could open his bent thumbs apart to make an entrance.

"Now look inside and see the bishop," and he wriggled a finger

[73]

which hung downward in the little pink darkness of his cupped palms.

I began to smile grudgingly.

"Why don't you try it?" he asked, and I began to fumble a cathedral into existence with my fingers, while Uncle Fritz corrected me and helped me until I too had a steeple, and church doors, and a bishop jigging upside down within.

By afternoon we were intensely friends, and later in the day one of his classmates came to visit, and the two talked Latin conversationally in front of all the family, until grown-up sisters and brothers looked at each other in marvelling pride which they did not try to conceal from the gratified seminarians. But I remember thinking, as I heard their florid rumbling Latin which sounded like nothing I had ever heard, "They are just making it all up."

Before supper, while the household gathered behind him on their knees, Uncle Fritz knelt by my grandmother's bed and led us in the recitation of the rosary. His voice rose and rang and fell in such power and style that everyone was more certain than ever that he must become the youngest bishop in the land.

But within a year he was no longer even a seminarian, for what reason nobody was told at home. But my grandfather must have known in patriarchal anger, for he never again spoke to that son, who in some way mortal to sanctity had betrayed the family vocation for the lordly office of bishop. Presently Uncle Fritz found his next vocation, which was for the theatre.

He went on the stage, as they used to say, and more rapidly than most young actors he attained to leading roles. The fact was, even in the seminary days, he had always been an actor. His devil-magic kept up, and on his return to Dorchester as leading man in *The Tudor Rose* he had his opportunity to achieve his masterpiece for me. For magic to succeed, there must be one who reveals and one who believes. I believed every word and every act he revealed to me.

On his arrival at our house that winter evening he had made me a king. How did he know that in my time of childhood my only proper companions were kings and queens, who lived in castles, went hunting, presided at tournaments, gave orders, and wore their crowns all day long? The make-believe was more plausible than the real, and it was so precious that I revealed bits of it only accidentally to my parents and to Anna. But Uncle Fritz needed to be told nothing about me. He knew who I really was.

"Are you about ready to go to sleep?" he asked when he came upstairs after waiting to greet my father.

"No."

"They will be furious with me if I keep you awake. You must go to sleep."

"You said a far kingdom."

"I did?"

"Yes, when you came. You said my far kingdom. But you didn't tell me what."

"Yes, of course." To invent was as easy for him as to be. "They are waiting for Your Majesty. The people go on long pilgrimages from castle to castle, hoping to find Your Majesty in each one, but they never do. I have heard them pray for your return. The Cardinal sings a Te Deum in the Cathedral every evening for you. The poor hold up their arms and beg in your name. The rich nobles laugh at them and say that as long as they have anything to say, Your Majesty will never return to the kingdom."

"Why?"

He gave a velvety, sardonic laugh.

"Because so long as you are the Young Lost King, they will be able to have all the jewels and the gold and the castles for themselves, and they do not care what happens to your poor people."

"They don't?"

I stirred under my covers with love of my poor people and my heart felt hot at the injustices visited upon them which I would redress.

"No. It is a beautiful kingdom and the wicked nobles have stolen it."

"Where is it?"

"Beyond the Sapphire Mountains and at the edge of the Emerald Sea. If you shut your eyes tight you might be able to see it, far away, far away, so that everything is tiny, but perfectly clear. The people will look five inches tall, and their castles will be no higher than a chair, and their hunting horns will sound like mosquitoes outside your ear. But they are all as real as real, like everybody and everything, only small, because they are far away. I think you will be able to see them if you become perfectly still and perhaps fall asleep."

"When?"

"Oh, we never know when these things will happen. We only know they will happen. We must be patient. The Young Lost King is always patient, and in the end, he always enters into his kingdom."

"He does?"

"But certainly."

"I see."

"And now before they make me go downstairs again, I must tell you about seeing a real king and queen."

I felt real, in my kingship, of course, but I knew, too, that we had been acting, and if he had seen a living king and queen I must hear about it.

"I have been in London, you know, playing at the Haymarket Theatre. I had a splendid part, and the critics were kind. We had a great success."

"What is a haymarket theatre?"

"Oh, you are not to think of cows and horses and barns, Richard. It is just an old name for a very old playhouse in London. Well, one day the company had word that the King and Queen of England were supposed to come to see our play, and sit in the royal box, and receive us afterward to say good evening."

"Did they come?"

"They came. The orchestra played *God Save the King* and everybody stood and faced the royal box and in they came, bowing right and left. I looked out through a peep-hole in the curtain. They were magnificent. When the curtain went up and the play began we all played better than we knew how to. I gave the performance of my life."

"What is that?"

"I acted my best."

"I see."

"All during the play we did not look directly at the King and Queen in the royal box, but just the same we kept seeing them, you know how you can do, out of the side of your eye? And when I was off the stage I could look from the wings. They loved us."

"They did?"

"Yes, and when the play was done, three or four of us were sent for to be congratulated, and of course I was one of them. The King shook hands and the Queen bowed. See this hand? It has shaken the hand of the King of England. Don't you want to shake it? Your Majesty is also a king. I am collecting quite a number of kings."

We shook hands seriously. I said,

"What did they look like?"

"Oh, like a real king and queen. He has a brown beard, and blue eyes, and he wore medals and stars, he looks like his cousin the Czar of Russia, and she has golden hair, dressed up high, and she glittered and sparkled with jewels like water in the sun. Her face is rosy pink. I am taller than both of them."

"Did they wear their crowns?"

"Not all the time. Sometimes they took them off and gave them to someone behind their chairs to hold for them. Crowns are very heavy, you know."

"Why?"

"Did you ever weigh a diamond?"

What a master he was—asking me this as though it would be the most natural thing on earth for me to weigh diamonds.

"No," I said, stirring with satisfaction.

"Open your hand," he commanded, and drew from his finger a large amethyst surrounded by small diamonds set in a gold ring. He dropped the ring from a little height into my palm where it struck with weight and force the most part of which I endowed it with. "You see how heavy this one amethyst and these eleven small diamonds are? Well: imagine one hundred and eighty-seven diamonds, and dozens of pearls, rubies, sapphires and emeralds all clustered together on a crown. Very heavy indeed."

"What did you do then?"

"Then? Oh, I simply bowed very deeply, and murmured something like this—*Your Majesties do us immense honor,* which made them glance at each other. I think they will remember me."

"Did they have a royal coach?"

"Of course. All glass and gold. It was waiting outside all that time."

"Did you watch them drive away?"

"Oh, no. I simply let them go. But it was a charming moment. And now, Sire, if I may have your permission to withdraw, it must be time for your royal slumbers?"

He bowed by my bed.

"Is that how you bowed to them?" I asked.

"Yes. Like this"—and he repeated his courtly grace. "Good night. You will have the royal box at my Wednesday matinee. Everything is arranged."

"Good night, Uncle Fritz."

"No, no, you should call me Prime Minister."

"Good night, Prime Minister."

"That's better. Good night, Your Majesty."

I was so drugged with golden visions and intimations of royal power and privilege that I could not stay awake for my father's usual bedtime visit.

※

In the morning I heard remarks at breakfast. It seemed that Uncle Fritz had stayed very late and had left for his hotel in a condition of extreme intoxication. They didn't see how he would ever be able to open his play tonight.

"I wonder when this started," said my mother.

"I saw it several years ago," said my father. "About the time he had that trouble with your father. He was drinking heavily then but he tried to hide it. Now he doesn't seem to care who knows."

"Do you suppose that was why the seminary had to—?"

"It could be. Anyhow, we don't know, and we won't find out by wondering, and furthermore, it is not our affair."

"Did you know he tried to see Papa this time?"

"No. What happened?"

"Papa refused to see him. Fritz then sent him tickets to the play. Papa returned them."

"It does seem rather hard, doesn't it."

"Oh, yes. But when Papa makes up his—"

"It isn't his mind. It is something else. Not his mind."

She sighed.

Much of what you hear means nothing until afterward, when events make it significant. Uncle Fritz remained for me the Prime Minister who alone in the world knew me for my true person and position—the Young Lost King, who would one day return to my people, and be acclaimed with bells, fireworks, prayers and fountains, ending with my marriage in the cathedral to the beautiful princess from the neighboring kingdom who need sorrow no more for my return.

※

On Wednesday morning when I awoke the day was lost in a blizzard. I ran to the window to see the wonder of it—wind made visible by long whistling veils of snow, and ice cunningly fixed upon every branch and twig of my bedroom window tree, and a gray light beating with the wind upon everything. And then I had a second thought which was anguished—what if we could not go to the matinee in weather like that?

And in fact, this was already the decision when I went down to breakfast.

"Unless the storm breaks," declared my father.

"Oh, no, this is going to last all day," said Anna, dreamily putting our plates before us. "I know the signs. You catch your death going out in this."

"Then will you stay home?" I asked my father with a pang of hope—for if he stayed home we could play together all day.

"Oh, no. I'll have to be at the office regardless. I'll get to the corner and see if a streetcar is running."

All morning I watched with desire for the storm to stop. About noon the light turned from silver to gold, and presently the phone rang. It was my father calling to say that if the livery stable could send a carriage for us, and wait all afternoon to bring us home, we could go to the Shubert Theatre.

It was still snowing, but gently, when we set out, and the day was now wet and raw where before it had been lashed with wind from the lake. At the theatre we were expected. A man in a cutaway coat led us to the right stage box.

"The royal box," he announced with a smile. "We were particularly told to have it ready for a certain young gentleman."

"Thank you," said my mother a little sharply. She was suspicious of Uncle Fritz's games with me; she was uneasy at the intensity of my imagined state.

We were alone in the box, whose high, red velvet drapings, caught up in thick loops of gold rope with heavy tassels, and golden armchairs cushioned in red velvet, and red velvet footstools, and a chandelier of crystals hanging directly above us, all seemed to me so fine that they made an excellent place to live, day and night, particularly for a king. In those days theatres imitated the airs of palaces, which had been their ancestors in society.

When the house went dark and the curtain rose releasing a bath of light from another world over all who watched and listened, I was lost even to my kingship. The play was full of great halls with leaded, mullioned windows, and ruffs and farthingales, and rapiers and daggers and small jewelled caskets of secret papers, and a traitorous cardinal, and a noble royal lady—played by the cat-nosed old actress who was the star—and a reckless hotblood of a young nobleman—my Uncle Fritz—who threw himself into risk of the king's wrath to serve her, if "he might but gain her lily hand to kiss."

I leaned on the red velvet rail of the box and poured myself to the stage. It was my first play. It gave me another life again. My uncle

[81]

was my uncle, that was clear; but he was also that raking young lord with his trimmed small mustaches and beard, just put on for the play, who could cross the floor of the great hall in four grand strides, and spring his rapier from its leather baldric while he tensed himself against the tapestry of the wall until he heard who came, and when who came was only a page boy dressed in white hose and white silk doublet bringing a letter heavy with red wax seals, a sudden new air of lovely ease came over all, and when they on the stage took a deep breath of gallant relief, so, obediently, did I.

The page fell to one knee and bent his head, showering his pale gold long hair forward by his cheeks, and surrendered his letter to my lord. I then and there became that page boy, for he must have been my age, and yet there he was, in white light and white court dress, nimbly using the stage with his slim elegantly covered legs, speaking in a clear light voice, inhabiting a Tudor palace, and taking all eyes to himself for the moments while he was before us. I was riven with stabs of love for the circumstance of such a life. I mourned that I was not a page boy exactly like that other one, and I thought that I must run away and become an actor. My mother felt my forehead. It was hot. She made a little breathy sigh, wondering if she should take me home.

At the curtain call after the first act, my uncle, with tender gallantry mixed with teasing comedy, led the star forward to the footlights; and when the applause swelled over them, he bowed not to the audience but exclusively to her, which drove the applause fuller and louder, so that when he came at last alone to bow, he was acclaimed as a great gentleman as well as a dashing actor. But he was not yet done with his people, for when they called him back again, he walked straight to the apron of the stage below the royal box and bowed to me the way he had bowed to the King of England.

"Oh! that monkey!" exclaimed my mother, who disliked for us to be conspicuous in any way not playfully devised by herself.

The audience clapped harder when they saw this, not knowing why they must do so. Some genius of the occasion filled me. I rose and bowed back to my uncle, and I was restored, in that gesture, in public, to my royal if secret estate. The curtain fell to a buzz of speculation. I went limp against the cushions of my chair.

"What is it, darling?" asked my mother.

"Nothing." I wanted only to be alone with my dreams.

"I think you're catching cold."

She felt my face.

"Why, Richard, you're burning up! Come, my dearie, we must go."

"Oh, no."

We had not seen all—the curtain promised to rise again, this time upon a forest glade by moonlight, for the program said so, and the golden page would return, and with him, whom I loved as myself, or who made me love myself as him, would return more of that power to create which stirred within me ever since the scene on the streetcar, a power which my Uncle Fritz—my Prime Minister—drove so strongly into action for me.

"I am afraid we must," said my mother. "You are coming down with something."

At this moment an usher of the theatre brought a folded note with a superscription written in a florid hand. It read, "To His Majesty." The usher handed the note to me but my mother took it from me and read it before I could try.

"Thank you," she said to the usher, "please say that we shall be unable to come backstage after the play as my little boy is ill and I must take him home."

"But I want to stay," I pleaded. "I want to meet the boy in the white clothes and ask him about things."

My mother smiled and dismissed the usher with a firm little nod.

Hurrying me to our carriage, she behaved as though she were rescuing me from evil.

By the time we reached home my fever was like a storm continuously breaking over my perception and wiping it out. I was put to bed, Doctor Grauer was summoned, and when my father reached home late in the evening through delayed traffic in the snow, there was even talk of sending for a nurse to stay by all night. But finally my parents took turns sitting by me in a deep armchair, dozing and listening all night while a little blue glass votive lamp with its candle cast a wavering light over the Holy Mother of God who was present in a delicate blue and gold statue on the wall opposite my bed.

※

That night was the first of many nights of high, clear, loving fantasy, when I felt weightless and insubstantial.

In the mornings I was exhausted but sane for a little while as the fever dropped with daylight. They would take me up soaking wet and bathe me with alcohol and change my pajamas and put me down again, and I would lie gazing at the complicated construction which stood on a low table beside my bed.

It was something I had made weeks earlier—a castle of cardboard overlaid with a thick coating of rock-grey plasticene. The walls and turrets, the battlements, great keep, deep court, and moat showed carefully marked lines of masonry, for with an orange stick given to me by my mother I had incised in the plasticene the shape of every stone in the castle. Painted banners hung from the towers and one wall could be swung aside to reveal the great hall where on a dais stood thrones for a king and queen.

Could the fever—could Uncle Fritz alone—wholly account for the vision of life which now rose so abundantly in me? They could only reveal what I had already created. For a whole week of my illness I could not say where the familiar truth of life ended or where the other world of my creative fever began.

For I was the host of a vision that persisted, and I knew that what I saw and what lived with me were my own creations—the children and the wards of my own fathering. I believed in them so hungrily that I dared to speak of them to my father and mother, certain that they must see as I saw.

"There, in the castle," I said. "Do you see them?"

"Who? What?" they asked fondly.

"The people," I said. "They are just the right size to live in the castle. They are there all the time. They talk to me and I talk to them. They go about doing things and I watch them. Don't you hear them? Don't you see them?"

They comforted me and gave me a drink of cool water and told me to be quiet and go to sleep, now, sleep now, Richard, Richard.

It made my head hurt with bewilderment that they refused to understand how what I told them of was actual, and dear beyond saying. My people. The castle was inhabited by a population of tiny creatures, all exquisitely lovely, all perfectly made in miniature as human beings, and all alive. I thought of them as elves, and in the dazzling and aching logic of my fever, I said to myself that I had read of elfland in many stories, all of which stated that elves lived long ago and did delightful deeds; and if they lived long ago, what was to prevent their living again right now? Imagined into being by myself, they populated the castle as king and queen, and courtiers, and men at arms, and ladies in tall cone-like headpieces from which long veils swept to the stone floor of the great hall, and pages in white who stood by the throne when the king and queen were seated there, and who otherwise played games and pranks up and down the stone stairways which led to the battlements within the walls.

I had only to turn my head on my pillow to see the life of the castle in all its intent glistening activity.

One night in the blue wavering light of Our Lady some of my exquisite little ones brought a long and narrow plank with which they made a bridge from the castle to my bed. They then marched across it to visit me. The king and queen came, and the ladies of the court, and spearmen and bannermen, and the pages with their tiny greyhounds as if they were going out to hunt, and a huntsman in green on a dancing grey horse who raised his horn and wound a call through the night. They spoke to me and I answered, they gave me love and I returned love, the love that had begot them. They told me to sleep peacefully and to get well, and I promised to. The king asked if I would sleep sooner and better if he ordered his knights to make a jousting play for me on my bedspread, and I nodded. In a twinkling the bed became a plain and the court took their places at one side under the shelter of my long legs. The knights entered the lists and in exquisite animation charged each other with lances forward. The clash when they met was like the distant breaking of thin glass, a music of elfland, and they charged and charged. Presently the meadow of the bedspread darkened until it seemed that a storm was coming and would break. At a gesture from the king, the company withdrew in brave display to the castle. The bridge was withdrawn; the castle wall closed after them; a few torches showed in the archers' deep lancet windows and then went out and the storm passed and moonlight like the lamp of Our Lady broke over the silent towers and when my people were all asleep and safe, it was safe for me then to go to sleep myself, feeling my mother's cool hand on my brow, and hearing her tell my father,

"The dream is gone. He is quiet again."

"It seemed like a happy dream."

"Yes. But exhausting, just the same."

But I knew that the world I made was not merely a dream that could be dismissed with a thankful word from relieved parents.

※

Toward the end of last week Uncle Fritz was allowed to come to see me for a few minutes. Evidently he had been cautioned not to excite my imagination with too much powerful suggestion of his own world. Even so I was still the Young Lost King, and sitting down beside me he nodded gravely over my castle, and said,

"That, of course, is where Your Majesty lives for the moment?"

"It is mine."

"You have many men at arms, and archers, and huntsmen?"

How did he know?

"Can you see them?" I asked eagerly. "They come to see me mostly at night. In the daytime the castle is closed."

"Very properly. Tell me, what are they like?"

I told him how high they stood—the king was the tallest, five inches high. They were all perfectly made, just like anyone big, but tiny, and perfectly dressed in the proper clothes for each. When they spoke to me they had to come close to my ear, but I could hear them clearly, and they told me of the treasure deep in the castle dungeons, which they promised to bring out and show me one night. They all wished to serve me, and begged me to say what I would have them do, but I had asked nothing of them but their loyalty, until now. But now I would tell them something very great which they must do for me.

[87]

If my father and mother refused to believe in them, I would ask them to prove they were real by showing themselves to someone else—to my Uncle Fritz.

"Open the castle," I said.

"But it is only afternoon," he protested.

"Yes, but, yes, but I want you to see the people."

"Won't they hide if they see me?"

"I will tell them not to."

"Has anybody else seen them?"

"My father and mother didn't see them. They don't believe they are there at all."

Uncle Fritz sighed fastidiously. His breath carried a sharp, sweet smell of whiskey across my bed.

"No," he said like one of the few in the world who understood the laws of creation, "how could they unless they saw them? And of course they wouldn't be able to see them unless they believed the tiny people were really there."

"But you do, don't you, Uncle Fritz?"

"But of course, if you tell me you have seen them. —Come, let us see."

Following my finger where I pointed, he leaned down to the castle and opened the wall. I saw my people, as usual.

"Do you see them?" I asked.

"But of course. —I must speak to the king."

He bent close to the great hall, making his stage face of excited interest, with his huge blue eyes wide open under a delighted scowl. He thinned his voice until it was just a thread of sound, quite suitable for conversing with elfin royalty, and said,

"I am immensely honored to be received by Your Majesties"—he turned to whisper swiftly to me that the queen was there too—"and I am deeply grateful for all you have done for my lord, the Young Lost King. He is not well at the moment, but when he is completely recovered, surely Your Majesties and your people will help him to find his kingdom again."

Such was his power that I watched him, instead of the king and queen in the castle, to whom he spoke. He turned his ear to hear their reply, and when he had it, he repeated it for me, saying,

"They say they will of course place all their treasure at your disposal, and all their warriors, to help Your Majesty come into his own kingdom. They say that until then you are welcome to live in the castle with them, where you will be treated with royal honors."

"Don't they think I am too big?"

"But if you went to live in the castle, you would be just as small as they are, while you were there."

"Oh," I cried, "let me go right now."

Burning with delight, I began to climb from my bed.

"Oh, no," he said, "I wouldn't do that just yet—the king meant that after you got well, you could decide to—"

"Right now!" I said loudly, and began to struggle against him as he held me in my bed.

"No, Richard, please—"

Our small commotion brought my mother.

"Oh, Fritz, what have you done to him! I told you not to excite him!—Here, darling," she said, taking me against her breast as she knelt by the bed, "be quiet and rest now. Uncle Fritz has been here long enough. He must go now and you must lie down and be quiet for Doctor Grauer when he comes."

"He told me I could go to live in the castle!" I insisted, weakly breaking into tears.

My mother gave her brother a look of worried annoyance and with a little imperious lift of her head, commanded him to leave the room.

"Yes, then," he said. "Goodbye, my lord," and made his bow, throwing his arm away and bending deep. "We are leaving town after the play tonight; but before I go I shall write to the King and Queen of England about you. You will hear from them."

"I will?"

"They will write to you."

"When?"

"Fritz—?" said my mother.

"Yes, I am hasted away," he said, with a glaring smile under a meaningless frown, "adieu, my lord. *Do not believe what they will say of me when I am gone!*"

He went to the door, turned, bowed again with his hand up like a statue's—and then even while I watched under his spell, he vanished. I did not see him so much as take a step or turn into the hall past the doorway—he was there one moment, and the next he was gone. My mother murmured,

"Lie down, my dearie, that was just what he used to call his vanishing trick when we were children at home. He practiced it for days on end. It was a terribly quick sidestep which was so fast you hardly saw him move. Now be easy and dear and do not think of magic any more, or things like that."

"When will the King and Queen of England write to me?"

She made a furious little sigh at the mischief her brother must plant in any mind he met, and said,

"How can I possibly say? Now sleep."

"But I want to know!"

"Hush."

※

I awoke during the night. I felt cool and tired but substantial. The fever was gone. I would soon be ready to enter the castle, assuming the proper size in which to live with my creatures who loved me and whom I loved.

I turned to the castle and opened the wall, eager to tell my people of my good fortune and theirs. There was no one there. The castle was empty. Everyone had gone.

All the rest of the night I lay awake, begging them to return. Where were they? Who had taken them away? In the morning my mother found me sitting up, quite restored to the world, but unhappy beyond telling.

"Oh, you are better—so much better!" she exclaimed. "But what is the matter?"

"They are all gone."

"Who?"

I motioned toward the castle which I could not bear to look at now.

"Ah, Richard, Richard, it was the fever, it was a dream. Never mind, darling. You will not miss them in a day or two."

"But they were mine!"

"Of course. —Now let us see about some lovely cold orange juice and breakfast. Doctor Grauer will be so pleased."

And so I continued all day to recover in my sorrow. It was Sunday, and my father was home. He said that we would all have a picnic lunch in my room. I ate very little, and soon felt drowsy, and lay down, and dozed, while my parents finished their lunch slowly, drinking Rhine wine with seltzer and talking gently. They were sitting in the bay window, which made a little sounding shell for their voices. They could not know how much I might hear.

I was alerted from my disconsolate nap when my father said impatiently,

"I am glad he has gone. He is a bad influence on Richard. It is one thing when a child makes up people and places, but to have some

[91]

grown man dazzle him with deliberate nonsense and unreality—this is dangerous."

"We always saw it in him at home," said my mother.

"And what's more, he drinks far too much."

"Yes, he told me that coming home to Dorchester always upset him. Mama's accident and her death. Papa's hardness. So much to forget. So much he couldn't forget."

"He ought to stop drinking," declared my father with an air of irritable virtue, "and get married, and settle down. If he doesn't, then I tell you, he's headed for no good end."

"Poor darling," sighed my mother. "He is so talented. Really, underneath it all, so sweet. He always was the one to do for everybody else. He wants so terribly to be loved."

"Well, the way to get me to love him is by not telling my son that elves are real, and that he will have the King and Queen of England write to him. —I must tell Richard not to expect anything from them." Bitterly he added, "Fritz has never been in England. Why did he lie to him?"

"Oh—oh, don't," said my mother in a pleading whisper. "Nothing will come, of course, and he will just forget about it, but please, dearie, don't spoil another dream for him just now. He isn't strong yet. Please."

"Oh, all right. I suppose I forget that seven years old is not entirely ready for the truth, the whole truth, and nothing but the truth, about everything. Perhaps you can start too soon with it. But I don't know. I keep feeling that Fritz—Fritz is some kind of a devil, who has to be fought against."

"Oh, no, no. There may be some of the imp in him—Mama used to shake her head sadly over him and say just that. But he is not the devil, himself. Please don't say that."

"Very well, I won't. We'll just let Richard gradually forget him and his imaginary kings and queens."

"Dearie:" said my mother gratefully.

The telephone bell rang downstairs in the front hall and my father went to answer it. I was falling really asleep when—it seemed a long afternoon while afterward—he returned and took my mother's hand and led her out of the room.

"What is it?" she asked, in a gust of fear at his serious air.

"I'll tell you downstairs, dearie. It is pretty terrible."

They went downstairs and I heard him speak against her cheek, and then I heard her lift a desolate cry and say in a storm of feeling to deny the impossible,

"No, oh, no, he couldn't have! Oh, what could we have done for him!"

My father comforted her for the dreadful news he had repeated from the telephone, the main fact of which was kept from me for a long while, until I was completely well; and which in its entirety I heard only many years later, and which told of the death of my Uncle Fritz.

※

The road company of *The Tudor Rose* closed its engagement at the Dorchester Shubert Theatre on Saturday night and with baggage and scenery was to leave by train in the small hours of Sunday morning. It was a snowy night. Everyone was tired, and if anyone looked out for anyone else, they paid attention only to the old star, whom they loved, and who was exhausted.

It was not until the train pulled into Cleveland the next afternoon that anyone noticed that my Uncle Fritz was not on board. The company manager telephoned his hotel in Dorchester. He had not checked out. The hotel desk called his room. There was no answer.

After a considered interval, the hotel detective broke open the door of his room and found him there.

He was dead. In habiliments out of the stock of a theatrical costumer, Uncle Fritz was lying in state on his hotel bed, wearing a bishop's mitre, and a scarlet chasuble over alb and cassock, and a pair of gold-embroidered scarlet gloves. His hands were folded upon his breast and on his right ring-finger his large amethyst edged with diamonds had now become a bishop's ring. Over his face was a faint smile, even though his brows were drawn upward in shadowy sorrow. *So young,* they would say when they found him, *so young to be a lord of the Church, and so handsome, even in death! Such a saintly man!* There was no evidence that anybody else had been in the room with him. Many empty whiskey bottles were neatly arranged on the desk. They soon found a pill box on the floor under the bed. The prescription label revealed that it had contained a sleeping drug to be taken sparingly. In his final act, Uncle Fritz had swallowed all of its contents. The coroner took charge, the verdict was suicide, and he was buried in Dorchester, though not in the family plot in the Catholic cemetery. My grandfather refused to attend the funeral but went at the funeral hour to his own parish church to pray for the repose of the soul of the son he had condemned.

When the news came which I was not immediately told, I felt that everything was different at home; but my mother winked back her tears and touched my face as if to praise life, and all the necessary observances of the funeral were carried out without my knowing anything of them until long afterward.

But Uncle Fritz was not yet quite gone. There was one more gesture from him. On Monday in the mail I received a picture postcard such as were then sold at newsstands showing King George V and Queen Mary of England standing side by side, he in full uniform as Admiral of the Fleet, wearing all his decorations and resting his hands upon a dress sword, and she in a prow-like crown of diamonds and many other jewels and a long gown shining with scabs of light. Addressed to me, the card bore this message on the back in flourished handwriting:

"To our Dear and Respected Cousin, fond wishes for early recovery and restoration to Your Majesty's Throne. George RI—Mary RI."

"You see!" I cried when this was delivered to me, "he was right! He was in England, and he does know them, and he did tell them to write to me!"

I reckoned nothing of the time of mails between England and America. My legacy from my Uncle Fritz was a reality to me until that time long later when I understood the circumstances of his end; and then it was clear that he must have bought the card and mailed it to me shortly before his fatal last scene.

But while it lasted, the illusion he willed to me was powerful, and one day when Anna, in a grumpy mood, serving my lunch in the kitchen, set my dish of cereal down noisily and rudely, I said to her,

"You must not do it that way. I am the Young Lost King!"

"Aah—" she growled, "you just think you are!"

Her scorn, not her words, offended me. After all, how did you know what was true except what you thought?

"How dare you!" I exclaimed.

Anna turned her grey, plate-like old face to the ceiling and shouted,

"Oh, my good God and Jesus!—Go on," she then grumbled, speaking for the real world in the weighty voice that she used in anger, "eat your farina or I'll *how-dare-you* myself!"

The powers which she represented must dethrone me in the end. I ate my farina.

⚜

CHAPTER V

Magic

Yet illusion—with its consolations and empowerments—never really dies in us all our lives long, for we have to keep it alive to conceal our true selves from us. If we seem to be less subject to it as we age, this is only a trick of the personality.

But as childhood is a pursuit of a self, illusion is first of all needed to find the powers of which the self is capable. When I lost my kingdom, I was for a time diffident about my own abilities in the simple tests of boyhood, especially those performed in public. I never expected to know someone worse off than I, from whom to learn how to return safely to the imagination, and thus find harmony with the common world.

⚜

"We go that way to the fort," said the boy in the lead, pointing ahead through the moldy woods.

We had just learned that his name was Jock and that as an older boy he had been told off to take the other boy and me to the fort on the mountain by ourselves because we were late in arriving at summer camp. All the others had already been to the fort and back.

"We always show the new fellows the fort on their first afternoon in camp," said Jock. "It gives everybody a lot of spirit. The camp is called Camp St. George and the fort is called Fort St. George. Only, the fort came first, you see, in the Revolutionary War."

He moved along the path like a forest animal. All of us were in the camp uniform which consisted only of sneakers and khaki shorts. We went in single file, and soon we lost far behind us the voices of boys back in camp. Gold light fell through the thick trees and touched to the leafy floor in silence. In my eighth summer it was the silence that I was most aware of as I met it among all the mysteries of the woods.

Jock striding ahead made almost no noise. The boy who followed me kept falling behind and then running to catch up. Jock wore a hunting knife in a leather sheath behind his right hip. Presently he reached for it, stopped us with his left hand, and threw the knife, which landed with a fine thick sound in the scarred trunk of a birch tree and stayed there like a ray of light.

"I always do that," he said, turning to smile at us, "to make people remember this place." He pointed to a fork of the trail. "That way, to the right, goes down to the lake, to Moccasin Cove. This way, to the left, goes on up the mountain to the fort. We'll rest a minute."

"Thank you," said the boy next to me with his forefinger diffidently on his mouth, as if to excuse the manners he had remembered to invoke.

Jock nodded to him kindly, then told me my name in order to be sure of it.

"You are Richard."

I nodded.

"I didn't get yours," he said to the other one.

"Yes," said the other boy, and then went miserably silent at who he was. We looked at him. He was a little taller than I, but the same age. He was thin and ivory white. His hair was silver yellow,

cut short. He hugged his visible ribs trying to conceal himself, smiling with his mouth but not with his large grey eyes. If I was lost in
hidden bewilderment at where I found myself on this first day
among competent young strangers, and conspicuous as a late arrival,
he seemed worse off than I. I betrayed him in his misery by turning
to Jock with a superior and knowing look. Jock saw me but did
not acknowledge my unkind appeal to make a league with him
against another. My spirits fell, for he was right and I was wrong.

"Suppose you just tell me and Richard, then," he said gently,
"what to call you."

"Yes, well," came the shivering reply as though he had been
chilled through by a long cold swim, "my name is Bayard."

"Where are you from, Bayard?" asked Jock to pass easily to other
matters from such an odd name.

"New York."

"Very good. —And you, Richard?"

"Dorchester."

"Very good.—All right, let's go, men, if we want to have some
daylight on the way back."

The woods at once seemed darker at his words. The heavy sweet
rot of humus hung in the air. Slender aisles of light strode away from
us in every direction. The sky was white above the pierced treetops.
Jock recovered his knife and led us up the mountain. We saw great
boulders and tiny meadows of moss hugging them to the ground.
The trail rose more sharply. Bayard and I began to pant. Jock
glanced around, but judged that we would do without another pause.

At last the ferns by the path stood in brighter green, and more
sky showed ahead, and the trees thinned, and we saw a rocky mound
up against clouds, and we broke out of the woods on a grassy crest
where brown walls of huge blocks of stone outlined the ruined fort.

Jock began to run crossing the slope and climbed a tumble of
fallen stones to reach the crown of an old battlement. He turned to

beckon us on, like one who had breached the walls. He was master of the mountain top, and the whole wooded side that stretched down to the long blue lake, where the forest war of wooden gunboats against scarlet-coated soldiers and painted Indians had won upper New York State for the colonies so long ago.

⁂

We joined him on the rim, and he gave us each a poke to commend us for taking the fort with him. He showed us the old overgrown gun-ports, and the dim rocky outline in the grass of where the powder magazine had been, and the clever placing of the casemates to command a sweep up and down the lake. We could just see scattered in and out of the blue woods of the far shore the little white buildings of the village called Old Foundry, New York, with its sky-blue steeple, and a drift of smoke from its sawmill. That was where the roads ended, and the rain stopped, and the mail came. We had crossed from it earlier in the afternoon by the camp launch. Everything lay far away beyond it—all certainties now lost, the cities we came from, the families who had consigned us to our four weeks of wilderness in July and August.

"Look at this," said Jock, leaping down from the heights. We followed. Half-buried, an old iron howitzer with a crown cast in relief above its touch-hole lay like a lichened rock in a bay of the battlements pointing toward the lake. "How do you like this? They used to call it 'The Old Sow.'"

We stroked it, peered into its mouth where leaves and spider webs softened all edges, and in high spirits Jock like a boy younger than we drove his fist as an iron cannonball through the air and made a soft cavernous "Voom!" with his voice, and we imagined a blast of flame and a white puff of smoke and a plumy splash dying away over the lake. How much he knew.

"And look here," he cried, scrambling up a steep pile of huge blocks at one corner of the fort, "this is where they had the flagpole, and where we ran up our flag when we captured the fort from the British."

We went to follow him. I got to the top beside him and we both looked back for Bayard who was loyally reaching for block after block to join us. He was nearly there when he missed his footing and fell belly-down against the sharp edges of the blocks, slipped across several, and then ended at the bottom in a fall. We went to him.

He couldn't move or speak. His mouth was open like someone shocked into laughter but making no sound. His hands were hovering stiffly above his right leg. The whole shin was bared to the white bone and seeping blood. The pain he felt took his breath away. He was pale blue in his flesh. Jock bent down to him. Bayard looked up at him, and shook his head and shrugged his shoulders. It was a grown-up gesture that apologized for being a nuisance, and it made Jock laugh with pride in someone so brave in such agony.

"Can you straighten it out, Bayard?" he asked.

Bayard tried. His mouth was still open and we could hear his breath now. Jock examined him for fractures. There were none.

"Can you stand?"

He could not, so we lifted him taking an arm each around our necks.

"Hang on, and we'll get you back to camp."

Tears began to run down Bayard's cheeks. He tried to stop them with sharp shakes of his head. They were tears of pain, and had nothing to do with crying. He hoped we knew that. Using his left leg and holding up the other, he hopped along between us as we entered the trail going down from Fort St. George. It was already evening in the woods. The air was almost cold. We were in a misty blue tunnel. Though we had a sense of haste, we seemed to be barely advancing. When we paused to rest now and then we heard silences outside silences and they roared in our ears. I felt guilty because I was only eight, instead of fourteen, like Jock, and pallid instead of Indian brown like him, and because I was in the presence of such great pain, and because I waited to be told what to do in life instead of thinking of it by myself. It was easier for me to make a decision about an imagined problem than about a real one. I remember thinking that if Jock fell dead, and a bear came, I could take the hunting knife and defend Bayard who could not move.

※

It was nearly dark when we heard the music of games calling aloud from the clearing before the camp. Soon afterward we came out of the woods down by the lake. The infirmary was in a log-built lodge across the clearing from the half-moon of tents that followed the line of woods leading in from the shore.

Jock took us straight to the doctor, who was just done with his annual opening-day checkup on conditions at camp St. George. He was closing his bag to return across the lake to Old Foundry where he lived. He was an old man with hair like a dog, and something of a dog's friendly desire, yet inability, to express himself fully to mankind. After helping to lay Bayard down, he just gazed for a second at the white bone and seemed absolutely to see its wild emanations of pain. Then he touched Bayard with his old paw and said,

"Hurts pretty bad, 'm?"

Bayard shook his head but tears came back not only for pain but the idea of it.

"We're going to have to clean it out," said the doctor, now putting on a waggish old voice, "bits of leaf mold in it, and lichen, and this and that. —Want me to whiff you some chloroform?—Iodine'll sting like blazes, most likely, I'll have to pour it right out of the bottle."

Bayard looked at Jock, and then at me, and said in indrawn breath making a long word out of it, "No," and then added on the last gulp of air, "—thank you."

"Very well, sir, damn it," said the doctor, and spent no more time on anything but what needed doing. "You," he commanded Jock, "go find Mr Mac and tell him I want to see him here." Jock ran out. "You," he said to me, "hold on to my fine fellow here." And while the doctor worked adding pain to pain, the mystery of inexpressible friendship, born of these events that had befallen young strangers, sprang alive between Bayard and me.

When he was done, the doctor said,

"That's a young man without fear, isn't it?" and cuddled one of his old hands on Bayard's head.

※

And I thought so too, for quite some days, as the camp activities became habitual, and every day brought challenge. If they only knew, I thought, how different I am at home; how much I am loved there; how many times I am able to do splendid things in my own place and make everyone look across the top of my head to trade glances about me. Here, at camp, I could not make my own terms, but had to observe those already powerful and inexorable among the boys.

There were some boys younger than I, some older, and a few veterans, like Jock, who had been coming to camp every summer for four years or more. Jock was the lord of all. Mr Mac, the blue-eyed, white-haired director of the camp, puffing on his pipe, lurching a little like an elderly boy, was often seen walking thoughtfully with Jock, getting his advice on how to handle a difficult case among the "Tadpoles," as the littlest campers were called. And Jock always had something to tell him, with confident respect and yet an air of magnificent indifference, as if it meant nothing to him whether Mr Mac, or any of the councilors, took his advice. Even the boys soon understood that it was wise of Mr Mac to have Jock on his side. Jock had influence. All the boys wanted to be like him, and, such was the mercy that played over them at their stringy stage of life, many thought they were. He was tall, but not yet as tall as he was going to be. His skin was tanned light brown, his eyes were dark brown. His round face was always friendly, which was reassuring, in view of his admired bunches of muscle, and the intuitions of savage power they aroused in so many of us.

Bayard could not leave his cot for many days. He lived in the last tent, farthest from the lake, and nearest the mountain. There were six boys to a tent. His mates brought him his food, and Mr Mac, beaming upon him for recovering without complications, came and saw him every day, or if he could not come, sent Jock. I went whenever I was not obliged to attend "Activities." Alone with me, Bayard was easily communicative. I believed that he had special talk because he was a New York boy. Actually, he was only using expressions he had grown up hearing at home, which were special since he came from a special family, as we presently learned.

"What are they doing today?" he would ask, and I would tell him of the world outside his tent.

"I talked to Jock for quite a while."

"You did? Yes. Let me imagine what you talked about."

"You never will."

"Why? What rubbish. What was it."

"You."

"Me? Oh, what rubbishy rubbish."

"No, the day you got hurt, he said Mr Mac came running, and all Mr Mac could say over and over was, Why did it have to be *that* boy? Oh-my-God, why did it have to be *that* family? And baa-baa-baa, and Why did it have to be on the first day of camp? Baa-baa-baa."

When I told him this, Bayard sat up sharply and cried in a sort of over-bred horror,

"He didn't send for them, in heaven's name!"

"I don't know. But Jock said he was certainly scared about your family."

That was how it got around that Bayard came from one of the two or three richest families in America—so rich that they were public, and so helplessly public that their youngest son was what he was.

It was known that Mr Mac went across the lake to Old Foundry every day to make a long distance call about Bayard. The flaps on Bayard's tent were rolled up all day, and he would lie on his cot and stare at the path that came from the dock, dreading to see his father or his mother arriving to publish not only how frantic they were about him, but also how special he was, and how silly it was for him to hope that he might hide anywhere, which, in his lively intelligence, was most of all what he thought of in any situation.

But no family appeared, and he worked to prepare himself for the day when he must leave his cot and return to the lake-side world where everyone now knew who he was.

"What are they doing now?" he would ask.

"Activities," I would answer.

"In heaven's name, what kind?"

My heart sank as I told him, for, feeling my own doubts more than his, I lived over again all my shortcomings. But I tried loyally to sound enthusiastic.

"They climb the rope."

"Does everybody watch?"

"Oh, sure."

"How gash-ghastly." He tried to smile. "What else?"

"We have archery matches."

"I can do that."

"And we play baseball. They choose up different sides all the time."

He twisted on his cot, and said,

"They'll never choose me, and I don't care a tinker's damn.—Do they choose you?"

"Sometimes. Not always."

"What do you do if they don't?"

"I watch and yell for my side."

"I see.—What else?"

"And then they blow the whistle and everybody has to run lickety-split down to the lake, and then it is time for water games."

"I suppose it couldn't be more tiresome.—How do they do it?"

I told him, and remembering how I despised myself for being so awkward, so ill at ease in the water where everyone, where Jock especially, was so spectacular and brilliant, I became defensive and I boasted of the fun. When the whistle sounded, everybody stopped what they were doing no matter what, and ran for the shore. There in furious haste everyone tore off his sneakers and shorts and plunged into the lake "to get wet all over." Jock usually trotted out to the end of the dock to show off a few dives. Unlike all the rest of us, he wore trunks, to identify him with Mr Mac and the senior councilors, who also wore them.

After Jock's expert diving demonstration, two canoes were pushed out into the water. A boy stood in each, while another paddled, and a fight ensued between the canoes. The weapons were long poles padded at the ends with which the standing boys thrust at each other.

"Who does that?" asked Bayard.

"Everybody. You have to take turns."

"You mean with everybody else watching?"

Yes, everybody watched. And then there was follow-the-leader, when everybody lined up and came in turn to the end of the dock and had to do what Jock did first—various dives, jumps, and tricks.

"What do they do when they watch?"

"Haven't you ever been around a bunch of kids, Bayard?"

"No, no, I haven't, how should I know?"

"Well, they yell and whistle if you're good, and they splash and say pee-yu if you're not."

"No," he said, "my family sent me here to learn how to be with people. How absurd.—Does anybody tell you how to do it if you don't know how?"

"Yes. Jock helps everybody."

"I suppose he can do them all, the wretch?"

How treasonable, to call Jock a wretch—and how distinguished!

"Oh, yes."

We both saw him intensely in imagination for a moment.

"Look, Richard," said Bayard, "do you do all the things?"

"Y-yes," I lied. "Of course I do."

I denied him the companionship in failure which he had hoped for. He felt of his leg which was healing rapidly, and which would soon be well enough for him to join the outer life again. He licked his lips. He gulped.

"Oh, dear God," he said.

Full of what was the matter with me, I never wondered if the same thing was the matter with him.

The day finally came when Bayard was let out on crutches, and then the day when he could do without them. Mr Mac put his arm around Bayard's shoulders and said he was proud to see him ready now to take his place in the "wholesome, well-rounded activities which every boy enjoyed at Camp St. George."

"Can you swim, Bayard?"

Bayard nodded and swallowed.

"Fine. Fine."

The whistle blew, everyone raced to the shore. The water broke in diamond sprays about young thundering bodies. Echoing off the lake our voices rose into the woods, up to the rim of our mountain cup, as we broke the calm of the elements. Bayard was lost in the flashing turmoil when Jock dove off the pier and swam over to me.

"You take number one boat," he ordered, and in a friendly way ducked me under the water. The canoes were being swum out as I came up. I was hauled into one and given the pole. The bathers made a wide ring about the two canoes which now approached each other. Partisan cries arose. I saw the other pole searching toward me in the high sunshine. Holding my pole with a tortured grip I leaned forward in a grinding resolve to distinguish myself. The pole was long and trembled heavily because I held it too close to the near end. To keep in balance I had to lean back again and I leaned too far. The canoe skidded aside under me, I threw away the pole, and fell into the water in defeat. My boat lost even before it had engaged the enemy.

I felt my heart and my ears ready to burst under the water. I stayed under as long as I could, wavering dimly among the broken skeins of sunlight, the fronds of green that grew from the clear lake-floor, and a little troop of fish that I saw swim toward me and then all looking sideways flip away together in a darting glide.

I broke into air at last. My place was already filled in my canoe. A new battle was making. I was forgotten, when all I now wanted was another chance. If I got it, how I would—and I comforted myself with a cloudy picture of winning a naval engagement in a wooden frigate coming under the guns of Fort St. George with a glory of flame, smoke and thunder, to take the whole wooded mountain where fame had passed me by.

"Follow-the-leader!" yelled Jock in a little while. He harried the boys out of the water and up the dock, making them get in line. Among them he found Bayard. With brilliant happiness he dragged him past dozens of others and thrust him into the line near its head. It was a gesture that told everyone that Bayard had his esteem, and that he was glad to welcome him after his long and painful absence, and that he must have a preferred place at his first follow-the-leader. Then Jock went to the edge of the dock where the springboard was and made a perfect swan dive. The next boy, and the next followed him, doing as well as they could. Bayard was then at the springboard, and all eyes and voices turned on him.

With his arms hugged about his ribs he stood looking down, trying to vanish.

Yells arose to make him dive.

He stood lost. He was paralyzed. Those near enough could see him shivering.

Catcalls and jeers.

The ones waiting in line danced with impatience. He was exposed as the center of furious attention.

Finally he moved. He took a deep breath, he shrugged in his familiar way, and turned and walked away from the springboard, and down the line to the shore. Silence fell in amazement. At the edge of the wood he found his shorts and sneakers and put them on. Without glancing around at us, he went toward the tents.

Presently I followed him. Jock caught up with me. We both saw Bayard stumble to his knees. He vomited like a sick cat and at once rose and went on to his tent, where he threw himself on his cot. When he heard us come in, he turned and said, "I'm sorry," rapidly, in a grown-up, social way, and his teeth chattered.

Jock sat down next to him like a family doctor and looked at him in a long silence. Then he smiled, to remember that the world was fair, and all good things would come to pass, and not a man lived who would not in the end perceive the right.

"Never mind, Bayard," he said, "you'll do all right tomorrow."

Bayard rolled his head on his hard unpillowed cot.

"Oh, no, I won't," he said, deathly-white, "I want to, I want to, but I can't, I can't."

And he couldn't. He went each day to lose himself in the throng, but each time when he was thrust out before them all, his agony of shyness turned him rigid and he could not move. He was pushed off the dock by those who told him he was crazy. Promptly agreeing with them, he fell, he recovered himself, and ran away.

One day I followed him. He took the forest trail up the mountain, and at the fork, turned right, and ended up at Moccasin Cove. He did not hear or see me. Nobody ever went there alone. A water moccasin had been seen there years before, and in the imagination of the camp, much developed by speculation and joyful horror, it was now a fearsome place. Bayard, alone, climbed a rock in the cove, and there by himself performed the dives he could not do in public. Whatever he was afraid of, it was not physical.

It was necessary with a smile of professional understanding for Mr Mac, and even Jock, to conclude that Bayard was "a special case." Jock, already guardian of order and sanity in the affairs of life around him, had a quiet talk with Mr Mac. If the doctor might say that Bayard, in order not to risk infection in his recent wound, which though healed might rip open again some day, must not quite yet undertake violent exercise, then even if it came a little late, there would be a proper explanation of so much that bothered everyone. Bayard could thus be ordered not to do what he refused to do, which would restore health to authority. The other boys would hear a logical excuse for special arrangements accorded one of their number, and would thus have no grounds for resentment. Bayard himself might benefit by an official removal of pressure.

The whole plan was very much Jock, and Mr Mac, crinkling his face with thanks for manliness renewed once again in life through Jock, acted. An appointment was made for Bayard to cross the lake in the launch one afternoon to see the doctor at Old Foundry. I wanted to go with him, but was feverish from a thick map-like outbreak of poison oak all over me, and was supposed to lie in my tent covered with sugar of lead, that smelled of the sting it made when applied. Bayard stopped to see me on his way down to the dock.

"Is there anything you want from the village?"

"No. I wisht I was going along."

"So do I, by all means. Thank whatever gods there be they are not sending anyone with me, in charge of me, I mean.—I plan to do a little shopping."

"What are you going to get?"

"I haven't the faintest idea. Just look around, I expect, as soon as I've done with the absurd old leech."

I looked at him with an idea that came in a flash.

"You aren't going to run away, are you?" I asked.

"What rubbish. Of course not—" but I saw how the idea was not new to him. A look of hungry abashment came into his face, as though his innermost longings had been exposed. He nodded and went rapidly off to the dock. I got a lump in my throat at the idea of the freedom that lay beyond Old Foundry, New York, and Bayard gone into it forever.

I took a nap and on awakening saw that something odd was going on in Bayard's tent, the last one in the line of which mine was in the middle. The tents made a half-circle backed up by the woods. With flaps up, day and night, unless it rained, the tents were open to the forest breath. Now I could see Jock and Mr Mac and one of the councilors going through the lockers in the distant tent. There were no boys about. Soon the lockers in the next tent were inspected, and the next, until they came to my tent.

"It's all right, Richard," said Jock, "this is a routine check-up," but he winked his off-eye as if to say he had more to tell me, and would do so when the ancient adults were not about. If he was now enacting with them a role in the law, he was still nearer to boy than to man, and to me than to them. Later when Mr Mac and the other councilor were already entering the next tent, Jock lingered a second to whisper to me that some money had been stolen from Bayard's locker, and they were looking for what they could find. I was not to mention this to anyone for fear of alerting the thief. But with my poison oak, and all, he just thought it would make me feel better to know what was going on. Dazed with admiration for his leadership—a quality much discussed at Camp St. George—I thanked him in a mumble which he accepted with expert apprecia tion of its concealed worth.

"Jock—" I added, ready to show him my gratitude and also to make a sensation by telling him that Bayard had run away; but when he paused to hear me, I felt a stronger loyalty to Bayard, and I said, "Oh, nothing."

Jock made a gesture of comic obscenity at me and joined the others. I watched the inspection reach the other end of the row, and if it turned up any discoveries, there was no sign.

※

The lake was white with late afternoon light when the launch appeared from Old Foundry. It cut a fine, long, black curve in the surface of the still water, coming to the dock with exactly enough momentum to reach the soft wet timbers with a velvety nudge. I was astonished to see Bayard spring from it before it stopped moving. He went off toward Mr Mac's office in the lodge, and then in a few minutes headed for me. He carried three brown paper bags.

"What did you buy?" I asked.

"Oh, nothing.—Here," and he handed me one of the packages, "I got you something."

I tore open the bag, to reveal a violently colored photograph of Fort St. George at sunset, framed in mother of pearl with small gilded pine-cones tacked to the corners, and lettered in black across the bottom of the frame, "Souvenir of Old Foundry, New York."

"Do you like it?" he asked, looking at me with a puzzled air.

"Oh, yes, by all means," I replied, meaning to sound like him. "Thank you very much. It's a peach."

"But I thought you'd laugh," he said. "It's so gash-ghastly it's wonderful. I mean at home, we always try to find each other the most awful thing we can buy."

[113]

Embarrassed at missing the point, I said stubbornly,

"No, it's beautiful. I really like it." He shrugged. "What's in the other ones?" I asked.

He put one, a flat package, between his knees and opened the other, a large one bulging with interesting lumps, to reveal a dozen long fat cannon firecrackers.

"Don't tell anybody," he said. "We are not supposed to have any. I bought all they had, left over from the Fourth of July. We can use them sometime."

"What's in that one?" I demanded, pointing to the thin bag.

"Oh, that." He took it and waved it idly. "Nothing much. Just something I got."

But his efforts at sounding off-hand were not convincing. His teeth chattered once or twice till he clamped them together. Charged with excitement, he refused to show it. He changed the subject.

"I saw the absurd leech. He gave me a letter to take to Mr Mac. He says my leg won't let me do activities. He's crazy. My leg's all right. He was just overcome with his own importance."

The twilight was coming. Boys were drifting back to the tents to get ready for supper. Bayard went to his own. That evening after supper, while Mr Mac was reading aloud by the council fire out in the open, Jock drew aside some of the boys a couple at a time, and told them that everybody had a chance to show real leadership now, and help Bayard along, and not make fun of him because he wasn't allowed to do the things other people could do, because of his leg, for the doctor had said so, and nobody wanted anybody to come down with a terrible infection, like blood poisoning, and have a leg chopped off, or anything, did they? None questioned his right and power to create opinion, and all fell in with his program of mercy for Bayard, who would never again be asked to disgrace himself before all eyes. With this preparation, what happened next day at water games was all the more astounding.

My poison oak was better, and I was returned to activities. The canoe fights were over, and follow-the-leader was well along, when from the woods at the shore broke a running figure of a boy, stripped for swimming. It was nobody we recognized, for its face was covered by a large, stiff, rubberized mask with huge ears that stuck out on each side of a wide painted grin. It was the face, though wildly exaggerated, of someone I had seen somewhere long before—the face of a comic tramp. Its eyes bulged with white under heavy black eyebrows arched in indignant surprise. Its cheeks were shiny red. Its nose was like a tomato. Its jaws were painted in the heavy ash color of a tramp's unshaven beard. From one corner of its mouth protruded a brown cigar stub fixed in place. The zany head looked much too large for the young thin body which it crowned with wild hilarity.

Racing down the dock past the line of everybody who waited to follow the leader, the figure roughly pushed aside the next boy up, ran out on the springboard without pausing, and in an airy sprawl of complete abandon, threw itself off the board and fell into the water with an immense splash.

After a clap of amazed silence, a collective shout went up.

The tramp reappeared from the lake, climbed the ladder to the dock, took the board again, and with his outrageous grin lifted to the sky, performed a perfect swan dive.

We watched spellbound to see him come up, but he did not break the water where he had disappeared. How could anyone stay down that long? Yelling began. Jock dived off the dock to look for him, and came up without him. The excitement was furious, until we heard a muffled cry from another direction, and turned to see the tramp waving grotesquely from the other side of the dock, to which he had gone under water, and where having climbed up he now cawed like a crow for attention. As soon as he had it from everyone, he ran splay-legged along the dock and off into space as if he didn't know where the dock ended, and signalling mock-anguish in midair, hit with a resounding belly-flop and sank. With the most careless splendor, he could do anything.

Staring and yelling, we believed the mask, not the body. In brilliant sunshine, our familiar surroundings only made the visitor seem more wonderful and strange. A power beyond doubting was among us and we were dazzled even while our bellies ached with laughter. If I suspected in one box of my mind who it was who found magic release behind the mask, in another I was under the spell of a mystery as old as myth. When the tramp came up for air again, and this time was captured and dragged to the shore and thrown down on the sand, I was among those who crowded close to see who it was as Jock, choking with laughter, pulled off the mask to reveal Bayard's serious, excited face.

When the commotion was over and Bayard was let go, I walked back to his tent with him and saw him toss the mask carelessly into the locker at the foot of his cot.

"Was that the other thing you bought yesterday?" I asked.

"Yes, in the same store where I got that vile affair for you."

"Do they have any more?"

"No. This was the only one."

I was saddened by the news, and with many inner qualms came to my decision as the night fell and the camp gathered about the council fire. I completed my plans and when the camp was asleep in its tents with the flaps rolled open to the aromatic night, I carefully left my cot, stooped my way out of the rear of my tent into the edge of the woods, and went on the soft, loamy ground to the last tent in the line. I entered stilly, opened Bayard's locker, and stole his mask. I did not ask myself how, after the expensive gift he had given me, I could rob my friend. With his mask, I could go to Moccasin Cove alone, and wearing it I could find the power to perform in glory, amidst future acclaim, those feats at which I tried and failed before my fellows every day.

Retreating to the woods with the treasure which was still damp in my grasp, I was taken by hands and revealed by a flashlight.

"We've got him," whispered Mr Mac.

They took me away to the lodge, a thief.

"Where is the money?" they asked. "We knew whoever had stolen once would try it again. It was just a matter of watching for him. Where is it?"

But in the end, they believed me, and wondered why anybody would take such risks just to steal a mask. They kept the mask to return it to Bayard in the morning. Jock took me to my tent. On the way he made me promise many times never again to take anything that was not mine, and when he left me, he said that so long as I kept my promise, he—and he meant the wide, good world—would forget the whole thing.

❦

But with morning I knew great remorse, and went by myself up to Fort St. George to consider how I could make it up to Bayard for what I had done to him. Suppose I had never been caught, and Bayard's mask were gone? Without it, how could he again repeat his triumphs? So in just the stage of civilization to do so, I respected wholly the magic in the mask.

The morning was pungent all about the old fort. The silvery dampness of the night hung in rock shadows. Far up the lake lingered morning mist. All was quiet until I heard someone coming to the mouth of the trail. I dropped behind fallen stones to hide.

It was Bayard, carrying one of his paper bags. He looked all about. I heard him say, "I could have sworn on a Gutenberg Bible that he came up here," and he seemed perplexed and friendly. I stood up and called across the grassy cup of the fort.

"There you are," he said. "It's high time. Come here."

We met in the middle of the fort. He reached into the bag and hauled out the mask and held it toward me.

"Here," he said. "I won't need it any more."

"Oh, no," I said.

He had been brought up in the anguished enlightenment of his family to give away anything he had that someone else wanted. Possessions were not owned, but only held in trust.

"I can't," I said, and because in shame I could not then accept the mask, I felt the need of it for some years thereafter.

He shrugged, stuck it back in the bag, and said,

"They told me all about it. Nobody cares. What I did was much worse."

"What."

"I lied when I told them my money was stolen. Nobody stole any. I just said so, so they wouldn't think I had twenty-five dollars that I could run away on."

I regarded him gravely. An inkling of pity long later to be understood struggled to reach between us. What desperate plots lay dearly alive just under so many faces, and what relentless confessions fell in idle courage from the same lips that could smile and lie.

"So I told old Mr Mac this morning, and *he: was: furious.*"

"Then what happened?"

"Then," he said, dismissing all nuisances along with our separate crimes, "I went to the mess hall, and snagged a handful of matches, and look here."

He dumped the fat bag out on the stones, making a scarlet mound of cannon crackers. Taking one, he went to the half-buried howitzer called the "Old Sow." He put the cracker into its maw, lighted its fuse with a match, and we both flopped down behind the cannon which with gestures we pretended to aim out over the lake.

There was a breathless moment beaded with the sputter of the fuse, and then in a deep, hollow roar, the "Old Sow" spoke. Cannonading sounded again from Fort St. George in ruins on the mountain.

We loaded and fired again and again, making sport with our history that was all about us in the bright air. We shook the mountain and dominated the lake, capturing the future with heroic attitudes out of the past. We imagined gunboats under sail riding heavily below us, and blue tail-coats that showed white facings, and heavy fringed gold epaulettes falling across shoulders twisting in action, and the flash of cutlasses, and the hoot of commands; and on both shores of the lake, the long points of wooded land faded one beyond another paler and paler blue till in the distance all—lake, land, and sky—merged in airy white like a page that we would write on with our lives.

CHAPTER VI

❦

Black Snowflakes

So, it seemed, I most often learned from one thing what another was.

It was this way when we all went from Dorchester to New York to see my grandfather off for Europe, a year or two before the first World War broke out. His thoughts and longings returned more and more to his homeland as the years in America brought him loss and sorrow and ailings. His wife was gone, his youngest son, whom he had dedicated to glory, was dead in scandal, unforgiven, and desire itself must have seemed to turn toward an order in design which a sense of time wasting made urgent.

As I grew through boyhood, I was increasingly fearful of him, for I no longer took him for granted as in infancy. Large, splendidly formal in his dress, and majestic in manner, he yet led me to wonder about him with something like love, for he made me know in ways I cannot describe that he believed me someone worthwhile. At nine years old, I could now imagine being like him myself, with glossy white hair swept back from a broad pale brow, and white eyebrows above china-blue eyes, and rosy cheeks, a fine sweeping mustache and a full but well-trimmed beard which came to a point. Except for his smaller beard, he looked something like Johannes Brahms in his last phase. He sometimes wore eyeglasses with thin gold rims and I practiced in secret how to put these on and take them off. I suppose I had no real idea of what he was like, for I never imagined that my elders had feelings.

❧

There was something in the air about going to New York to see him off that troubled me. I did not want to go.

"Why not, my darling?" asked my mother the night before we were to leave. Before going down to dinner, she busily came in to see me, to kiss me goodnight, to turn down the night-light, to glance about my room with her air of giving charm to all that she saw, and to whisper a prayer with me, looking toward Our Lady, that God would keep us.

"I don't want to leave Anna."

"What a silly boy. Anna will be here when we return, doing the laundry in the basement or making Apfelkuchen just as she always does. And while we are gone, she will have a little vacation. Won't that be nice for her? You must not be selfish."

"I don't want to leave Mr Schmitt and Ted."

My mother made a little breath of comic exasperation, looking upward for a second.

"You really are killing," she said in the racy slang of the time, "why should you mind leaving the iceman and his old horse Ted for a few days? They only come down our street twice a week. What is so precious about Mr Schmitt and Ted?"

"They are friends of mine."

"Ah. Then I understand. We all hate to leave our friends. Well, they too will be here when we return. Don't you want to see Grosspa take the great ship, you can even go on board the liner to say goodbye, you have no idea how huge those ships are, and how fine? This one"—she let a comic effect come into her voice as she often did when pronouncing German words—"is called the *Doppelschrauben Schnelldampfer Kronprinzessin Cecilie.*"

"Why can't I go the next time he sails for Germany?"

At this my mother's eyes began to shine with a sudden new light, and I thought she might be about to cry, but that did not seem possible, for she was also smiling. She leaned down to hug me and said,

"This is one time we must all go, Richard. If we love him, we must go. Now you must not keep me. People are coming for dinner. Your father is waiting for me downstairs. You know how he looks up the stairs to see me come down. Now sleep. You will love the train as you always do. And yes: in New York you may buy a little present for each one of your friends and bring them back to them."

It was a lustrous thought to leave with me as she went, making a silky rustle with her long dinner dress that dragged on the floor after her. I lay awake thinking of my friends and planning my gifts.

※

Anna came to us four days a week from the Lithuanian quarter of town and I spent much time in her kitchen or basement laundry listening to her rambling stories of life on the "East Side." I remember wondering if everybody on the "East Side" had deep pock marks like those in her coarse face, and one day, with inoffensive candor, I asked her about them, and she replied with the dread word, "Smallpox."

"They thought I was going to die. They thought I was dead."

"But you weren't?"

"Oh, no," quite as serious as I, "I fooled them all. But look at me. There was a time when I thought I would have been better off dead."

"Why, Anna?"

"Who wants a girl looking like this?"

"Did they care?"

"Oh, my man came along, and I forgot about it."

"What is it like to be dead, Anna?"

"Oh, dear saints, who can tell that who is alive?"

It was all I could find out, but the question was often with me. Sometimes in late still afternoons, when I was supposed to be taking my nap, I would think about it, and I would hear Anna singing, way below in the laundry, and her voice was like something hooting far away up the chimney. It always seemed the same song that she sang, and I think now that she simply made up a tune long ago, and was satisfied with it, and so hooted it over and over, with words I never understood. Drowsily I wondered if the song were about dying. What should I buy for Anna in New York?

And for Mr Schmitt, the iceman. He was a heavy-waisted German-American with a face wider at the bottom than at the top, and when he walked he had to lumber his huge belly from side to side to make room for his great jellying thighs as he stepped. He had a big, hard voice, and we could hear him coming blocks away, as he called out the word "Ice!' in a long cry. Other icemen used a bell, but not Mr Schmitt. I waited for him when he came, and we always exchanged words, while he stabbed at the high cakes of ice in his hooded wagon, chopping off the pieces we always took—two chunks of fifty pounds each. His skill with his tongs was magnificent, and he would swing his cake up on his shoulder, over which he wore a sort of rubber chasuble, and wag his way in heavy grace, hanging his free hand out in the air to balance his burdened progress up the walk along the side of our house to the kitchen porch. He made two trips, one for each cake of ice, and he blew his breath with extra effort to interest me.

"Do you want to ride today?" he would ask, meaning that I was welcome to ride to the end of the block on the seat towering above Ted's rump, where the shiny, rubbed reins lay in a loose knot, because Ted needed no guidance, but could be trusted to stop at all the right houses and start up again when he felt Mr Schmitt's heavy vaulting rise to the seat. I often rode to the end of the block, and Ted, in his moments of pause, would look around at me, first from one side, and then the other, and stamp a leg, and shudder his rattling harness against flies, and in general treat me as one of the ice company, for which I was grateful.

What to buy for Ted? Perhaps in New York they had horse stores. My father would give me what money I would need, when I told him what I wanted to buy, and for whom. I resolved to ask him, provided I could stay awake until the dinner party was over, and everybody had gone, when my father would come in on his way to bed to see if all was well in the nursery. At such times I might hear him and awaken and answer him still dreaming. He called me "Doc" because he believed that I would one day study medicine and carry a narrow black bag full of delicious colored pills like coarse sand in little phials, like the ones in the toy doctor's kit which I owned. How much love there was all about me, and how greedy I was for even more of it.

❊

Having no voice in the decision, I was with everyone else the next day when we assembled at the station to take the Empire State Express. It was a heavy, grey, cold day, and everybody wore fur but me and my great-aunt Barbara—Tante Bep, as she was called. She was returning to Germany with my grandfather, her brother.

This was an amazing thing in itself, for first of all, he always went everywhere alone, and second, Tante Bep was so different from her magnificent brother that she was generally kept out of sight. She lived across town on the East Side in a convent of German nuns who received money for her board and room from Grosspa. I always thought she resembled an ornamental cork which my grandfather often used to stopper a wine bottle opened but not yet emptied. Carved out of crisp soft wood and painted in bright colors, the cap of the cork represented a Bavarian peasant woman with a blue shawl over her flat-painted grey hair. The eyes were tiny dots of bright blue lost in deep wooden wrinkles, and the nose was a heavy wooden lump hanging over a toothless mouth sunk deep in an old woman's poor smile. Despite the smile the carved face showed anxiety. The same was true of Tante Bep. Left alone in Germany many years ago, she might have starved, if her splendid brother, who had become prosperous in America, had not saved her. He sent for her and gave her what American life she knew with the German nuns who reassuringly kept the ways of the old country. Her gratitude was anguish to behold. Now, wearing her jet-spangled black bonnet with chin-ribbons, and her black shawl and heavy skirts which smelled rather like dog hair, she was returning to Germany with her brother, and I did not know why.

But her going was part of the strangeness which I felt in all the circumstances of our journey. In the Empire State Express my grandfather retired at once to a drawing room at the end of our car. My mother went with him. Tante Bep and I occupied swivelled arm chairs in the open part of the parlor car, and my father came and went between us and the private room up ahead.

"Ach Gott!" exclaimed Tante Bep many times that day, looking out the window at the passing snowy landscape, and then at me, moving her tongue inside her sunken mouth, as she smiled to console me and blinked both eyes to encourage me—for what? Tante Bep prayed her rosary, trying to hide her beads in the voluminous folds of her skirt. But I could see the rosewood beads and the worn, heavy crucifix now and then as she progressed by Hail Marys, using her work-toughened old thumbs to advance the stages of her chain of mercy.

In the afternoon I fell asleep after the splendors of lunch in the dining car. Grosspa's lunch went into his room on a tray, and my mother shared it with him. I hardly saw her all day, but when we drew into New York, she came to awaken me, saying,

"Now, Richard, all the lovely exciting things begin! Tonight the hotel, tomorrow the ship! Come, let me wash your face and comb your hair."

"And the shopping?" I said.

"Shopping?"

"For my presents."

"What presents?"

"Mother, Mother, you have forgotten."

"I'm afraid I have, but we can speak of it later."

It was true that people did forget at times, and I knew how they tried then to render unimportant what they should have remembered. Would this happen to my plans for Anna, and Mr Schmitt, and Ted? My concern was great—but just as my mother had told, there were excitements waiting, and even I forgot, for the while, what it had seemed treacherous of her to forget.

We drove from the station in two limousine taxis, like high glass cages on wheels. I worked all the straps and handles in our cab. My father rode with me and Tante Bep. He pointed out famous sights as we went. It was snowing lightly, and the street lamps were rubbed out of shape by the snow, as if I had painted them with my water colors at home. We went to the Waldorf-Astoria Hotel on

[126]

Fifth Avenue. Soon after I had been put into my room, which I was to share with Tante Bep, my father came with an announcement.

"Well, Doc," he said, lifting me up under my arms until my face was level with his and his beautifully brushed hair which shone under the chandelier, and letting his voice sound the way his smile looked, "we are going to have a dinner party downstairs in the main dining room."

I did not know what a main dining room was, but it sounded superb, and I looked pathetic at the news, for I knew enough of dinner parties at home to know that they always occurred after my nightly banishment.

"It won't be like at home, will it," I said, "it will be too far away for me to listen."

"Listen? You are coming with us. What did you think?"

"Well, I thought—."

"No. And do you know why you are coming with us?"

"Why?"

"Grosspa specially wants you there."

"Ach Gott," murmured Tante Bep in the shadows, and my father gave her a frowning look to warn her not to show so much feeling.

❦

A few minutes later we went downstairs. I was in a daze of happiness at the grand room of the hotel, the thick textures, the velvety lights, the distances of golden air, and most of all at the sound of music coming and coming from somewhere. In a corner of the famous main dining room there was a round table sparkling with light on silver, ice, glass, china and flowers, and in a high armchair sat my grandfather—rosy face, blue eyes and white beard. He inclined himself forward to greet us and seated us about him. My mother was at his right, in one of her prettiest gowns, with jewels. I was on his left.

"Hup-hup!" said my grandfather, clapping his hands to summon waiters now that we were assembled. "Tonight nothing but a happy family party, and Richard shall drink wine with me, for I want him to remember that his first glass of wine was poured for him by his *alter Münchner Freund, der Grossvater*."

At this a wet sound began with Tante Bep, but a look from my father quelled it, and my mother, blinking both eyes rapidly, which made them look prettier than ever when she stopped, put her hand on her father's and leaned and kissed his cheek above the crystal edge of his beard.

"Listen to the music!" commanded Grosspa, "and be quiet, if every word I say is to be a signal for emotion!"

It was a command in the style of his household terror, and everybody straightened up and looked consciously pleasant, except me. For me it was no effort. The music came from within a bower of gold lattice screens and potted palms—two violins, a 'cello, and a harp. I could see the players clearly, for they were in the corner just across from us. The leading violinist stood, the others sat. He was alive with his music, bending to it, marking the beat with his glossy head on which his sparse hair was combed flat. The restaurant was full of people whose talk made a thick hum, and to rise over this, and to stimulate it further, the orchestra had to work with extra effort.

The rosy lamp shades on the tables, the silver vases full of flowers, the slowly sparkling movements of the ladies and gentlemen, and the swallow-like dartings of the waiters transported me. I felt a lump of excitement where I swallowed. My eyes kept returning to

[128]

the orchestra leader, who conducted with side-jerks of his nearly bald head, for what he played and what he did seemed to me to command the meaning of the astonishing fact that I was at a dinner party in public with my family.

"What music are they playing?" I asked.

"It is called *Il Bacio*," answered Grosspa.

"What does that mean?"

"It means *The Kiss*."

What an odd name for a piece of music, I thought, as I watched the musicians who went at their work with a kind of sloping ardor. All through dinner—which did not last as long as it might have—I inquired about pieces played by the quartet, and in addition to the Arditi waltz, I remember one called *Simple Aveu* and the Boccherini *Minuet*. The violins had a sweetish mosquito-like sound, and the harp sounded breathless, and the 'cello mooed like a distant cow, and it was all entrancing. Watching the orchestra, I ate absently, with my head turned away from my fork until my father, time and again, had to turn me to face my plate. And then a waiter came with a silver tub on legs which he put at my grandfather's left, and showed him the wine bottle which he took from its nest of sparkling ice. The label was approved, a sip was poured for my grandfather to taste, he held it to the light and twirled his glass slowly, he sniffed it, and then he tasted it.

"Yes," he declared, "it will do."

My mother watched him in this ritual, and over her lovely heart-shaped face, with its silky crown of rolled tresses, I saw memories pass like shadows, as she thought of all the times she had attended the business of ordering and serving wine with her father. Blinking both eyes rapidly, she opened a little jewelled lorgnon she wore on a fine chain and bent forward to read the menu which stood in a little silver frame beside her plate. But I could see that she was not reading, and again I wondered what was the matter with everybody.

"For my grandson," said Grosspa, taking a wineglass and filling it half full with water, and then pouring it full with wine. The yellow pour turned pale in my glass. There was too much ceremony about it for me not to be impressed. I took the glass he handed me, and when he raised his, I raised mine, and while all the others watched, we drank together. And then he recited a proverb in German which meant something like,

> *When comrades drink red wine or white*
> *They stand as one for what is right,*

and an effect of intimate applause went around the table at this stage of my growing up.

I was suddenly embarrassed, for the music stopped, and I thought all the other diners were looking at me; and, in fact, many were, and I had a picture-like impression of how all smiled at a boy of nine, ruddy with excitement and confusion, drinking a solemn pledge of some sort with a pink and white old gentleman.

Mercifully the music began again and we were released from our poses, as it were, and my grandfather drew out of one vest pocket his great gold watch with its hunting case, and unhooked from a vest button the fob which held the heavy gold chain in place across his splendid middle. Repeating an old game we had played when I was still a baby, he held the watch toward my lips, and I knew what was expected of me. I blew upon it, and—though long ago I had penetrated the secret of the magic—the gold lid of the watch flew open. My grandfather laughed softly in a deep wheezing breath, and then shut the watch with a lovely cushioned click, saying,

"Do children ever know that what we do to please them pleases us more than it does them?"

"Ach Gott," whispered Tante Bep, and nobody reproved her, and then he said,

"Richard, I give you this watch and chain to keep all your life, and by it you will remember me."

"Oh, no!" exclaimed my mother in an uncontrollable waft of feeling.

He looked gravely at her and said,

"Yes, now, rather than later," and put the heavy wonderful golden objects into my hand.

I regarded them in silence. Mine! I could hear the wiry ticking of the watch, and I knew that now and forever I myself could press my thumb on the winding stem and myself make the gold lid fly open. The chain slid like a small weighty serpent across my fingers.

"Well," urged my father gently, "Richard, what do you say?"

"Yes, thank you, Grosspa, thank you."

I leaned up out of my chair and put my arm around his great head and kissed his cheek. Up close, I could see tiny blue and scarlet veins like something woven under his skin.

"That will do, my boy," he said. Then he took the watch from me and handed it to my father. "I hand it to your father to keep for you until you are twenty-one. But remember that it is yours and you must ask to see it any time you wish."

Disappointment spread heavily through my entrails, but I knew how sensible it was for the treasure to be held for me instead of given into my care.

"Any time you wish. You wish. Any time," repeated my grandfather, but in a changed voice, a hollow, windy sound that was terrible to hear. He was gripping the arm of his chair and now he shut his eyes behind his gold-framed lenses, and sweat broke out on his forehead which was suddenly dead white. "Any time," he tried to say again through his suffering, to preserve a social air. But stricken with pain too merciless to hide, he lost his pretenses and staggered to his feet. My mother quickly supported him, and my father left my side and hurried to him. Together they helped him from the table, while other diners watched, staring with neither curiosity nor pity. I thought the musicians played harder all of a sudden to distract the people from the sight of an old man in trouble being led out of the main dining room of the Waldorf-Astoria.

"What is the matter?" I asked Tante Bep, who had been ordered with a glance to remain behind with me.

"Ach, Grosspa is not feeling well."

"Should we go with him?"

"But your ice cream."

"Yes, the ice cream."

Though we waited, my family did not return from upstairs. Finally, hot with wine and excitement, I was in my turn led to the elevator and to my room where Tante Bep saw me to bed. Nobody else came to see me, or if anyone did, long later, I did not know it.

❈

During the night more snow fell. When I woke up and ran to my hotel window the world was covered and the air was thick with snow still falling. Word was sent to me to dress quickly, for we were to go to the ship almost at once. I was now eager to see the great ship that would cross the ocean.

Again we went in two taxicabs, I with my father. The others had gone ahead of us. My father pulled me to him to look out the cab window at the spiralling snow-fall. We went through narrow dark streets to the west side of Manhattan, where we boarded the ferry-boat that would take us across the North River to Hoboken. The cab rumbled its way to the deck and into the cold damp interior of the ferry.

"Let's get out and stand out on the deck," said my father.

We went forward into the clear space at the bow just as the boat moved into the blowing curtains of snow. All I could see was the dark green water where we sailed, a little sideways, across to the Jersey shore. The city disappeared. We might have been at sea, as Grosspa would soon be. I felt something like loneliness, to be closed away by the storm from sight of what I knew. Yet I noticed how the ferryboat seemed like a great duck, and the trundling action of her power under water seemed like the engine-work of huge webbed feet. At a moment I could not exactly fix, the other shore began to show through the snow, and we docked with wet, grudging blows against the old timbers of the slip.

When we returned to the cab to disembark, my father said,

"We are going to the piers of the North German Lloyd."

"What is that?"

"The steamship company where Grosspa's ship is docked. The *Kronprinzessen Cecilie*."

"Can I go inside her?"

"Certainly. Grosspa wants to see you in his cabin."

"Is he there?"

"Yes, by now. The doctor wanted him to go right to bed."

"Is he sick?"

"Yes."

"Did he eat something?—" a family explanation often used to account for my various illnesses at their onset.

"Not exactly. It is something else."

"Will he get well soon?"

"We hope so."

He looked away as he said this. I thought, He does not sound like my father.

[133]

The cab was running along the Hoboken docks now. Above the snowy sheds rose in silent grandeur the funnels and masts of ocean ships, and now I could see how huge they were. They made me ache with a bowel-changing longing. The streets were furious with noise —horses, cars, porters calling and running, and suddenly a white tower of steam that rose from the front of one of the funnels, to be followed in a second by a deep roaring hoot.

"There she is," said my father. "That's her first signal for sailing."

It was our ship. I stared up at her three masts with pennons pulled about by the blowing snow, and her four tall ochre funnels, spaced separately in pairs.

As we went from the taxi into the freezing air of the long pier, all I could see of the *Kronprinzessen Cecilie* were glimpses through the pier shed of white cabins, rows of portholes, regiments of rivet heads on the black hull, and an occasional door of polished mahogany. A hollow roar of confused sound filled the long shed. We went up a canvas covered gangway and then we were on board, and I felt immediately the invisible but real lift and slide and settle of a ship tied to a dock. There was an elegant creaking from the shining woodwork. I felt that a ship was built for boys, because the ceilings were so low, and made me feel so tall.

Holding my hand to keep me by him in the thronged decks, my father led me up a stairway whose curve was like the gesture of a sweeping arm. At the top we came to an open lobby with a skylight whose panes were colored—pale yellow, pale blue, pale green, orange—in a fancy design. From there we entered a narrow corridor that seemed to reach toward infinity. Its walls were of dark shining wood, glowing under weak yellow lights overhead. Its floor sloped down and then up again far away, telling of the ship's construction. Cabin doors opened on each side. There was a curious odor in the air—something like soda crackers dipped in milk, and distantly, or was it right here, in every inch of the ship around us, a soft throbbing sound kept up. It seemed impossible that anything so immense as this ship would presently detach itself from the land and go away.

"Here we are," said my father at a cabin door half-open.

We entered my grandfather's room, which was not like a room in a house, for none of its lines squared with the others, but met only to reflect the curvature of the ship's form.

At the wall across the stateroom, under two portholes whose silk curtains were closed, lay my grandfather in a narrow brass bed. He lay at a slight slope, with his arms outside the covers, and evidently he wore a voluminous white nightgown. I had never before seen him in anything but his formal day or evening clothes. He looked white—there was hardly a change in color between his beard and his cheeks and his brow. Seeing us, he did not turn his head, only his eyes. He seemed all of a sudden dreadfully small, and he gave the effect of being cautious in the world where before he had magnificently gone his way ignoring whatever might threaten him with inconvenience, rudeness, or disadvantage. My mother stood by his side and Tante Bep was at the foot of the bed in her black crocheted shawl and full peasant skirts.

"Yes, come, Richard," said Grosspa in a faint wheezy voice, searching for me with his eyes anxiously turned.

I went to his side and he put his hand an inch or two toward me —not enough to risk effort which would revive such a pain as had thrown him down the night before, but enough to call for my response. I set my hand in his and he lightly tightened his fingers over mine.

"Will you come to see me?" he asked in gallant playfulness.

"Where?" I asked in a loud clear tone which made my parents look at each other, as if to inquire how in the world the chasms which divided age from youth, and pain from health, and sorrow from innocence, could ever be bridged?

"In Germany," he whispered. He shut his eyes and held my hand and I had a vision of Germany which may have been sweetly near to his own; for what I saw in mind were the pieces of cardboard scenery, lithographed in dusty color, which belonged to the toy theatre he had brought to me from Germany on one of his returns from his journeys abroad—the Rhine in printed blue haziness with a castle high on a wooded crag; a deep green forest with an open glade in the far distance where gold lithographed light played through the leaves; a medieval street with half-timbered houses; a throne room with a deep perspective of white and gold pillars, a golden throne on a dais under a dark red canopy.

"Yes," I replied, "Grosspa, in Germany."

"Yes," he whispered, opening his eyes and making the sign of the Cross on my hand with his thumb. Then he looked at my mother. She understood him at once.

"You go now with Daddy," she said, "and wait for me on deck. We must leave the ship soon. Yes, Richard, *schnell*, now, skip!"

My father took me along the corridor and down the grand stairway. The ship's orchestra was playing somewhere—it sounded like the Waldorf. We went out to the deck just as the ship's siren let go again, and now it shook us gloriously and terribly. I covered my ears but still I was in the power of that immense deep voice. When it stopped, the ordinary sounds around us did not come close again for a moment. I leaned over the top of the railing and looked down at the narrow gap of water between us and the dock, where the spill and filth, the snake-like glide of small eddies, so far down below, gave me a chill of desire and fear. Snow was still falling—heavy, slow, thick flakes, each like several flakes stuck together, the way they used to stick in my eyelashes when I went out to play in winter.

A cabin boy came along beating a brass cymbal, calling out for all visitors to leave the ship.

I began to wonder if my mother would be taken away to sea while my father and I were forced to go ashore. Looking carefully, I saw her at last. She came toward us with a rapid, light step, and saying nothing, she turned us to the gangway and we went down. She held my father's arm when we reached the pier. She was wearing a spotted veil, and with one hand she now lifted this up just under her eyes and put her handkerchief to her mouth. She was weeping. I was abashed by her grief.

We hurried to the dock street, and there we lingered to watch the sailing of the *Kronprinzessen Cecilie.*

※

We did not talk. It was bitter cold. Wind came strongly from the North, and then, after a third shaking blast from her voice, the ship slowly began to change—she moved like water itself, leaving the dock, guided by three tugboats which made heavy black smoke in the thick air. Everything went by in a trance-like slowness, but at last I could see the ship, all of her, at one time.

I was amazed how tall and narrow she was as she stood out to the river at a long angle, stern first. Her four funnels seemed to rise like a city against the blowy sky. I could squint at her and know just how I would make a model of her when I got home. In midstream she slowly turned to face the lower bay. Her masts were like lines I drew with my pencils. Her smoke began to blow forward. She looked gaunt and proud and topheavy. At a moment which no one could fix she ceased backing and turning and began to steam clear and straight down the river and away.

"Oh, Dan!" cried my mother in a caught sob, and put her face against my father's shoulder. He folded his arm around her. Their faces were stretched with sorrow.

Just then a break in the sky across the river let light open on the snowy day and I stared in wonder at the change. I was the only one who saw it, for my father, watching after the departed liner in his thoughts, said to my mother,

"Like some old wounded lion crawling home to die."

"Oh, Dan," she sobbed, "don't, don't!"

I could not imagine what they were talking about. In my own interest and wonder, I tugged at my mother's arm and said with excitement, pointing to the thick flakes everywhere about us, and against the light beyond,

"Look, look, the snowflakes are all black!"

My mother suddenly could bear no more. My witless excitement released all her feelings. She leaned down and shook me and said in a voice now strong with anger,

"Richard, why do you say black! What nonsense. Stop it. Snow-flakes are white, Richard. White! White! When will you ever see things as they are! Oh!"

Her grief gave birth to her rage.

"Come, everybody," said my father. "I have the car waiting."

"But they *are* black!" I cried.

"Quiet!" commanded my father.

We rode to the hotel in silence.

❦

We were to return to Dorchester on the night train. All day I was too proud to mention what I alone seemed to remember, but after my nap, during which on principle I refused to sleep, my mother came to me, and said,

"You think I have forgotten. Well, I remember. We will go and arrange your presents."

[138]

My world was full of joy again. The first two presents were easy to find—there was a little shop full of novelties a block from the hotel, and there I bought for Anna a folding package of views of New York, and for Mr Schmitt a cast iron model of the Statue of Liberty. It was more difficult to think of something Ted would like. My mother let me consider by myself many possibilities among the variety available in the novelty shop, but the one thing I thought of for Ted I did not see. Finally, with an inquiring look at my mother to gain courage, I asked the shopkeeper,

"Do you have any straw hats for horses?"

"*What?*"

"Straw hats for horses, with holes for their ears to come through. They wear them in summer."

"Oh. I know what you mean. No, we don't."

My mother took charge.

"Then, Richard, I don't think this gentleman has what we need for Ted. Let us go back to the hotel. I think we may find it there."

"What will it be?"

"You'll see."

When tea was served in her room, she poured a cup for each of us, and asked,

"What do horses love?"

"Hay. Oats."

"Yes. What else."

Her eyes sparkled playfully across the tea table. I followed her glance.

"I know! Sugar!"

"Exactly"—and she made a little packet of sugar cubes in an envelope of Waldorf stationery from the desk in the corner, and my main concern in the trip to New York was satisfied. My father returned with all the tickets and arrangements to go home.

At home, in the next few days, I could not wait to present my gifts.

Would they like them? In two cases I never really knew. Anna accepted her folder of views and opened it up to let the pleated pages fall in one sweep, and remarked,

"When we came to New York from the old country, I was a baby, and I do not remember one thing about it."

Mr Schmitt took his Statue of Liberty in hand, turned it over carefully, and said,

"Well—."

But Ted—Ted clearly loved my gift, for he nibbled the sugar cubes off my outstretched palm until there was not one left, and then bumped me with his hard itchy head making me laugh and hurt at the same time.

"He likes sugar," I said to Mr Schmitt.

"*Ja.* Do you want to ride?"

❧

Life, then, was much as before until the day a few weeks later when we received a cablegram telling that my grandfather was dead in Munich. My father came home from the office to comfort my mother. They told me the news with solemnity in our long living room where the curtains were now closed against the light of the world. I listened, and I had a lump of pity in my throat for the look on my mother's face, but I did not feel anything else.

"He dearly loved you," they said.

"May I go now?" I asked.

They were shocked. What an unfeeling child. Did he have no heart? How could the loss of so great and dear a figure in the family not move him?

But I had never seen death, I had no idea of what death was like.

Grosspa had gone away before now and I had soon ceased to miss him, what if they did say now that I could never see him again, as I had never again seen John Burley next door in all these years? I could show nothing. They shook their heads and let me go.

Anna was more offhand than my parents about the whole matter.

"You know," she said, letting me watch her at her deep zinc laundry tubs in the dark, steamy, confidential basement, "that your Grosspa went home to Germany to die, you know that, don't you?"

"Is that why he went?"

"That's why."

"Did he know it?"

"Oh, yes, sure he knew it."

"Why couldn't he die right here?"

"Well, when our time comes, maybe we all want to go back where we came from."

Her voice, speaking of death, contained a doleful pleasure. The greatest mystery in the world was still closed to me. When I left her she raised her old tune under the furnace pipes and I wished I were as happy and full of knowledge as she.

※

My time soon came.

On the following Saturday I was watching for Mr Schmitt and Ted when I heard heavy footsteps running up the front porch and someone shaking the door knob forgetting to ring the bell. I went to see. It was Mr Schmitt. He was panting and he looked wild. When I opened the door he ran past me into the front hall calling out,

"Telephone! Let me have the telephone!"

I pointed to it in the bend of the hall where it stood on a gilded wicker taboret. He picked up the receiver and began frantically to click the receiver hook. I was amazed to see tears roll from his eyes and down on his cheeks which looked ready to burst with redness and fullness.

"What's the matter, Mr Schmitt?" I asked.

I heard my mother coming along the hallway upstairs from her sitting room.

Mr Schmitt suddenly put down the phone and pulled off his hat and shook his head.

"What's the use," he said. "I know it is too late already. I was calling the ice plant to send someone to help."

"Good morning, Mr Schmitt," said my mother coming downstairs. "What on earth is the matter?"

"My poor old Ted," he said, waving his hat toward the street. "He fell down and just died in front of the Weiners' house."

"Oh—" and my mother spoke words of sympathy.

I ran out of the house and up the sidewalk to the Weiners' house, and sure enough, there was the ice wagon, and in the shafts, lying heavy and gone on his fat side, was Ted. There lay death on the asphalt paving. I confronted the mystery at last.

Ted's one eye that I could see was open. A fly walked across it and there was no blink. His teeth gaped apart letting his long tongue lie out on the street. His body seemed twice as big and heavy as before. Without even trying to lift it I knew how mortally heavy it was. His front legs were crossed, and the great horn cup of the upper hoof was slightly tipped, the way he used to rest it at ease, bent over the pavement. From under his belly flooded a pool of pale yellow fluid—his urine—and from beneath his tail flowed the last of his excrement, in which I could see oats. In his fall he had twisted the shafts which he had pulled for so many years. His harness was awry. Melting ice dripped at the back of the hooded wagon. Its wheels looked as if they had never turned. What would ever turn them?

"Never," I said, half aloud. I knew the meaning of this word now.

In another moment my mother came and took me back to our house, and Mr Schmitt settled down on the curbstone to wait for people and services to arrive and take away the leavings of his changed world.

I went and told Anna what I knew. She listened with her head on the side, her eyes half-closed, and she nodded at my news and sighed.

"Poor old Ted," she said, "he couldn't even crawl home to die."

This made my mouth fall open, for it reminded me of something I had heard before, somewhere, and all day I was subdued and private, quite unlike myself, as I heard later, and late that night, I awoke in a storm of grief so noisy in its gusts that my parents came to me asking what was the trouble?

I could not speak at first, for their tender, warm, bed-sweet presences doubled my emotion, and I sobbed against them as together they held me. But at last when they said again,

"What's this all about, Richard, Richard?" I was able to say,

"It's all about Ted."

This was true, if not all the truth, for I was thinking also of Grosspa now, crawling home to die, and I knew what that meant, and what death was like. I imagined Grosspa's heavy death, with his open eye, and his loss of his fluids, and his sameness and his difference all mingled, and I wept for him at last, and for myself if I should die, and for my ardent mother and my sovereign father, and for the iceman's old horse, and for everyone.

"Hush, dear, hush, Richard," they said, and it was all they could say, for who could soften or change the fact of death?

A pain in my head began to throb remotely as my outburst diminished, and another thought entered with rueful persistence, and I said in bitterness,

"But they were black! Really they were!"

They looked at each other and then at me, but I was too spent to continue, and I fell to my pillow, and even if they might insist that snowflakes were white, I knew that when seen against the light, falling out of the sky into the sliding water all about the *Kronprinzessen Cecilie,* they were black. To children—as to artists—all life is metaphor. Black snowflakes against the sky. Why could they not see that? Black.

CHAPTER VII

꾫

Center of Interest

Summer was the time when the world seemed to open itself distance upon distance ahead. Some things that happened in growing summers were stranger and stranger afterward, as though created afar by distance itself, and never to be seen close to.

On our first evening at the United States Hotel in Saratoga in the following summer, I heard a man and a woman talking behind a lattice twined with vines and electric lights that divided one section of the long piazza from another.

I was already washed and dressed for dinner after the whole day's drive from Dorchester. We were on our way to a vacation in the Adirondack Mountains on a little island which my father had leased. Saratoga was magical to my eyes. The evening was warm, and shadows were falling in the groves of the deep park behind the hotel. Colored lights were everywhere, even in the fountain of the courtyard, where they changed the hues of the ever-arching waters as I watched. The vast corridors with their moon-like lamps and the endless piazzas with their platoons of rocking chairs and the deep carpeting inside and the gallantry of guests all dressed up for evening held great appeal for me at ten years of age. They said a band was going to play in the court during dinner and afterward.

I was so full of curiosity about this place where we planned to rest for two or three days on our motor trip to the mountains that when I came downstairs before my parents were ready, I left behind me in my room my new toy sailboat which I had carried in my hands all the way from home. She was bound for her launching in the mountain lake where our island—Thunder Island—awaited us.

After exploring the main floor and the grounds of the United States Hotel, I settled into a rocking chair by the lattice to watch the fountain where the water was playing with sounds like whispers of laughter repeated over and over. Against this I heard from beyond the vines the conversation whose meaning I reconstruct here.

"He was with them when they arrived," said a man's voice. "I was in the lobby at the time."

"Yes," said the woman, "I saw him. They make a nice little family. She is a pretty thing."

"I hardly noticed. I could hardly take my eyes off him."

"Who—the father?"

"No—the boy."

"Oh. Oh, yes. I see." Her voice flattened. "Of course. He is a sweet looking little fellow."

"Sweet looking?" The man laughed in a muted horn-like tone. "Marjorie, you never really see what you look at, you know."

"Oh, I don't know. Sometimes I don't want to."

"Ah. Thank you. Though perhaps you don't mean what it sounded like."

"No, really. I meant nothing."

"No, I hoped not. But his eyes are so deeply blue, and he has all that dark gold hair brushed so thickly, it falls over his forehead on one side. And his cheeks are ruddy without being hot-looking— really, I wish I knew them so they would let me paint him. I would paint a wonderful thing. He stands beautifully, too. How old do you suppose he is?"

"Oh, perhaps eleven or so."

"It is the last of the age of innocence, isn't it. You can say what you like as a school teacher, Miss Marjorie, but true beauty disappears when knowledge arrives."

The woman laughed scoffingly, and with affection.

"Oh, Hubert, you're no good at philosophy. Every time we meet for our summer holiday together I wonder what your new tack is going to be."

"Always trust a New England female friend to be handy with the disagreeable truth," said the man with a comic sigh.

I held my rocking chair still so I could hear this exchange. Their voices interested me. They did not sound like anything in Dorchester. Marjorie's was dry, her words were clipped, and her accent, I know now, suggested Boston. Hubert sounded like a New Yorker, perhaps a grown-up Bayard, though his tone was richer and more mellow than you heard generally in New York. He had a mocking sort of elegance in the way he said things. What did they look like?

※

Leaving my chair so carefully that it did not even creak, I went to the lattice and peered through the vines. By the bright fountain light I saw that Marjorie looked old enough to be Hubert's mother—grey-haired, thin-faced, and wearing a black lace shawl over her grey silk evening dress. Hubert sat facing me. He was perhaps my father's age, very slim, with black eyes that had a hard gaze in his thin face. His nose was odd—once broken, it was still bent, like a parrot's bill, I thought, and when he spoke, his voice sounded bent. Revealed by a constant, downward smile, his teeth were irregular in shape and color. A tired, if humorous, look of perpetual disappointment and hope came out of all these elements. Since most people dressed for dinner at the United States Hotel, he was in a dinner jacket. He held his narrow shoulders stiff and high.

"How would you paint him, then?" asked Marjorie.

"As I first saw him, I think. He was wearing a blue serge jacket with brass buttons and white ducks and he was holding a toy sailboat and he was looking at the boat with his head a little to one side, and dreaming the boat into life. You know?"

"Oh, yes, yes, I see it."

I held my breath. They were talking about me.

I felt an obscure thrust of pleasure and love—self-love, I suppose. It was an exalting feeling. I longed to hear more, but just then I recognized sharp little footsteps behind me on the bare wood between the carpeting inside and the raffia runners on the planking of the piazza, and my mother called, generally toward the fountain,

"Hoo-hoo, Richard! Here we are!"

She didn't see me until I turned and went to her. She looked particularly lovely in her evening dress with her bits of jewellery. Her color was high. She was in love with my father and with me. It was a comfortable state for our family at that time. My father, feeling as charming as he looked in his dinner jacket, took my right hand formally and said,

"Good evening, Doctor. I believe we are to enjoy your company at dinner?"

My mother bridled at his comedy, as she always did, in case anybody might be about who would not understand our jokes.

"Oh, you two," she said. "Do come. I'm starving. I adore this place. I must never leave it."

My father put his arm around my shoulders and said,

"Doc, how about trying the boat in the fountain tomorrow? Do you think she'd work?"

"I don't know. There's a lot of spray. She might get her sails wet."

"And then she would tip over, I believe," he said.

[148]

"Yes."

"Well, if your mother wants to stay here in Saratoga, she can simply stay, and you and I will go on to the lake, and sail that pretty boat all day long."

"Very well," she said gaily, "I'll stay. You two can go on at any time. I won't be bored. I never saw so many attractive men anywhere."

"Well, of course," declared my father, putting on a stern look which fooled nobody, "that settles it. We'll all leave in the morning."

My mother decided to be fooled.

"Why Dan, how can you talk like that. We promised ourselves two or three days here. We wanted to find another couple and play bridge in the evenings. I've already asked the lady from Elmira. Really. Your jealousy is such a bore."

She began to use the word that summer.

"Oh, so I am a bore?" said my father.

"I didn't say that. I said—."

"I know what you said. We're scaring Doc, now. Let's forget it and go to dinner and have two cocktails each."

And in truth, I was uneasy about their mock quarrel, for who could ever be sure when grown-up people meant what they said or not? Laughing together, they put me between them and we went to the vast dining room which even then just before the first World War looked old-fashioned enough to be interesting.

※

During dinner the band began to sound from the fountain court. The lights, the water and the music all made me sleepy and cloudy in mind. I felt everything in a mist of formless pleasure, as though once again all had been devised for my own particular enjoyment.

[149]

When we left the table, it was time for me to go to bed, but as a special observance of the first evening of our family holiday, we all strolled together in the fountain court and out through an arch of tall trees into the park where flowering bushes and little groves grew darker and more mysterious and inviting the farther we walked from the music and the lights.

"What a place for a honeymoon," said my father huskily.

There was an occasional ornamental iron lamp among the leaves to guide lovers along the paths, but these served only to make little coves of darkness and summery sweetness where bushes or trees grew like enclosing walls.

We soon turned around and went back to the court and up the steps to the piazza. There I saw Hubert with Marjorie. As we passed him, I heard him say to her, for his voice followed me as his eyes did,

"I know it's your bedtime, Marjie, so I'll just look around for a table of bridge. Let's meet late for breakfast."

She nodded and went indoors.

After a few steps, my father said,

"Why don't I go ask him if he will join us, and make a fourth?"

"Yes, do," replied my mother. "I'll take Richard upstairs and pop him into beddy-bye, and be right down. Where will I find you?"

"There's a big red card room off the sun porch. Look for me there."

He gave me a punching sort of hug and sent me off with her. I watched as long as I could to see him go to speak to Hubert, and the last I saw was a delighted, astonished look on Hubert's face, and a rapid nod of agreement to join a table of bridge.

At breakfast, they talked about him with me.

"Well, Doc," said my father, "how would you like to be famous?"

"Oh, Dan, don't spoil him so," murmured my mother.

"How?" I asked.

"We met a man last night," said my father, "who is famous. His name is Hubert Monckton. He is a famous portrait painter. Even I have heard of him."

I already knew more than my parents about all this but I kept silent. My father continued,

"We played bridge with him and the lady from Elmira, and what do you think. He wants to paint your picture."

I looked at my mother to find out how I should think about this.

"Yes, he really does," she said. "Of course, I told Daddy it was all nonsense. But Mr Monckton did rave about you."

"He says you are like a Sir Thomas Lawrence. Eighteenth century. English."

"I still think," mused my mother idly, "that it is most odd that he would try to interest perfect strangers in letting him paint their child."

"He wasn't angling for a commission," replied my father with maddening reasonableness, "he doesn't have to do that. He said—you heard him say—that wherever he found a fine subject he always tried to establish some connection so that he could work it up into a sketch, and maybe a painting."

"Well, we'll only be here a little while longer," said my mother, "and he would never get a picture done in that time."

"He asked me where we were going. When I told him Thunder Island, he said he had friends up at our lake and might come there."

[151]

"Well," said my mother, "I am sure it is all very flattering and exciting and I can think of nothing that would bore Richard more horribly than posing for his portrait. You ought to see how he acts when I take him to the photographer's! Pity he didn't ask me to pose for him."

It was a strange, disturbing feeling to be the center of such unexpected interest, and I wished that my parents regarded Hubert Monckton's request as more than a breakfast joke.

"Well, anyway," said my father, "he plays a splendid game of bridge and I look forward to this evening again."

"Oh, yes, he really played brilliantly, didn't he," answered my mother. "He's really the most charming man I've met in years. Isn't it odd. He's not good looking. But he has great charm. I suppose it is the way he has of looking at somebody as if he never saw anyone as charming as they are."

"No," said my father, "it's more than that. He talks well. He seems to know everything about everybody and more than enough about everything else. So, when he says *anything,* he draws on so much that *whatever* he says it is interesting. I hope I make myself clear?"

"Who was that old lady with him?" I asked.

"Why? Did you see her?"

"Yes"—but I did not explain where I first saw her.

"She's his mother's best friend," explained my mother. "Miss Hobson. She teaches at a ladies' college in Boston. His mother is dead, but they used to have their vacations together all three, and now the two of them keep it up, in memory of his mother. He says he wouldn't know what to do without Miss Hobson.—Richard, you have not eaten a thing. Sit up now and come to the party."

My cereal spoon began to travel its appointed course in an abstracted sort of way. I felt powers and mysteries behind all that my parents discussed so lightly, and I tried to think what could be the meaning of what I had overheard the evening before. But there were limiting blurs at the edge of my thought, and it made my head ache slightly to try to pierce beyond them, and I was happy and relieved when my father said at the end of breakfast,

"Come on, Doc, let's try the boat in the fountain."

Action in sunlight and spray was a joy. We sailed my sloop along the edge of the fountain basin, keeping the sails dry, and if you put your cheek down on the cold wet stone of the basin and half closed your eyes and watched the sloop from that unaccustomed angle of vision, you could have her at sea, tipping before the breeze, and you could make her little darting turns slow down and become grand long tacks of a full-sized vessel with yourself on board at the wheel.

"Good morning," said a voice I knew.

"Oh, hello, Monckton," said my father. "We're trying out a new sailboat."

"She's a beauty," said Hubert.

"Richard," said my father, "get up and speak to Mr Monckton."

Hubert and I shook hands. He looked as though he couldn't stop smiling if he tried.

"Well, I'm glad to know all the family now," he said to me. "Your father and mother and I became great friends last night over the bridge table. I hope you and I will be too."

Again I had the feeling of knowing more than any of them, though I couldn't say what about.

My father answered for me.

"Richard makes friends easily wherever he goes. We're very

glad of it, since he is an only child.—Look, look, Doc!" he exclaimed, turning me around to the fountain, "she's getting away
from us!"

I went back to my sailing. After a few more words with my father,
Hubert strolled away.

※

I did not see him again until early evening. Then he came idling
along the gravel walk and found me sitting on the grass in the
lighted fountain court, writing postcards to my friends at home. He
was, I thought, dressed up like a society artist on a resort holiday.
His hat was a straw sailor. He wore a white silk shirt with a loosely
knotted tie, and a blue and black striped blazer. Tapering with his
slender legs, his trousers were of white flannel, and he wore white
buckskin shoes, and he carried a light, whiplike cane of bamboo.

"I'm out for a little walk," he said. "Would you like to join me?"

I wanted to finish what I thought of as my correspondence, but
invitations from adults were really commands, and I scrambled to
my feet and put my postcards into my jacket pocket.

We walked into the park. It was already dark under the trees and
the lanterns were glowing. The damp ground gave off a musty
fragrance that made your breath feel heavy. Crickets sounded in the
bushes. From very far away, it seemed, the hushed laughter of the
fountain water came and went behind us on the wafts of air. We
saw nobody else in the park—people were indoors changing for dinner.

"Richard," asked Hubert as we walked driftingly into the deepest
part of the gardens, "how old are you?"

"Ten."

"No! I would have thought a year or two older. You seem such a grown-up boy in many ways."

"I wish I was."

He laughed.

"The irony of it. All too soon you will be wishing you were a boy again."

"No, I won't."

"You will see.—Would you mind if I smoked?"

"No."—Why would he ask me that? I had heard men ask women the same question, but why ask me?

He lighted a cigarette from a gold case. His hands trembled slightly as he managed the matches.

"Richard," he asked then, "do you have a happy life?"

"I guess so."

"You have such charming parents. So beautiful, both of them."

My mother was beautiful, but how could he say that of my father, or any man?

"I am sure," he added, "that they are very good to you."

"Oh, yes. They are."

"And do you make them happy?"

"I don't know.—They know I love them."

"Do you tell them everything?"

"What do you mean, everything?"

"Oh, you know—everything you do. Or do you keep some things to yourself?"

"I guess I tell them everything I remember. But sometimes I have so many things that I forget some."

"How delightful. How delightfully you put it.—Tell me, what is it like, at home, in Dorchester?"

Under his brief, prodding questions, I told him of our house, and Anna, who had gloomily helped me to grow up, and of our leafy neighborhood, and of my school, and of our church.

"Then, you go to Mass regularly, all of you?"

"Yes."

"Do you like it?"

Who ever thought of that before? I neither liked it nor disliked it. It was beauty and it was faith and it was like the day or the night, enclosing all. Lamely I replied,

"I like to see the candles all lighted and the colors of the vestments and hear the music."

"Yes, I know. I know exactly what you mean.—Tell me, Richard, have you everything you want?"

"I suppose so."

"No, I mean, is there some particular thing you don't have that you'd love to have, that somebody could give you?"

He induced a luxurious greed in my thought, and I began to think hotly of a real motor boat, not a toy, and a live pony, and a full-sized cavalry sabre. But a great part of love was secrecy, and I could not speak of these objects of my desire—the only sort of desire my years could reveal to me.

"No," I said.

"What a wonderful, strange boy.—I hope you don't mind—I've been looking at you from a distance all day." His voice was full of extra breath. He spoke near to me. "Let's sit down here—there's a little bench in the bushes."

We sat side by side and I let my legs swing.

"What will you be when you grow up, Richard?"

"My father calls me Doc. I am going to be a surgeon."

"How fine. To save lives. I am sure you will make a wonderful surgeon. Let me see your hands." He threw away his cigarette and took my hands and turned them over. "Yes. They are the hands of an artist or a surgeon. Long fingers. Sensitive fingers." He pressed my hands damply and then released them. "Imagine how it will be when you have your own office, and those wonderful little pinpoint lamps to use for examining people, and all the clean, bright instruments, and everybody coming because they need you."

I said,

"My father says there are great discoveries that have to be made. He says medicine has the greatest things to find out for people. I think I will try to find out all sorts of things and tell all the other doctors so they can use them too. I will never ask poor people for a single dollar, but I will take care of them free, and I will make them get well. My father says a man should always love his work, and he says I will love my work as a doctor, but he says that a doctor loves his work, yes, but more than that, he has to love *people, all* people, he says, and has to work for them, because he has to relieve suffering! That is what I am going to do! I am going to do it, when I grow up!"

My thoughts, suddenly opening into this pour of words, gave me a feeling of power. Imagination made the future immediate and real for me. I was already a great surgeon. I spoke with commanding certainty. I was physically alive with passion. My face felt hot with passion. My body quivered with passion. It destroyed Hubert.

"Ah, Richard," he said with a sound like a swallowed sigh. Then, with movement so slow that he seemed to watch his gesture as if helplessly betrayed by it, even as he gazed at himself, he succumbed. Subject to the rustling night, with the far band music beginning its evening waltzes, and against a distant shimmer of fountain light reflected on the topmost and farthest trees, and enclosed by shadows like substance in the grove, and under the night scent, and pierced by the prickling song of the crickets in the bushes, he closed his arms about me and his lips searched for me in a moaning intensity which carried with it the breath of his recent cigarette. I had no idea of what he meant as he grasped me with a sinewy nervousness against which I struggled on principle like a young cat who refuses to be held.

As the cat always does, I gained my freedom, and I burst into a loud mocking laugh.

Fear, pleasure, shock, disgust—he might have anticipated these and perhaps could have met them out of experience. But hilarity? It was the last response he expected. Stricken away from his embrace, he asked in an urgent whisper,

"What are you laughing at?"

"You!"

"What for? It may have been a lot of other things, but it wasn't funny!"

"Oh, yes it was!"

"Why was it?" He sounded full of anguish and hope.

"Because only girls kiss!"

The hearty conventionality of this ended his hope and started his panic.

"Richard!" he said, standing up suddenly to impress me the more, "please, please forget what happened, and please, please, don't tell anybody about it. Will you promise? You said there are some things you forget to tell. Oh, forget this, will you? You don't know how important it is, Richard? I didn't mean anything!"

Only then did I become frightened of what had happened and of him.

"No," I said heartlessly, "I'll tell anybody I want to!"

"Oh, anything—if you will promise, and keep your promise, I will get you anything you want!"

Without answering I ran away down the path. I heard him running after me. He must have been in terror. He called my name in soft gasps, pleading with me to wait and listen before we should be overhead. But I ran and he dared not overtake me as I reached the fountain court where the light was so full and the music so loud. He remained in the shadows, surely in anguish.

My father and mother were on the piazza steps.

"Where on earth have you been?" asked my mother.

"What have you been doing, Doc?" asked my father.

Something in their faces made a secret of what I could have told them. How little do parents really know of the lives they have given to the world. Panting from my run, I said,

"Nothing. I was in the woods, and I thought it must be time for dinner, and I ran."

"Well, it is indeed, we have been looking everywhere for you. Go up and wash your paws and come down as soon as you can. We're going to play bridge again and we're already a little late to start the evening."

❦

We were just finishing dinner when Miss Hobson came to our table and my father and I rose to greet her.

"The strangest thing," she said. "My friend Hubert Monckton, you know? He has been most unexpectedly called away. He has already packed and gone. He asked me to make his excuses to you for not making a fourth at bridge with you this evening."

"Oh, what a shame," said my father. "I hope he did not hear some bad news?"

"I cannot say. He was much agitated, and only spoke to me briefly. My holiday is quite ruined. But I am sure he had good reason—he is a most conscientious man."

"Oh, we liked him so much," said my mother.

"He took quite a shine to our boy," said my father with a proud, innocent smile.

"Yes, I know. He spoke of wanting to paint him."

I stood under all this with bowed head and private knowledge. I resolved never to tell anyone what I knew and I never have.

After Miss Hobson made her way upstairs, my mother sighed prettily and said,

"What a bore. Now we must find another fourth."

CHAPTER VIII

❊

The Spoiled Priest

With what wonderful ease a boy could live in two worlds at the same moment—the world of whatever books he might be reading, and that other world believed in by the people about him.

❊

The snow hardly stopped falling on Paris in the winter of 1451. It clung to all the roofs and towers like great featherbeds. In the narrow, crazy, medieval streets, snow lodged against doorways and piled sloping banks against one side of the passageways between houses. By night the wind staggered the snow off roofs in a stinging shower and if you happened to be passing that way you felt it on your cheeks and against your eyes, especially if you went before dawn, when all was so dark. The cold breathed inside your clothes and against your prickled skin. You pressed your lips tight because a draught of air made your teeth ache. There were few lights to be seen. The sky was only just lighter than the city. People were dying of plague in certain houses and children who went to sleep a few hours ago might never awaken, but would forever be like waxen angels with their eyelids closed over blue chicken-eye shadows. The poor were starving and the rich—even the king and queen and the royal princes in their stone towers above the freezing river—had little enough to eat and drink. They all prayed to the Blessed Infant of Prague for food and safety. If you had to be out at night hurrying on some adventure or act of duty you heard sounds that froze the blood in your veins. The wind tore itself around chimney tops and towers, now crying like a child, again shrieking like an evil spirit. You hurried to be indoors, not daring to pause until you came where you must be. If you stopped you heard the most terrible sound of all hurrying after you along the driving air. It was the howling of wolves on the very outskirts of Paris. Some said they even ventured into the town, for they too were starving, and would be glad enough to come upon someone, especially a boy, who went alone before daylight through the streets of Paris until he could reach the narrow sacristy door set under its deep pointed arch in the grey stone of the cathedral. When you came at last to the cathedral close and in spite of the whipping snow saw the door dimly dark against the wintry walls, you hurried still faster out of relief, and also out of final respect for the wolves who lived on snow and wind and who called out their angry hunger as if they knew you were there to be taken and who if they stood upright would be as tall as your father. Sometimes there was a sweet crack of light showing under the door but sometimes all was yet dark. In any case you must throw yourself against the heavy iron ring of the door hoping that the sexton had already come to unlock it from within. Then you could let yourself in, stamping the snow off your feet and saying a prayer of thanks that once again you had come safely past the night and the wolves of Paris to serve the early Mass at Holy Angels Cathedral where the curate, Father Coach, in his languid and muscular way, would be the celebrant at the high altar. Only then, safely indoors, did you know with the other part of your mind that the winter

darkness and the sharp cold before daylight and the empty streets
were those of Dorchester, New York, in the year 1915.

※

And then I was of course safely in the world of everybody else,
and the streets had held no wolves, but only distant streetcars which
made occasional flashes of blue electric light as their trolleys jumped
gaps in the power lines overhead. I always remembered the grinding
song of their wheels on the ice-cold rails when they turned a corner.
I had to walk seven blocks from my house to the cathedral, which
was our parish church. I must have come to the sacristy with my
vision of medieval Paris still in my eyes, for Father Coach said when
he saw me,

"Richard, what are you so excited about?"

"Nothing, Father."

"You look as if you had seen a ghost or a tiger."

It was a temptation to say, "No, Father, a wolf," but I knew
enough not to expect anybody that much older to see what I saw,
even though Father Coach was only in his early thirties, and seemed
more like a boy than most men I knew.

"Never mind," he said, "you have one minute and sixteen seconds
to get into your cassock and surplice. I have already lighted the
candles myself. I would like some day to be able to count on a boy
not to be late to whom I have cheerfully given my whole and entire
trust."

"Yes, Father. My clock almost didn't go off at all."

"I think with one or two simple questions I could demolish that
statement.—Are you ready?"

He put on his biretta, took up his veiled chalice and the taber-
nacle key with its golden chain and real gold tassel, dipped his hand

in the holy water font and gave me his wet fingertips to take a few drops for myself, we crossed ourselves, and went forth to the almost empty church to celebrate together the Holy Sacrifice.

As I did each time, I felt a hollow, carved-out sensation at my stomach, wondering if I would make any mistakes this morning, and whether if I did so, God, and Father Coach, would forgive me. My worst usual mistake was to move too fast, whipping the skirts of my cassock with my legs, and audibly bumping the carpeted floor and steps of the altar with my knee as I genuflected. True reverence, I remembered, was never hasty. On the other hand, it was worse to be lazy or dull. But who could exactly match that wonderful combination of ease and intensity which Father Coach showed in all he did? Move like an athlete who need never hurry because he knew exactly how to do all? Stroll with the effect of marching, and turn like a sail in the wind? He was my model and my despair, both of which he intended to be, for the good of my soul and for the purpose which he had sought within me.

※

Who that was there could forget the day when he came to our classroom to look us over and assure us that he had no hope at all of finding the sort of boy among us whom he searched for?

Without warning the classroom door opened and there he stood, glaring and smiling at our teacher, Miss Mendtzy, and nodding his head as if to say "I thought so" about nothing.

Miss Mendtzy all but genuflected as though he were the Blessèd Sacrament or a bishop, and cried,

"Oh! Father! We are so honored! Pray come in!"

Still nodding silently he lounged through the door ignoring us who all rose as we had been trained to do when a priest entered the room. He took off his biretta and unbuttoned the long black coat he wore over his cassock and finally said,

"What grade are these boys in, Miss Mendtzy?"

"Fifth grade, Father," she answered, motioning us to be seated.

"A pretty ragged crew, I suppose?"

"Oh, no—they are bright, splendid, hard-working boys, Father. Just ask them questions. You will see."

We dreaded "questions." Everything we ever knew flew out of our heads like sparrows when a visitor asked a question.

"No. No questions," said Father Coach. "I know without asking that I won't find what I want in here. God knows where I will find it if I ever do. When I think," he said slowly, nodding sorrowfully and yet with courage at Miss Mendtzy, "when I think how Our Lord is patiently waiting, and how hard it is to find anybody to come and serve Him, and how if you think you have found someone they almost always let you down, and what is worse, let *Him* down, why, then, I almost give up."

"Oh, no, Father!"

"Yes, Miss Mendtzy. But of course we have to go on, we both know that. But honestly, now, Miss Mendtzy, can you stand there and tell me that you really and truly think there are boys, there's even two boys, no, wait, even *one* boy, in this room who could ever do what Our Lord has to ask him to do to serve Mass?"

"Oh, Father."

"No, I know it is hard for you to say. But when you think of what it takes, you just have to wonder."

"Yes, yes," murmured Miss Mendtzy, hypnotised by his fervor and his strong, slow speech, "to be neat and prompt!"—the prime virtues she stressed for us in the classroom.

[165]

"Ho. If that were all." He seemed almost to menace her with his keen gaze as he addressed her for our benefit. "Do you know, Miss Mendtzy, what it is to hear the alarm go off in pitch darkness, *yangggg!*,—we jumped in our seats at the sudden violence of this —"and how cold it is in winter, and then to get up shivering and strip off your nice warm pajamas and go like a man to take your cold shower"—she cast her glance away in modesty at the idea of male nakedness in the shower "—and then without breakfast to pull on your earmuffs and your mittens and your mackinaw and set out through the empty dark streets where who knows what danger may be lurking? And do you know that if you are in a state of sin how Our Lord grieves at seeing you come to serve Him with a black mark on your soul? Do you know that if you have a headache, or ate something the night before that don't set so well this morning, you still have to get up and go before anybody else is awake and stirring? Our Lord never sleeps. Is it so much to ask if someone will get up after a good night's sleep to be with Him?"

"Oh, I know, yes, Father, my gracious."

He still did not look at us but he gave one hand in a slow, wide gesture indicating us all.

"You know, Miss Mendtzy, and *I* know, but do *they!"*

Respectful of him, she was also loyal to us. She loved us. We teased her sometimes, but we loved her, too.

"Oh, yes, Father, I believe they know." She turned to us. "Don't you, boys?"

"Yes, Miss Mendtzy." We sang out our dictated answer instantly in unison, in the pattern of our schoolroom manners.

Only now did Father Coach face toward us. He scowled. His wide pink young face went darker. His pale eyes burned with light. His short-cropped blond hair seemed to stand up more stiffly. He positively threw his spirit at us, and we thought, "Coach!", for his ideal for the priesthood was to make it take on the manner of the athletic

[166]

coach, and in fact he insisted that his name be pronounced as if it were spelled Father Coach, though actually it was Koch.

"All right!" he cried loudly, with a whirl of his arms, "I don't think any of you have got what it takes. I think you're all yellow! I think you would rather lie in bed and keep snug and think about breakfast and pretend to be still asleep and take naps like a cat until your mother comes and says—" he imitated a woman's voice inexpertly—" 'Come on, now, Willie, time to get up out of your bedsy-wedsy!' "

We writhed with shame. How did he know exactly how we felt in bed?

"You!" he shouted at the boy in front of me. "If you had the stomach-ache and absolutely knew you couldn't get out of bed that day, would you have the guts to ignore how you felt, and get up, and get dressed, and go out in the snow, and hurry to the cathedral in time to serve six o'clock Mass for me?"

"I don't know, Father," said the boy out of honest confusion.

Father Coach threw his hands and let them fall against his long thighs and said,

"What did I tell you? Is there *anyone* here with the heart of a soldier and the will of an athlete who thinks he *could* serve Our Lord however hard it might be?"

We threw ourselves forward against our desks and reached our hands toward him, snapping our fingers in the air to be noticed individually, aching to be chosen.

"Me, Father," "Yes, Father, here, here," "Me, me, Father!"

He let us snap and pant for a long moment in the agony of our desire to prove him wrong about us. Then slowly he began to nod. He murmured aloud as though to himself, and we heard Greatness musing.

"Well, who knows. Perhaps I am wrong. Perhaps there *is* a boy here who would literally rather lie down and die than miss his duty

[167]

at six o'clock every morning, rain or shine, winter or summer. Where is he?" He roved our faces with his stern, light-lashed gaze to make us die for him if he would ask. Suddenly he pointed at me and I had a strike of certainty that he had meant to pick me all along. "You. Who are you?"

I rose and told him.

"All right, Richard. How far is it from your house to Holy Angels?"

"Seven blocks, Father."

"Does the street car run by that way?"

"No, Father, it runs downtown instead."

"So you'd have to walk, is that it?"

" 'S, Father."

"Are you a good walker—Is he a pretty good walker, class?" he asked, turning to us all, now radiantly genial, so that if we loved Father Coach when he was furious at us, we must worship him when he liked us.

"Yes, Father—" but somebody hidden in back made a tongue and lip noise of derision. A sacred silence fell. Then Father Coach said in deep quiet,

"Whoever did that will tell about it when he goes to Confession on Saturday. I feel sorry for him. He is full of envy because he was not chosen. He is in the grip of one of the Seven Deadly Sins. I will ask Richard to pray for him at the foot of the altar. Richard: you: are: chosen. Report to me today and every day after school for instruction. I will telephone your mother to congratulate her on the great honor you have won today. Thank you, Miss Mendtzy. Please do not punish the individual who made that disgusting noise. His punishment will come from Somewhere Else."

Resuming his biretta with a lazy bend of his head sideways, and squaring his shoulders, he left the room with an exhibition of physi-

[168]

cal power under control which made us desire to be exactly like him in every way.

And yet I was now cast down by my new eminence. How could I ever measure up to Father Coach's standards? Matters were not helped for me with my classmates when Miss Mendtzy, sparkling with happiness behind her pince-nez, declared,

"Class, I am sure we are all very pleased for Richard, and very proud that this great honor has fallen on one of our own boys. To be almost a preesst! To think of the good of it for his soul!"

An atmosphere of gloom settled over the rows of desks and with a heavy heart I prepared to enter the service I had striven for. I wondered if my soul had begun to feel different.

⚘

For a long time in my childhood I thought my soul—and there-fore every soul—was a small, flattish lump of wax lodged obscurely in the spinal column. It was there, but nobody could see or touch it. My image of it was derived from the holy object called the Agnus Dei, which was a small square or oval packet of velvet or fine baize or silk, edged with fancy tatting by nuns, and showing a colored picture of the Lamb of God on its front. It was slightly padded, and the padding was a piece of blessed bees' wax which could not be seen but whose thickness could be felt. The Agnus Dei was pinned to the underside of a boy's lapel or to some hidden fold of a girl's dress. The blessing it carried was a protection against the world. Mine—I wore one for a little while in the third grade—almost made me rich.

For one day while I was playing with a friend at his house in our neighborhood his grandmother came to smile upon us. She was a thin, tall woman with a face, I thought, like that of a chipmunk who gazed through frail golden eyeglasses. From the wrists of her black silk dress lace cuffs fell over her hands, which she carried crossed at her waist. Finding my jacket where I had thrown it carelessly, she picked it up to fold and smooth it and set it away more properly, and she saw my Agnus Dei under my lapel.

"Richard, what is this?" she called.

"It is my Agnus Dei."

"What is it for?"

"It was blessed by the priest and so you wear it to be protected."

Her cheek pouches seemed to fill and quiver with horror. I had never thought about it, but my friends in that house were not Catholics. Now the grandmother put down my jacket with a shudder. She was thinking about something. In a moment she called,

"Richard, do you believe all those things that the priest tells you? And the sisters?"

"Yes."

"Do you believe in God?"

"Certainly."

"But you do not read the Bible, do you?"

"No. They read it to us in church."

"But how can you know God if you don't read the Bible? It is the only way to know Him. All the rest that they do to you has nothing to do with God. It is just for the sake of the Church and themselves. Don't you know that?"

"I don't believe you."

She smiled with bitter patience.

"You are too young to know, Richard.—Would you like to have a dollar?"

"Yes."

"I will give you a dollar every week if you will do something for me. For yourself."

"What is that?"

"If you will read the Bible every day for five minutes I will give you a dollar every Saturday, after you tell me what you have read. Here. Wait." She hurried to her room and returned with a small black limp Bible with edges stained red. "Take this with you and oh, my poor boy, be faithful! How I wish I could save you!"

Save me? I who had a guardian angel who was beside me at that moment though nobody could see him? I smiled and took the Bible.

"All right," I said.

"Dear, good Richard. Here is a dollar in advance. I just know you will earn it between now and Saturday and then we will talk and I will explain what you did not understand in the Bible and then you will have another dollar."

"Well, gosh, Grandma," said my friend, complaining because he had no such swift rise to fortune. She silenced him with a colorless glance of unexpected force.

❦

That evening my father came to say goodnight in my room.

"How's the Doctor?" he asked.

"Fine."

"What did you do today?"

"I played after school at Dodie's."

"What did you play?"

"We played soldiers. He has a thousand hundred of them."

"Did you have a battle?"

"Yes."

"Who won?"

"He did."

"Why."

"It was his house."

"I see. Was anybody else there?"

"His grandma."

"Oh, Lord. Yes, I suppose so. Poor old soul."

"Why is she poor old soul?"

"Why, you know, they're Presbyterians. They never have any fun out of life."

"They don't?"

"No."

"Why not?"

"It's too hard to explain."

"But she's very, very nice."

"Of course. They're all nice.—Why is she very, very nice?"

"She gave me a dollar. I put it in my bank."

"Why did she give you a dollar?"

He was getting that keen softened look he got when finding out something. His eyes narrowed and his mouth went thin sideways a little. I began to be sorry I had mentioned the dollar. He didn't seem to like the idea.

"She gave it to me to read something."

"You mean if you promised to read something she would give you a dollar?"

"Yes. A dollar every week."

"*What?*" He stood up from my bed. "And what is it you are supposed to read to earn a dollar every week at your age?"

"The Bible. She gave me one. She said it was the only way to know God, and to save me."

He took a step backward. His mouth fell open. On his brow came a frown like that of God the Father. His eyes rayed blue fire. I never saw him so angry. He made a fist of his right hand which trembled at the punishment he would inflict upon the meddling old

[172]

woman who sought to corrupt his son away from his Faith.

"And for *money!*" he shouted hoarsely, completing his thought. "To take an innocent child and tempt him with what no child could resist!—Where is that Bible?" he demanded.

"On the dresser."

He went and took it up.

"And where is that bank?"

"Behind my Book of Knowledge."

He went to my bookshelf and thr   n several volumes of the Book of Knowledge until he foun   nk which was made of cast iron in the shape of a spanie   whose ears lifted up to receive deposits of money. He th   bank to the floor with force. It broke. A folded green do   y among small coins.

"Is this her dollar?" he asked.

"Yes."

"Say goodbye to it. And don't   ever accept money from her, or anybody else, unless you c   isk me first whether you may do so. Is that clear?"

"Yes, Father."

"Do you know what she tried to do to you?"

"No."

"She tried to take you away from our Holy Mother Church. Would you want that?"

"No."

"I should hope not." He sickened a little as his anger subsided from its first power. "My poor old Doc. First he got rich and then he got poor. Never mind, boysie, your father will take care of you. I'll get you a new bank. Now you ask God to forgive you if you had any idea of what you were doing, and ask Him to keep you, and say a prayer of thanks to your guardian angel for how this turned out, and go to sleep."

"What are you going to do?"

"I am going to return her Bible and her dollar and tell her that you will not be allowed to go to their house again."

"Can't I ever play with Dodie again?"

"Yes. Over here. Not at his house so long as that old buttinsky is there."

"Well, gosh."

"I know. But I don't want you near her. She will go to Hell for this."

"She will?"

It was an awesome thought made the more so because he delivered it with shocked regret.

"Yes," he said, "and so would you, if she had her way. I'm going right over there."

A few minutes later I heard the front door thunder and tremble gently with its great oval pane of plate glass. As I went to sleep I spoke to my guardian angel as usual, who answered me, not in words, for he never used words, but in thoughts or ideas which came in return for my prayers to him. It was a momentous exchange that night, for as clear and lovely as light on water the idea came to me that in return for my escape from Hell I would do well to give my life to God by becoming a priest. Wonder and greatness, all in explicit detail, enfolded me as I went to sleep an ordained priest that night.

In the morning when I awoke my idea was still with me, and it remained with me in secret all that year, and when Dodie's grandmother died one night, I sorrowed for where she had gone. Presently I drew nearer to my vocation when Father Coach chose me as server for his six o'clock. In my own eyes, I was a miniature priest, already close to the Divine Mysteries, and I was impatient to come closer still.

One morning after Mass I lingered alone in the sacristy. It would be half an hour before the rector of the Cathedral, our pastor, old Monsignor Tremaine, came to vest himself for his own Mass at seven. His vestments were all laid out for him on a wide deep counter above ranks of tray-like drawers. His black biretta was there too, with its silky pom-pom of red violet.

How would I look if I were a priest and wore it? And that maniple and stole of white heavy watered silk with hard thick gold embroidery over which the light zipped when you turned to give a blessing? The chasuble had a heavy, rich design of rose vines in gold, tracing the shape of the cross. It was too large for me to wear, and I fingered it hungrily; but I could manage the other things. I put the stole around my neck and slipped the maniple over my left arm. The counter was about the height of an altar. It became my altar.

I put the biretta on my head. It was only slightly too large. I put it on and off several times as though observing the sacred name during the *Gloria* or the *Credo,* and then I set it down on the counter and bent over and kissed the altar and then raising my arms to God I recited, "Benedicat vos omnipotens Deus," preparing to turn and bless the people, "Pater et Filius et Spiritus Sanctus," and I turned, and there watching me stood Monsignor Tremaine in the doorway of the sacristy.

My blessing died away in midair.

He came forward slowly, looking at me with keen and serious brown eyes in his creamy pink face. He usually smiled and hummed a continuous tune, but now he came silently and gravely to me.

"Richard, what is the meaning of this?"

"Nothing, M'nsígnor," I said.

"Have you forgotten your instructions that servers are never, never to handle the vestments except to assist Father?"

"No, M'nsígnor."

"Then why did you dress yourself up in them? Don't you know they are holy objects, with sacred meaning? They have been blessed. Don't you know that?"

"Yes, M'nsígnor."

He took the stole and maniple from me and laid them on the counter and picked up his biretta and put it on. He wore it toward the back of his head. It gave him at once a look of Old Testament strangeness and authority.

"Did you mean to desecrate these things?"

"No, M'nsígnor."

"What were you *doing,* then. Playacting?"

"No, M'nsígnor."

Usually patient and kind, he now grew exasperated.

"Don't be such a dunce. What *were* you doing, then?"

"I was trying to feel how it would feel to be a priest, and say Mass."

"You weren't making fun of it?"

"Oh, no, M'nsígnor."

"I see. Well. Richard. Let me see."

He became solemn and gentle. He leaned down and put his hand on my shoulder. He let it rest there heavily as to impress me with the seriousness of what I might say.

"Why did you want to feel that, Richard?"

"I don't know."

"I think you do. Tell me truly, now. Do you think you want to become a priest?"

It must be, I thought, that there are simply no secrets which children can keep from their elders.

"Yes, M'nsígnor."

"Then this makes a great difference. Come with me."

He led me to the sanctuary and he knelt down on the lowest step of the high altar and had me kneel beside him and he said,

"Let us ask Our Lord to help us to know if this a true vocation you have or not. If it is, you shall have all the help we can give you. It is the greatest thing I could hope for you. *Our Father Who art in Heaven,*" he prayed, and *"Hail Mary full of grace,"* and *"Glory be to the Father,"* and I prayed with him, giving the responses aloud to each prayer.

Then it was time for him to vest himself for his Mass, and he sent me off to breakfast and school, for the world went on and he must go with it, and so must I.

※

The next morning after Mass Father Coach said to me,

"So there's some sort of idea running around in that empty head of yours."

"I don't know, Father."

"Yes, you do. Monsígnor told me. He has put me in charge of your vocation. How old are you?"

I told him.

"Ten years more, and five or six years on top of that. Do you think you can last that long?"

"I don't know, Father."

"Do you want to know something?"

"What, Father?"

"It gets harder all the way. Do you know that?"

"Yes, Father."

"No, you don't. You don't know the first thing about it. Well, I'll try to give you some idea. If you can take the first hurdles maybe you can last the race. We'll see. Beginning tomorrow morning, I'm going to say a Mass at five-thirty, and you're going to serve it, and we'll see just how much you mean all this wearing of vestments and saying 'Dominus vobiscum.'"

"Yes, Father."

"After that we'll think of other ways for you to prove yourself. Nobody ever claimed the way was easy. It wasn't for me. Well, I made it. We're going to find out if you're man enough."

"'S, Father."

"Skiddoo."

How he would have loved to have his own son whom he could train as an athlete from the first hour of life, in the image of one who had no thought but to serve God. He believed he had the most solemnly great reason in the world for putting me through an ordeal which would have been difficult for a man. He became a tyrant as he tested me in all ways he could imagine. He taunted me with mockery and weakened me with harsh criticism. Nothing I did could ever satisfy him. When I faltered at serving Mass, or left without saying the extra prayers of thanksgiving after Mass which he had set me as exercises proper to one who thought he was a priest, or had a cold and could not swallow my sneezes, or missed Communion on a weekday because of sins I could not confess until Saturday, he rose over me with lazy contempt, slowly nodding at how much of a fool he had been to give his time and trust to someone so faithless. He began to make me twist and flee him in my dreams, so that I awoke exhausted, and audibly yawned at Mass, for which I would again know his scorn.

I decided that he hated me, but—a master of the change of pace, like any good coach—every now and then he would suddenly ease up in my training, and take me with him to get books at the Catholic Union Library, or do some extra shopping for the rectory table; and then he would be easy and confidential with me, letting me have bits of gossip or even a sarcastic comment or two on the life of the rectory, quite as though I already belonged to his sacred brotherhood whose members, being human, had opinions and sometimes vented them.

"Monsígnor, you know?" he would say, raising an eyebrow at me, "God bless him, Monsígnor thinks of himself as a musician. Can you beat it? Thinks he can play the piano. Gave up a concert career to be a priest."

"Well, can he play?"

"All thumbs. They say the Bishop calls him Maestro. They were classmates."

Or,

"If you want cookies and milk after Mass, you'll have to get in good with the housekeeper at the rectory. But I advise against it."

"Why, Father?"

"The price is too great."

"Well, what is it?"

"You know that gasping, smelly old dog of hers, the one she calls Scruffy?"

"'S, Father."

"Offer to give Scruffy a bath, or walk him around the block. She'll give you the moon. But if you start it, you'll have to keep it up. Lay off, is my advice. She's—" and he made a finger go round and round like a little wheel at his temple. "The only reason His Nibs keeps her on is that she can bake the best mince pie in Upstate New York. And I'll tell you another thing, if you ever come around me smelling of Scruffy, *we're through*. Get me?"

Threatening to end our league, he handsomely established its existence for me, and I kindled warmly to his fondness. At such moments I would think my troubles were over.

[179]

But they never were. One morning he said,

"I suppose you think you believe in God?"

"Oh, yes, Father."

"Who is your favorite in the Holy Family?"

"Jesus."

"Which statue do you pray before?"

"The Infant of Prague."

"Why?"

"He is a boy."

"He is a King."

"I know. He has a crown."

"And an orb, which means the world, which He holds in His very own hand, and He blesses the world with His other hand. Well, this King, then. Do you pray to Him about your vocation?"

I had honestly to admit that I had never done so.

"And yet," he scoffed, "you say you believe in Him."

"But I do."

"No, you don't. If you did, you'd ask Him every day and every night to tell you to be true to Him and go all the way to become one of His priests."

"How could He tell me?"

"How could He tell you? Don't you ever get the feeling that your prayers are being heard and answered?"

"I don't know, Father."

He scratched his head in knuckly despair at such a boy.

"I suppose," he said with almost a lisping drawl of sarcasm, "you won't be satisfied until He appears to you in a vision and says, 'Hello, Richard, how's the boy! Great news I hear about you. Keep up the old fight!' Go on. Get out of here. Don't be late in the morning."

They noticed at home how restless I was, and unable to eat. I looked thin and felt thinner. Nobody knew what I was suffering and why. If only I could be sure that I must suffer, then I believed I could suffer all that might have to come to me. But how could I know?

I woke up one night remembering Father Coach's taunt about expecting a vision. My heart jumped against my bony chest to mark the moment of a great discovery. Why should I not ask for a miracle? If I could make the Infant of Prague hear me and believe how I loved Him and wished to serve Him, then I could make Him appear to me and give me the answer I needed. Once again I slept at peace, for I knew what I must do, however dangerous and difficult it might be to arrange.

Since Dodie's grandmother had died, I was allowed to go to his house again. Sometimes I went to stay all night with him.

I now got him to ask me to spend the night and then I reported this to my mother. She gave permission. I went to Dodie's for supper and then told his family I suddenly had to go home. They protested, and for a moment Dodie's mother meant to telephone my mother to ask if I might not stay? But quickly I said she must not do this, as I had not brought my plaid bag full of homework, which was true, and they let me go.

I was free for the night and my great purpose lay before me.

※

I went to the Cathedral of the Holy Angels and entered by one of the four side doors. It was about half-past seven. The doors would be locked at eight. As I knew, all the doors—even the sacristy door— had bolts which were secured from within by heavy keys which the sexton would carry away with him on their iron ring.

Three or four people—women and a man—were kneeling far

[181]

apart from each other in the cavernous twilight of the church. The only illumination came from two immense bronze lanterns high in the transepts.

All was so still that now and then when a little draught stirred the wick of a votive lamp this became a large event. The soaring vaults of the ceiling seemed as far away as the sky. Like cloth woven of darkness itself, long rows of shadows hung as pillars from the arches of the aisles.

The smallest sound—a creak of a bench under one of the praying people, a door opening or closing far off in the sacristy, the beady click of a rosary against a pew—set up echoes in the high vaults with the sound of a whispered voice saying, "H-o-w-w-w?" in a long sigh that seemed to take forever to die away.

The sanctuary lamp threw no light but only hung in the air like a red star, how near or far who could say? The altars were dark. Before some of the statues burned little wicks in colored glass. One of these was my goal—the Infant of Prague, whose crown, orb and blessing I could barely discern from the rear pew where I crouched.

I kept my eyes upon Him because I must come to Him later; and also because if my eyes roamed, they might be drawn to certain objects which even in broad daylight always gave me a heavy fear in my soul—that flat wax lump caged within me—and which in this sighing darkness made my mouth dry up at the thought of them.

These were the tombs of the two previous bishops of Dorchester which stood against the rear wall of the sanctuary, one on each side of the high altar. Marble sarcophagi which rose high as a man, they were carved and indented with miniature Gothic colonnades on all sides. Carved marble mitres and heraldic devices rested on the massive lids. Bishops, I knew, were buried in their vestments. It was sorrowful and terrifying to think of them as richly robed they lay there in those great boxes of marble, unlike all the other dead who were part of the earth in green cemeteries.

The presence of the dead bishops almost made me give up my resolve to stay the whole night in the locked cathedral, kneeling before the image of my patron the Infant of Prague, Who before daylight came and the doors were unbolted must appear to me in a vision. If He would do this, no doubt would remain about my vocation, and perhaps I would be left in peace by Father Coach.

At a few minutes before eight the sexton came around and told the people it was time for them to leave. They all seemed to be old people who rose heavily to their feet and one by one made their aching way down the aisle and out the main door, while I cowered in the dark under my pew. I was in a panic to run out after them, but already it was too late for escape. The sexton had already secured the side doors, and now after the last visitors of the night had left God to go down the outside steps, he rang home the heavy bolts in the bronze main door. Going up the center aisle to the sanctuary where he paused to look around for a last duty that night, the sexton, himself an old man, genuflected in a rapid little cringe and went on to the sacristy. In a moment, out of sight, he turned off the two lanterns in the vaults of the transepts. Leaving the sacristy for the rectory where he would hang up his key-ring in the kitchen, he left me alone behind him. Only the distant, pure points of flame in the votive lights in their ranks of blue, red and yellow glass, and a few other candle lamps before certain statues, remained to define the darkness.

"H-o-w-w-w . . ." sighed the vaults so far above me. The church was cold. In the darkness where I could not see I felt huge for a moment, and then small—smaller than I was.

Perhaps he had forgotten to lock one of the doors. I went to each of the side doors, and even to the main doors, but all were securely locked. My footsteps sounded like those of someone else following me. I looked to see who it might be and could not see who was there. Far at the end of a side aisle was the shrine of the Infant of

Prague. I hurried there and knelt down in the first pew before it. A candle lamp with red glass burned at His feet. The light flowing upward over Him made His eyes look empty in cups of shadow above His plump young cheeks. I said,

"Blessèd Infant of Prague, have mercy on me,

"Blessèd Infant of Prague, have mercy on me,

"Blessèd Infant of Prague, have mercy on me," and I felt myself losing command of my imagination, as happened in times of intense feeling.

※

You could see in the red glass how the fires of Hell always looked, except that this glass was only one little pool of fiery light, and those fires were everywhere all about you. You could not count the bodies of the damned. In their legions, they were thrown upon each other, fixed in writhen positions upon red-hot rocks, and they were naked, men and women alike, as you had seen in your grandfather's copy of Dante's *Inferno* with plates by Gustave Doré. Their mouths were open and silent. Their eyes were gazing and empty.

You had seen fires burn—wood, leaves, refuse; and it was the law of fire that after a little while in the flames nothing was left of anything except ash. But in Hell nothing ever burned away, it simply kept on existing in the fire, and it would do so forever and ever. You thought that if fire would only burn those condemned bodies up once and for all this would have been terrible but it could be accepted as an idea: short, frightful suffering, and then the end of feeling. But you forgot when you thought in that way how the very law of Hell was to provide suffering that had no end. And so you saw those quadrillions of men and women burning forever and yet never consumed.

[184]

In a moment you saw someone you knew. She tried to cover herself from your wondering gaze. She said nothing, her mouth hung open, and her hollow eyes looked and looked at you, and she bowed her head slowly and sadly at you, and you recognized Dodie's grandmother. She made you feel responsible for sending her there. Would she have gone if you had not told about her? It was something you would never know. Not knowing was another kind of punishment if it was something you absolutely had to know.

Did you know anybody else in Hell? Your grandfather had died in Germany. Was he in the fires or was he in Heaven? He must be in Heaven.

The bishops in their marble boxes—how was it with them, and their golden croziers and their jewelled rings and crosses and the zipping light over all the silks and embroideries of their vestments? When the cathedral vaulting whispered "H-o-w-w-w . . ." it might have been their voices that you heard, for they were to lie there forever, and there was no way for you to get out either. You would rather be a martyr in an open place in ancient Rome than die here and be enclosed forever in white marble darkened by night.

The catacombs must be like a whole train of tombs. You knew how their corridors wound along underground like the burrowed tracks of great worms. There the early Christians had found safety with their single candles and their hidden Masses. You thought probably they too had been afraid but they went on praying under the ground as if they lived and would die in their own graves. You knew how courageous they were, and what great examples, but you did not want to live in your own grave until you died and had to use it forever. Who knew? Perhaps, you thought, they too may have wanted to live in the open air?

Pity for the longings which lay buried with all the dead of the world rose within you and made your throat thicken and your eyes smart. You knew about rising from the dead. Why was it so terrifying? Because it was contrary to nature. It would be something happening that simply could not happen. But if enough wishing took place, perhaps by all the dead of the world, then they might rise again, even if this was contrary to nature?

Now because your eyes were used to the darkness you could see most faintly the shapes of familiar objects in the cathedral. You could see the tombs of the two bishops. If the marble lids, which weighed tons, began to open slowly, perhaps twisting sidewise smoothly and silently as if oiled, you would be able to see this happen.

The lids opened, it seemed, during a passage of hours, but at last in either sarcophagus there was enough open space in the shape of a wedge of pitch darkness to allow the dead to rise into view. You could see rising first the coiled and jewelled head of the golden crozier which was buried alongside the bishop; and then his hand, wearing scarlet gloves, embroidered in gold, with his episcopal ring on the outside of his glove, grasping the marble edge of the box, and then the white pod-shaped crown of his mitre lifting up. And then he would come into the air of the church he had loved, where he had sat on his throne so many times amidst incense and candle-light and air mightily shaken by the voices of organ and choir, and if he turned and looked at you without eyes and spoke to you, you would have to answer in proper singsong, "Yes, Right Reverend Bishop." What if he looked like Uncle Fritz who died to become a bishop? You would love to see Uncle Fritz again—but alive, not dead. And then what if—as you had read somewhere—the bishop's body might in an instant fall down in dust on its encounter with the air of the living world after so long a time in the breathless dark of the tomb?

And yes: if that could happen, then the statues in the locked cathedral might also move on their altars, and you would be surrounded by others risen from the dead, for the saints were all once alive.

[186]

"Blessèd Infant of Prague," you prayed, suddenly remembering Him, "let them stay dead!"

You shook as if you were freezing. Your teeth clattered in your skull. In the dark it was difficult for your hands to find each other in order to join in prayer. Terror exhausted you so that you thought you might fall asleep at any minute, as if you could not endure any more of the night of the dead.

And just then you could hardly believe what began to happen. You watched it with your eyes wide open.

※

The statue of the Infant of Prague began to glow with light. The light came from all around it and inside it and in front of it. It was a kind of light that did not light up anything else around. It lighted only the statue in still radiance. Kneeling before the light, you put your arms wide back with your hands opened to it as if to receive it. You were no longer frightened; only too amazed to say anything.

The Infant of Prague opened His arms aside as if to say, "Yes, it is true, Richard, this is a vision, I am appearing to you," and then brought them back to their usual position holding His right hand up in blessing, carrying the orb in His left. His face was like a real child's, alive with joy.

For a long time nobody said anything, but just exchanged their gaze. Then the little painted plaster mouth of the Infant of Prague, moving like the mouth of a real child, said, clearly,

"Never fear, Richard. They will stay dead."

Though He was only a child, He spoke like someone grown to all knowledge.

[187]

"They will?" you asked in wonderful relief.

"Yes. Now was there anything else?"

But if you had something else to ask Him, you did not remember what it was. Happiness and safety put such peace over you that you began to fall asleep not out of fear now but out of ease. The last thing you recalled was how the Infant of Prague, who always held His right hand with His fingers fixed to make a blessing, now actually moved His hand again and blessed you. His light then vanished. The statue was dark again above its red lamp.

When I felt a rough grasp on my shoulder I awoke throwing myself hard against the back of the pew. Father Coach was there. At the windows faint light was announcing the day.

"Get up," commanded Father Coach. "Come with me."

His voice was level and hard. I rubbed myself awake and found out where I was.

"Get going," he added. There was no comfort to be had from his sound. I went rapidly ahead of him to the sacristy where we could talk out loud without disrespect to the Blessèd Sacrament.

"Now explain yourself," he said.

I looked down tongue-tied.

"How long have you been in the cathedral?"

"All night."

"I see. I am not ready to explain your presence all night as an act of piety. How do *you* account for it? What leads me, when I arise before five o'clock to come here and perform my usual early morning devotions, to find a delinquent intruder? Do your parents know you are here?"

"No, Father."

"So you had no thought of how they must be frantic with worry?"

"No, Father. I mean, yes, Father. They thought I went to stay all night at Dodie's."

"But instead, you stayed here. Is that it?"

"Yes, Father."

"So you are a liar as well as a trespasser."

"No, Father."

"You aren't?"

"Yes, Father."

"And I had the stupid belief that here was a boy who would some day be a man, and that man a priest. How do you like that."

"Yes, Father, that's why I came."

"Why you came?"

"Yes, Father. You said the Infant of Prague would have to appear to me and tell me about being a priest."

"I never did. Watch your tongue, young man."

"Yes, Father. But you did. So I came and stayed before Him all night."

"And I suppose He took the trouble to come down from Heaven and appear to you? What makes you think you would be worthy of such a thing?"

"I'm not, Father. But He did."

"Did what:"

"He did appear to me."

"Now just you look out, young fellow, I won't take much of this. I don't have to stand here and listen to blasphemy!"

"But He did. I saw Him. He talked to me. He was as bright as an electric light."

"And what, if I may make so bold as to ask, did He say to you?"

I saw then that my case was about to be lost, for in truth, the Infant of Prague said nothing to me about becoming a priest, which was what I was supposed to discuss with Him. Miracles, I saw for the first time, were not always clear in their meaning.

"Richard?" prompted Father Coach with an edge of threat in his voice. I knew how flat it must sound when I had to reply,

"He told me not to be afraid."

"Afraid? Of what:"

"He said all the dead people would stay dead."

Father Coach folded his arms and set his head to one side and looked at me with his eyes drowsily half-closed as if to see me for the first time. Then he began to nod slowly like a man who has had to accept an unwelcome fact.

"All right, Richard," he said with ominous patience, "you get along home. I'll telephone your parents you are on your way. I'll report what you have told me. They will know best how to deal with it. I'm just sorry that all my faith in you, and my confidence, the hours I have given over to your training, the thought I put in day after day on how to toughen you up for your future, I'm just sorry all this has been for nothing."

"But Father, I have to serve your five-thirty."

"Not any more, you don't. Not after all this record of breaking every rule in the cathedral, and lying to your parents, and trumping up this crazy vision you had, and thinking I would accept all this."

"I never meant anybody to know. I just wanted to know myself."

"Well, you know now, and what's more important, so do I. I hate to tell Monsignor all about this. It will merely break his heart, that's all. Go on, get going."

When I came home the sun was not yet up. All the lights in our house were on. After Father Coach's call, my father was on the porch waiting for me. In silence he grasped me by the arm, hurried me upstairs to my mother's room where she lay with witch-hazel on a handkerchief cooling her throbbing brow while tears welled out of her eyes. When she saw me she reached for me and pulled me to her breast.

"All night long!" she murmured against my cheek. "We have been frantic. The police are looking for you! Your father has been driving around through the streets all night long, looking and looking, between here and Dodie's. How could you do this to us!"

"Is that my son?" asked my father coldly. "To act out a lie to his parents? Only by accident did I find out. I saw your plaid homework bag under the hall bench and I drove over with it to Dodie's so you could do your homework, and they said you had gone home." He turned to my mother. "That will do. Let him go. It is time he came with me."

"Oh, no, Dan," she said. "Don't."

"Let him go. He has to learn. Come with me, Richard. And all that talk about a vision of the Infant of Prague. You simply fell asleep and had a dream. Come on."

This was what Father Coach meant by having my parents deal with me. My father whipped me with his mahogany-colored razor strop and then sent me to bed. In an effort to resolve one kind of trouble I had thrown myself into another kind. Was that how life went? Once again I took refuge in sleep and slept all day until late afternoon. Then I was awakened by a delegation.

My father came bringing Monsignor Tremaine. I shrank in my bed toward the wall.

"No, my boy," said Monsignor Tremaine, "I have not come to scold you. Sit up."

My father put a chair for him and he sat down, leaning toward me. He sparkled with freshness—his white starched collar, his trim black suit, the thread of red-violet showing above his high-buttoned vest, his pink and white head.

"You are feeling rested, now, Richard?" he asked gently. His kindness made me want to cry for the first time that day.

"Yes, M'nsígnor."

"Well, you have given us all more to talk about than we've had for years. Some people want to punish you. Others think you are perhaps a little over-sensitive to some things, and perhaps you need a little while of getting more sleep and eating well and putting some flesh on your bones. I don't really know why you did what you did. I think maybe you don't know why, yourself, really." (But I did.) "But now that it's over, no real harm has been done, and I came to see you and tell you not to worry. It may be too soon for many things, Richard. I myself, you know, I didn't know until I was in college that I was meant to be a priest. And even then it took me a mighty long time, and not a happy time, altogether, I can tell you, until I knew."

"Yes, M'nsígnor."

I did not understand at the time what he was trying to tell me; I felt only his warm humanity, and the forgiveness it was made of. He turned to my father and said, as though I had ears but would hear not,

"You know, Daniel, the whole thing looks like boyish nonsense, somewhat overwrought and feather-headed, and of course, it may be just that. But never forget the chance in a thousand that there may be real holiness somewhere in it. Only God knows which it might be. But what if He meant it the way Richard received it? See what I mean?"

My father looked at the floor like a young man and nodded silently. Monsignor Tremaine turned back to me and said, as he arose,

"Get yourself rested and healthy again, my boy, and your imagination won't give you as much trouble. But if it does, don't be sorry for yourself. God gave us all our faculties, including that one. It may lead you to Him to serve Him for life, or it may lead you to bring something to your fellow-men as an artist of some sort. For the present, try to be just a boy. God bless you."

CHAPTER IX

❦

A Discharge of Electricity

A summer later, a bond of fear was broken for me in honor of another bondage—perhaps one more tyrannical.

❦

"Do you think—?" asked my mother, looking at the sky above the darkening mountains across the mottling lake.

"It may," said my father. "What do you say, Miles?" he asked Miles O'Connor who with his wife Nell and their son Billy—a boy in my class at school—had come to spend the weekend with us at our cottage on Thunder Island in the small Adirondack lake where we were again spending the summer.

"What if it does?" replied Miles in his loud voice which always gave what he said a furious sound, despite what he may have felt. "We would only get wet."

We were on the rustic porch of the cottage where the air was already chilled by the rain that began to sweep toward us across the lake. Our picnic was all packed in hampers, we had extra cushions waiting in a heap, and Miles O'Connor had his banjo by the throat, ready to bring it along so that after we had eaten and the embers were renewed with under-scrub from the woods where we were going in a cove on the mainland he could sing for us to his own accompaniment. There was an unexpected sweetness in his voice when he sang, a hint of a self the world never otherwise knew. But all secrets ask to be heard, and my mother once said that next to making money, Miles O'Connor would rather sing than anything.

The wind reached us and as it did the sky opened in a sustained rip of white lightning. There was a short horrifying pause as if all breath were cut off and then the thunder cracked over us and the rain came down like a waterfall repeated endlessly in a sky-wide mirror. In one moment we could see our white launch, the *Arrow*, sliding and rocking at our dock below the cottage, and in another she was erased by the rain. It suddenly seemed hours ago instead of minutes that we had been ready to board her gaily to ride across the lake for our Friday evening picnic.

"This won't last," shouted Miles to my father.

※

I heard no more, for I ran into the house and down the damp hallway whose raw wooden walls released the smell of pitch-pine, and into my room where Billy was to sleep with me. I slammed the door and went to my clothes closet and shut myself in and sat on the floor with my hands over my ears. My heart shook me with a slow pounding stab at every beat. I prayed for my life, as the air cracked like mountains about our island in the storm.

"My Jesus, mercy!" I thought at every bolt. "Hail Mary full of grace," I said in between times, and "Oh, my God, I am heartily sorry for having offended Thee"—for I knew from nuns, and from

Anna, and from the bravely concealed winces of my mother every time it lightninged and thundered how I might be struck dead by God's rage, which was surely what sounded out of the sky.

I felt rather than heard a banging on my closet door. I uncovered my ears to hear.

"Come out of there!" called my father, pulling at the closet door. I tried to hold it fast. He sounded disgusted but full of control.

"Please: Dan:" said my mother. "There is no use making him even more afraid." She talked across his shoulder.

"In front of those people," said my father. How could his son so fully have humiliated him before his business partner, whose boy Billy was never afraid of anything? "It's time he had this nonsense whaled out of him once and for all."

"I know," said my mother. "But just please, dear, leave this to me."

The storm struck again and I hid my senses in the frail darkness of the closet. When again I listened my father had gone back to the O'Connors on the porch, where they stood silently staring at the storm which though lessened in force still held on and slashed them with rain, which they endured because Miles refused to budge.

The door of my closet opened when my mother gently pulled at its rusty iron latch.

"Richard:" she said. "Don't you think you might decide to live, and come out, now?"

I regarded her in silence.

"The storm is going away," she said.

As though to contradict her, a bolt struck a tree at the tip of our island and the crack of it seemed to set all things in the world an inch or two aside. My mother shrugged in exasperation.

"Oh, I don't like it either," she scolded, "I hate it. But really: my dear: we have guests: we *must*—"

Her social spirit was stronger than her own nervousness (I had often seen her cross herself secretly during thunder and lightning)

[196]

and she now tried to make me into the son of her braver self by adding,

"When this clears, it may still be light enough to see, and we will go in the *Arrow,* and you can bring your new airplane kite that Daddy brought you from town, and you can show Billy how to fly it."

"I don't want to show Billy how to fly it. It's mine."

"Then don't, don't, oh, my God, why am I given such a boy!" But she knelt down and embraced me, and said, "What geese we all are, *everybody* is afraid of *something,* only they don't show it."

"My father isn't," I said resentfully.

"Oh! If you knew! But he is brave. Don't you want to be brave?"

"I don't care."

"Oh, yes you do. Every man does."

"I never cry any more."

"I know you don't, my darling. You are very brave."

"My father said a man does not cry."

"He did? Of course he did. Well, then, you must believe him."

But her voice seemed to carry some sad knowledge otherwise. She sighed and pulled me to stand, saying,

"Come, Richard, we simply must go back to the others."

"I don't want to"—for now I was ashamed of myself. She knew why. She said,

"Yes, one of the things about behaving badly in front of others is that the time always comes when we must be with them again. The only way is to go back immediately. So come. Miles is furious at having his picnic spoiled by the storm. We mustn't spoil it even more."

We returned to the porch.

[197]

The thunder was now hiding behind the mountains and the rain was hanging in open curtains instead of in solid falls. Outspoken like his father, Billy O'Connor said to me,

"What's the matter with you?"

"Now Billy," said Nell O'Connor, with a smile of complicit understanding at my mother, "don't be rude. Richard has come back to us, and we're all going to have a scrumptious time."

I know from old photographs how pretty she was, and how much at that time her son looked like her. He had her high, round, flushed cheeks, and her blue-grey eyes, and her petal mouth, always smiling over nothing. She made a great point of being sensible. She seemed not to want to change anything in the conditions about her in the world. She hardly ever stopped talking, which may have explained why when they said anything her husband and her son shouted.

Looking at me, Miles O'Connor said to my father,

"If he were my boy I'd never let him get away with anything like that."

"He isn't your boy," replied my father with his widest smile, and yet with a wrinkle of warning in his brow.

"Now Miles," chaffed Nell, "everybody is trying to calm things down, don't you stir them up again."

"Lightning," declared Billy, with his stocky little chest stuck out, "is only a discharge of electricity."

"That's right," said his father with approval. "You'd better teach Richard a few lessons."

"Quit it, will you, please, Miles?" said my father.

"Oh, all right, what the hell," muttered Miles causing my mother to wince at the ugly word. "We might as well give up the whole show. It's getting dark. If we went, we might see a little heat lightning, and then we'd have another scene."

He kicked his way into the house and put his banjo back into its black case which was lined in blue plush.

"It's really better this way," said Nell to my father. "You and Miles have a lot of business to talk over this weekend, he told me so, you can get started tonight, and get it out of the way, we can have supper right here, everything is ready anyway, we brought the most delicious piccalilli, my cook makes it, and I said to her, They will die when they taste it, it's so good, just that pinch of red pepper makes all the difference, and I said, it's so good, we must take them a couple of jars, I said, and we. . . ."

Her voice trailed after her as she and my mother went inside to unpack the hampers and get supper ready at home.

To show whose side he was on, my father pulled me over against him with his strong thin arm. He squeezed my shoulder silently a few times, trying to tell me he was sorry for scolding me when I was frightened by something I could not yet control. He was all refuge for me then. He was honor and forgiveness. He was a man who would never say *that word* in front of women and children.

"Well, what sh'we do?" asked Billy, impatiently jigging his members by the porch railing.

"The rain is stopping," said my father. "Do you boys want to take a lantern and go down to the end of the island and see if a tree got struck? You might see one of the beavers, too. Sometimes they come out at twilight."

"Come on, Richard," said Billy.

In a few minutes, carrying the coal oil lantern my father had lighted for me, I led Billy toward the other end of the island, which was only about six hundred yards away. The ground was covered with wet pine needles. The smell of cold wet cedar was in the air. Within the woods that rose from the middle of the island, darkness was already immense and foreign. The lake was quiet after the storm. We could hear lappets of shallow waves whispering up the narrow edge of white sand where the island sloped into the water. There was no other cottage but ours on the island. The only way to reach the other side of the lake, at the village of Aetna, was by boat, either in the *Arrow,* or by the mail boat, the *Mollie,* which touched at the private docks all about the lake every day during the vacation season. Removed from everywhere, the island seemed my kingdom. It was now doubly fine because I had a friend there with whom to share it.

"Let me carry the lantern," demanded Billy. "I know how."

"So do I."

"But I can do it better."

"Why can you?"

"Because my father says I can."

"When did he say you could?"

"Never mind. Give it to me."

"You won't know where to go. You'll get lost. I know the way."

We were slipping along the hidden path inside the woods.

"Anybody can see where to go. Give it to me."

I gave it to him and he took the lead. The path turned suddenly to avoid a moss-covered boulder higher than either of us. Billy missed the path and struck the boulder. He dropped the lantern, which tipped over. Its dim yellow flame was smothered out. We were in complete darkness. The house at the other end of the island was concealed by the woods.

"Well, why didn't you tell me?" asked Billy.

"Tell you what?"

"Not to run into that rock."

"You could see it."

"I couldn't either."

"You wanted the lantern."

"Well, anyway, it's out. Have you got a match?"

"No."

"We better go back."

I reached around on the ground for the lantern, felt its dying heat, and took up its wire handle.

"Can you see?" I asked.

"No. Can you?"

"No."

"Which way do we go?"

"I don't know."

"Well, *which?*" he asked, angrily. After all, it was my island and I must know. We stood and listened. The trees dripped. The lake came and came up to the sand with a sound like a sleeper's breath. Suddenly there was a slow clatter somewhere under branches on the woods floor.

"What was that!" asked Billy in a hush.

"I don't know."

"You don't know. You don't know. What *do* you know? This is your island!"

His voice carried into the trees. With a clap like boards struck flatly together, a great bird left the topmost tree near us and went heavily into the air.

"What was that!" cried Billy in a tight whisper.

"It was the owl."

"What owl?"

"There is an old owl who lives at this end of the island. You scared him away."

"I did not."

"Yes, you did. He scared you, too."

"He did not."

"He did too."

"Come on," said Billy, "let's get back to the house."

We started out. Billy held on to my shirt because he could not see to follow.

※

You felt your way tree by tree, but in the dripping nightfall you did not know where you were. If seconds were days, and days years, and the woods a forest, and the island a continent, and the hour an unending midnight, in your anxiety and hunger you knew the doubtfulness of men lost in wilderness. The overland march from the interior of Thunder Island to find the lights of civilization after the torrential rain was without time and measure. You slid and fell on the wet pine needle carpet of the forest and you bruised your arms and knees and brow against unseen rocks and trees. All sounds were compounded by the drumming of blood in your ears. The whole history of courage as you knew it was focussed into a few minutes. The explorer's instinct came alive in you as leader of the expedition, and you believed that if you struck out for the coast you would come to the shoreline which would lead you by a longer and possibly more arduous but sure route to the settlements. But in the hemispheric darkness there was no way to know with any certainty which way to turn. Man could only persist against the unknown by making the movements it was his habit to make.

"Let's yell," said Billy.

"Why?"

"They might hear us."

"I don't want to."

"Why?"

"I'm not scared yet."

This was not true. It was only that I did not want so soon again to show myself afraid before him.

"Who's scared?" he said. "I'm hungry."

"So'm I."

"What's that!"

We heard the faraway engine whistle of the short freight train which drew into Aetna every night. Its sound, so familiar and so homely, called us home. We hurried again blindly. Then we stood each other still with a grasp and listened again. There came a sound. It was nearer than seemed possible without our having heard it before.

". . . And really, my dear, if I ever saw anyone look completely ridiculous," it said, "the way she wore it, and the hat itself, and besides, when you consider how old she. . . ."

It was Nell O'Connor. In another second we saw a flashlight ray wandering about just as her mind wandered, and I heard my mother murmur, "I know, I know," and then they came upon us.

"Where have you been? Supper is waiting and waiting. Come, darling," said my mother. She and Nell, wearing yellow sou'wester raincoats, had come for a little stroll along the wet path to find us.

When we came back to the cottage our fathers were seated at right angles to each other at the far end of the table, beneath a Coleman lantern. They were arguing.

"Oh, you crazy things," scoffed Nell. "Wrangle, wrangle. Still at it. It's time to eat."

The fathers drew in their elbows and we all sat down, but not to a meal in the social sense. The discussion kept up at the end of the table. Its energy became disagreeable. It had to do with details of a new enterprise they had incorporated outside of their general partnership in the insurance business. Who would get what percentage of the profits?—for Miles had thought of the idea behind the new business and believed he should have the greater share; but it was my father who had the most energy and imagination to bring to its operation, and all he asked was an equal share.

"All right," yelled Miles, drowning out everything we tried to say to each other at our end of the table, "just answer me this. If it weren't for my idea, just how much added income of any sort would you get?"

"Not a cent, of course," replied my father, speaking slowly in a calm rage, "but that is not the issue. The issue is whether you'd make a dime out of your idea if someone didn't come along and run it for you."

"Oh, it is, eh. I see. I may have a lot of brainy ideas but when it comes to carrying them out, I am an incompetent, is that what you're getting at?"

"Now Miles. For God's sake be reasonable."

My father was suddenly pleading through a sort of sickened gentleness in his voice. How could matters go so perversely wrong between him and his best friend and partner?

"Reasonable! Now I'm unreasonable!" shouted Miles. "I'm sick and tired of being in the wrong, day in and day out. I came up here to have a nice, quiet talk with you, and get affairs in order, and I run into this. Well, let me tell you something. I'm just about through!"

"Oh, Miles," said Nell, looking at my mother to register shock and good sense for all concerned, "you don't mean that."

"Try me and see!" snapped Miles.

My father leaned back and gazed at him for a long while, and then said,

"You know something? I think you came up here with your mind all made up to have a row. What for, I can't imagine. But from the minute we began to talk—."

Miles jumped up and slammed his hands flat on the table. He flushed a dark Irish purple. I remember now how the truth must have hurt worse than an empty insult. He could not bear it, for he knew it would one day be known that already, and in secret, he had made an arrangement with another businessman to take over my father's interest in the new company. Threatened with failure in accomplishing the separation which was the private object of his visit, he responded with all his might. He looked very young and as handsome as a fine animal in danger. We all saw him with fear and admiration. Billy watched his father with eyes like blue-burning steel—bright reflectors of energy and personality. Nell shivered as if remembering an instant of Miles's love-making. He could hardly speak through his fury.

"I don't have to sit here and listen to this! Come on, Nell. Billy. Get your things! We're leaving."

My father stood up and reached his hand to Miles's shoulder. Miles flung it off.

"Miles," said my father. "For the love of God. We're only trying to talk business. You can't leave. There's no train till tomorrow. There's no place to stay in the village. Let's forget all this and get together with cooler heads in the morning. Good Lord, don't you remember? *We're partners!"*

The white-hot core of Miles's anger began to cool to red and then dulled itself further. But something had been burned out forever, it seemed, in his guilty heart. Coldly, now, he said,

"I've been thinking for a long time that there might be a more sensible thing for us to be than partners."

"Oh, Miles!" exclaimed my mother. She knew how much the business association with Miles O'Connor meant to my father in personal as well as financial terms. "Don't say things, my dear, that will be hard to think of and take back tomorrow!"

"Are you coming, Nell?" he said. "I'm going to bed. We'll leave tomorrow. What time is the train?" he suddenly asked me, as though he would rather not have any exchanges with my parents.

"At noon," I said, "if it leaves on time."

He turned and went to the bedroom prepared for him and Nell. My father walked alone out to the porch and down to the shore. I could hear his long, trudging steps. Billy and I were forgotten for the moment.

"Really," said Nell, "aren't they ridiculous! They really, you know, love each other like brothers. That's probably just the trouble."

"Yes," said my mother, "in some ways they're too much alike."

"Why, they couldn't *do* without each other. If Miles has said it once he's said it a thousand times, that he wouldn't know what to *do* if anything ever happened to Dan, he leans on him so much, why, they're ideal partners, think of how well they're doing, I know *I* never expected to be living so well so early in our married life. . . ."

"Nell, I'm frightened."

"Oh, now, don't, after all, it's just a flare-up."

"I don't know." My mother suddenly saw me listening. "Whiii —off to bed with you boys. Trot along now. Come give me a hug, both of you."

[206]

I did and Billy did and we went to my room and because the evening was now late and the air cold off the lake our teeth chattered as we undressed and got into our pajamas and climbed into bed where the sheets were heavy with cold and damp.

Through the thin board partition we could hear Miles O'Connor still fighting as he heaved and turned himself in the bed next to my room trying to get to sleep but unable to deny himself the consoling and bitter joy of remembering what had been said all through the quarrel.

Where was my father? Outside, alone, doing the same thing, down by the narrow shore of Thunder Island. I see now how comely they both were as men and fathers, as husbands and friends and doers in the world, and how frightening they became in their sudden bad blood. If men could go that way who loved each other, how then could it be with families, and playmates, nations, and all mankind? I learned more about all this the next morning.

※

The O'Connors slept late, or pretended to.

Billy and I were up soon after sunrise.

"Let's go down to the lake," I said during the morning. "I know a place."

"What for:"

"We can build something."

"What:"

"A harbor."

"Like Dorchester?"

"Yes. We can put the docks and the freight boats and the cranes. I've already got a little tugboat I made that floats, and a freighter, too."

"I'll build the breakwater."

"There are lots of little stones to put for it."

We worked without much talk for over an hour, quite as though nothing serious had happened the night before. Our model of Dorchester harbor took form in a miniature cove a few yards from the house. The sun crowned us with golden nap on our heads. We were half in, half out of the water, wearing our swimming trunks. Billy was a stocky little reproduction of Miles, with a high, challenging lift to his chest and an aggressive thickness about his shoulders. He was adroit with his hands and built his breakwater with swift, light touches. The water was clear as air, and almost as warm. Those little breathing waves broke at us and washed the sugary sand off our toasting skin. The pines on the island gave out the waft of their scent. Across the lake we could see Aetna as clear as if it were a carved model of a village made inside a glass shadow-box by an old sailor. I erected a grain elevator beside a dock where my long freight boat, assembled from a length of two-by-four and little square blocks of wood for the deck houses fore and aft, was tied up. My tug-boat lay at her bow. In the wetted sand of the shoreline I traced with a stick a set of lines like railroad tracks and I ran to the house to get my toy engine to set along the dock. Freight from all over the United States came to the dock by the railroad, and was transferred to the freighter, which when loaded would turn slowly away from the dock and head out beyond the breakwater built of sparkling pebbles, and sail across the lake to Europe.

My mother was on the porch having coffee with Nell. She waved to me as I ran by to fetch my train.

"What are you boys doing?" she called idly.

"Playing," I yelled over my shoulder, impatient at the idiotic questions of parents. My father and Miles O'Connor were nowhere to be seen.

[208]

When I returned to the harbor, I found that Billy had turned the freight boat around end for end.

"What did you do that for?" I demanded.

"It's better that way."

"It isn't the right way. I had it the right way." I began to turn it back the other way. He watched me with scowling eyes.

"No," he said, "you see, the way you have it, she can't go out past my breakwater unless she turns all the way around. My way is better."

"No. My way. Besides, I saw real ships do it the way I have it."

"Oh, hell. Who cares."

Last night's bad feeling began to show through. It had never been dissipated.

"You needn't swear," I said.

"I'll swear if I want to. Hell, hell, hell!" he added, as if dared. Then, wondering if he had gone too far, he said in a hurry to restore our mood of play, "It's a fine harbor. I wish I could take it home."

"Well," I said, "you can't. It's mine."

"I know I can't. But not because it's yours. But because you can't move a lake and take it home with you. But the harbor is not yours. It is ours. We both made it."

"But it is here, on my lake, so it's mine."

"We'll see whose it is," he said, and waded with a heavy splash into the harbor and kicked it apart, destroying the breakwater, and the dock, and the railroad lines along the edge, and lofting the freighter with his bare foot into the air and up to the needly edge of the woods, where it crashed to pieces. "There's your old harbor!"

Because our fathers fought, we fought. I threw myself upon him in the shallow water, shouting,

"Your father is wrong, my father says so."

"He is not."

"He is too."

"You damn thing you," gasped Billy, rolling in the water where I held on to him.

"Don't you swear at me."

"I will too."

"You're a rotten old b.m.," I cried, in an access of daring, while I tore and beat at Billy in a passion to invade and despoil his body. I was slighter than he, and he began to pound me against the wet sand till my head made sounds of cracking and I saw odd lights. Kicking and clawing, we rolled up the shore to be pierced by pine needles and choked with leafy mud. Our noise brought our mothers running, but not until we knew blood, and nose-run, and tears mixed with sand, and mouths full of stinging bits of earth, and rubbed bones that would ache all day and night. Panting, we were drawn apart amidst dim impulses of unspoken insults much better than those we had given.

"What on earth got into you two?" asked Nell O'Connor. "Why, Billy, you're a sight!"

"He wrecked my harbor," I said.

"It was our harbor," said Billy. "Not just his."

"Richard," said my mother, "apologise to Billy. He is your guest. You must give way to him if you have to."

"I don't have to."

"Ah, but you do."

"I don't want his old damn apologise," said Billy.

His mother shook him dutifully in punishment, at the same time saying to my mother,

"Just like their fathers. *Men! Oh!*"

She took her son away to clean him up and get him dressed. My mother said gravely,

"I am ashamed of you."

"He was wrong."

"Who knows?" she sighed. "All I know is, we cannot let them all go away feeling like this. They are to take the mail boat when she comes by at eleven-thirty and go home on the noon train. Sometimes I wonder why I even try. . . ."

But try what, she did not, or could not, say.

"Well, where's my father?" I asked

"In our room. He tried to talk to Miles but Miles wouldn't talk to him, so he wrote a note and put it under Miles's door an hour ago. It's still there, you can see it sticking out a little, he won't touch it. I feel dreadful about it all. There must be some way to keep them here until everybody feels better. Then they can go if they have to. But not this way. Not this way. It would do something awful to Daddy."

Her distress made her seem young and pretty and very close to me. I longed to help. I said,

"Well, why don't I go and get Billy, and say we will fly my airplane kite, and once she's in the air we can run with the string down to the dock and tie it there and watch it above the lake?"

Her eyes filled a little at all the feelings of the past hours.

"Thank you, my darling. Perhaps they would stay. Yes. Ask him."

"And another thing," I said. "If he likes it, I will *give* the kite to Billy."

"Oh, would you give it up?"

"I would, if you want me to."

"Then try! Your Daddy would feel so good about it if Miles would let them stay!"

I had a fine surge of feeling that we were acting as a family, and that I had as great a part as anyone else in making our world. I ran off to get my kite and then to find Billy and show it to him as the great peace offering I meant it to be. The kite had not yet even been assembled out of its long flat box. I knocked at the door of the O'Connor bedroom, calling,

[211]

"Well, say, Billy?"

I was not aware of voices within until they went silent as I waited. My father's folded note was gone from under the door. Nell must have picked it up when she went to wash Billy with water from the blue and white pitcher and basin on the corner washstand of the guest room.

"Don't answer him," said Miles O'Connor within.

"Billy?" I said, "come on out and we can assemble my new airplane kite and we can go down to the dock and fly it. You can have it for keeps if you like it."

"Billy?" said his father in warning.

I knew of no weapon then, and know of none now, against silence. I waited until I felt small and idiotic, and then I returned to the porch where my father and mother were both waiting for me.

"Well?" asked my father. His face was drawn and sick-looking.

"I did, but they won't," I said.

He shrugged at my mother and she touched his arm consolingly.

"There comes the *Mollie*," I said. The mail boat was rounding across to us in a long shining path on the water. Every morning I ran down to the dock to meet her. Unless she was to bring or take passengers, she merely slowed down, passing the end of the dock in a movement expertly steered by Dick Burlington, the postmaster's twenty-year-old son from Aetna. To me he was the captain of an ocean liner and a brave man of noble parts including wisdom, who threw the canvas mail bag to the dock as he went by with a wide, lazy wave of his hand. I pretended that I resembled him, who—though I did not know it—was only like any just-grown incurious country boy with a ripe body.

"Run down to the dock," said my father, "and tell Dick to stop for passengers."

"Oh, Dan," said my mother, "then you really will let them go?"

"Let them? What can I do about it?"

"Oh, no," she said against her fingers. "Oh, no."

⁂

I ran down and waited for Dick. I began to wave before he could hear me call. He understood my signal and brought the *Mollie* sweetly against the dock with hardly an inch or two of headway. As he docked he gave two short toots on her pressure whistle.

"Hi, Richard," he called from the awning shadow over his cockpit where he moved in his summery competence amidst dials and gauges and his boat's wheel.

I nodded. He threw me the mail bag. It was light. I threw back our empty which he would use on the next round.

"Well, there they are," he said, nodding past my shoulder up the little slope of the island. I turned to see.

The O'Connors were coming along in single file, Miles in the lead carrying two suitcases. Nell followed and then Billy. None of them looked at any of us. My father and mother walked slowly after them in silence. Dick expertly kept the *Mollie* bumped against the dock by the use of his engine. He put up his hand to help Nell and Billy over to the deck. Miles jumped in after them. The atmosphere of rage and dignity reached Dick and he raised his fuzzy eyebrows at me.

"All right, come on, come on, let's go, let's go," snapped Miles at Dick Burlington. Nell looked then searchingly at each of us as the *Mollie,* with a silky ruffle of her exhaust, drew away from us into the blinding sparkle of the morning sun on the blue water.

Turning his back on my mother and me, my father made a huge choking sob. He sounded just like me when I used to cry. To see his

[213]

father cry who had said men don't cry! What son who had given up crying would not know fear at this? My father drew back his right arm and then smashed his fist against the tall piling at the end of the dock.

"God damn him!" he wept, "God damn him to hell!" while he smashed his hand again and again on the old piling.

"Dan! Don't!" cried my mother, coming to him to restrain his driven arm. She lifted his hand. It was bleeding and torn. His hand was broken. The physical pain of it now began to reach him through the pain of losing his trusted friend and partner. He let his head down to my mother's shoulder and with her arm around him she took him to the house.

⚕

In a few minutes she called to me.

"You know how to start up the *Arrow*, don't you, Richard?"

"Oh, yes!"—but I was not sure without trying.

"We must get Daddy to the doctor. He has hurt himself badly. Go get some clothes on and go down and get the boat started. We'll be right down."

Soon I was on board the *Arrow*. If Dick Burlington had his ship, I had mine. Fiercely I remembered how my father always started the engine by setting the spark, putting the gears in neutral, and whirling the heavy flywheel. The *Arrow* was a white launch with a canopy over all her length and red plush seat cushions on her side benches. Her engine was exposed amidships. The pilot sat in the stern and steered by the wheel which was set in the planking at his side. We had a flag at the bow and another at the stern. With my father by, I had often steered her in the open lake, but I had never taken her out. Now I was in command.

After several heaves I got the engine to run. I reset the spark. I cast off the bow line and held us to the dock by boat hook. Soon my parents came to board us. My father, cradling his hurt hand with the other, looked at me in pallid abashment and said,

"Can you take her out, Doc?"

I nodded and threw off the stern line and I said to myself, "Now let me see," thinking about what to do next. But before I could do much thinking, I had the *Arrow* on her way across the lake to Aetna.

From halfway across we saw the last gesture that spoke of the O'Connors. We saw the noon train couple her engine and in a few minutes start off Down State. We heard her steam whistle and her bell and saw her rich blooms of black smoke go blowing upward against the bright air as the O'Connors once more left us with our trouble.

Coming to the dock at Aetna was the great test. My father came to sit beside me as we neared shore.

"Cut her now," he said. "Take a long curve to come in. Better to lose too much power and start up again than keep too much and have to crash or go by."

I begged silently that he would not take the wheel with his good hand at the last minute. He seemed to hear me, for he made no move. I docked the *Arrow* for the first time by myself. We made a hard bump and then a long scrape, but we caught the pilings and we tied up and my heart rose. In my selfish joy of achievement, I tried,

"Everything's going to be all right, now!"

"God help us," groaned my father hardly audible.

"You wait here, Richard," said my mother. "We'll be back as soon as the doctor can take care of Daddy. You did beautifully. Come, dear," she said lightly to my father, as if taking him to a party to which he did not particularly want to go.

[215]

"Yes," he said, "yes, it hurts like the devil, thanks to nobody but myself."

"Hush. Come."

They went up the dock to the village and I worked on the *Arrow*, as I had seen Dick Burlington do on the *Mollie* in port, putting her to rights. In an hour or so we all returned to Thunder Island. My father's hand was in a plaster cast.

※

Then began for him a period of long chastening, of sorrowful self-judgement, of mourning for his friend. In about a week a letter came from a lawyer at home in Dorchester to institute proceedings to dissolve the partnership between Miles O'Connor and my father. In the same mail came a letter from another friend in town who said he had heard how Miles O'Connor and somebody or other were getting together on a scheme they had been working on for several months: was this the same scheme my father and Miles had long talked of? So my father learned of his betrayal. White about the jaws and mouth, he dictated to my mother whatever was needed in written form to do his part in the dissolution. With that he began to lose some quality of his health forever.

My mother said to me in a private moment,

"Richard, don't ever get so involved."

"In what?"

She shrugged and sighed. Anything. Everything.

※

The summer was almost over and I was glad, for my holiday happiness was ruined anyway, since this must depend on whether or not my father and mother were happy. But before we went home for the start of school and the changes to be made in my father's office, I once again was crowded toward darkness by fear, though this time with new results.

During lunch one day a particularly violent thunderstorm broke over us almost without warning.

I made a move.

My father said sternly,

"Richard!"

Thunder and lightning seemed to spring at us from the very trees at our door.

Fear drove me from the table in spite of the commands of my father. I ran to hide with my heart beating out the ejaculatory prayers of safety. "My Jesus, mercy!" said my bones at every house-cracking crash.

In a few moments the door of my closet was pulled open. My mother was there, wearing her heavy stiff yellow raincoat and holding my smaller one.

"Richard? Come?"

"No!"

"Come with me, my darling. *Schnell?* Come?"

Her voice was sharp and commanding. She reached for my arm and pulled me from the closet and held out my sou'wester. "Put this on! Quick!"

The storm was making the house cry in its wooden ribs.

"No! No!"

She slapped me hard on the cheek, which she had never done before. Appalled by shock, I put on my raincoat. She took my arm and led me to the porch.

"Where are we going?"

"We are going to meet the storm, not run away from it."

"No!"

She took me down the steps, down the island slope, down to the dock, down to the far end of the dock where there was no refuge —where there was much actual danger from lightning bolts. We were soaked through in a second, for the wind tore at our raincoats. The lake danced wildly with waves. The far shore was lost except when the lightning flashed over there and here above us and everywhere. Calling to me above the wind, my mother said,

"Richard, look!" She shook me and pointed to the wild sky, the sweeps of rain on the lake, and then at the tearing strikes of lightning amidst the clouds. "Richard! Look! Why be afraid? *It is so beautiful!*"

She put her arm about my shoulders and when the lightning struck I could feel how she too trembled before the power of God. But how new was her idea that this power was beautiful! I stared at the new idea as I stared at a world I had never been able to see before. I met an entirely fresh way to regard the thing that had terrorized my childhood. About to be convinced, I shouted,

"But it's dangerous!"

"Of course it's dangerous," she replied. The wind tried to hollow out her words and sweep them away, but I heard her meaning even so. "There is something dangerous about all beauty, and it is still beautiful! I don't know what it is, but—."

We stood there and the thunder and lightning broke over us, here, and afar, and my vision cleared, and I knew that what she said was true. After the great gift of life itself, it was the finest gift she made me, this means of losing fear. In immediate terms, then, and afterward, any storm was charged, for me, as much with beauty as with danger.

We stayed on the dock until the worst of it had passed over us, and the thunder went tumbling farther and farther away behind the mountains on the other shore. The light came changing in a calm of gold while an aromatic breeze was left behind by the spent ozone of the retreating storm. The moving air took my thoughts aloft.

"My kite!" I cried.

"Yes, but first go dry off and change your clothes," said my mother, sending me safely to my own affairs.

At the far end of Thunder Island was a miniature meadow edged by tall trees. There I took my airplane kite and assembled it and ran with it across the meadow until it caught the breeze and went aloft, pulling at the string which played burningly through my fingers. The kite was fashioned like a biplane aircraft. It had a wooden propeller at the nose and fine Japanese rice paper over its wing structures and tail fin. Up, up, it went, taking the very sky and giving it to me.

When the string played out as far as it could go, I tied the end to a stump and sat down leaning my back against the stump and I looked up, and all that existed turned into the ever-lasting present.

Above me is my ship in the sky. It takes me with it, I travel in the wind, the propeller is I, I cunningly use the air, I see all from there, and my vision is that of God. And yet I am of course sitting here below, looking upward, upward, feeling the mossy damp beneath my rump bones, and breathing the island earth, and I discover somewhere within me how I am, like everyone, a creature of bone and breath, of rock and air, of earth and heaven, of sorrow and joy, of body and soul.

CHAPTER X

✻

Parma Violets

When children love, they do not give, they only receive. It is a love that creates only a self. The aching desire to give, to create life beyond the self, calls boy into man. Gratified, this love creates an analogue of heaven on earth. Denied or betrayed, it sets forth the terms of hell in the very stuff of life, unless it can be resolved by sanctity.

During the first World War, imprisoned as I was in the last year of childhood, I knew intuitions of what people meant when they spoke of love.

At that time, the most frequent and beloved visitor at our house in Dorchester was a lady I called Aunt Bunch. I had given her this name because so very often she wore a bunch of Parma violets, now pinned to her grey fur coat, now to an ermine muff she carried, or again at her waist in the style of the period. She was not a real aunt. The title was merely a possessive courtesy.

I loved her with tyranny and excitement. I believed her to exist for me alone, and I behaved accordingly. When she came to see us, I rudely interposed myself between her and all other persons and relationships, until general laughter resulted, and I was returned to the childhood which I was ready to lose—which, in fact, I had forgotten.

There lay the key to my worship. She treated me not like a youngster in black ribbed cotton stockings, itchy knee breeches, a jacket whose sleeves never seemed long enough, and a starched collar, but like a young man to whom she could send silent messages confident that they would be received and understood, no matter what the world might hear her say or see her do in ostensible propriety.

She was I now think in her early thirties. Her hair was so blonde as to seem silvery. She wore it loosely in a maddening way—I wanted to put my hands into it and make it all fall down, heavily sliding like gold and silver treasure whose surrender would mean everything that I could not precisely imagine. Her eyes were violet-blue, which must have accounted for her bunches of violets, and the effect she knew they made. Dark lashes shadowed her gaze in which great liquid purities shone forth right into your heart. Her mouth fascinated me. The lips were full, yet ever so delicate in their scrolling, and when she smiled, they flattened slightly against her white teeth. Her cheeks always looked warm, but felt cool, as I knew.

I knew, because our ardent relationship included embraces. She would come in from a winter day with snowflakes on her furs, her violets, her lashes, her veil, and let me climb against her until we both hurt. She would kiss me, put her cheek on mine, press me in her arms a few times, and I smelt snow, and violets, and felt the exquisite tickle of melting snowflakes between our faces. Her face was always softly glowing as though in the light of a rose-shaded lamp. If she ever looked archly and humorously just over my head at other adults I never saw her do it.

She belonged to me. How could I doubt it? She always called me "My dear," as she might call a man, and in that winter we became acknowledged as a cunning joke, "lovers," with quotation marks, and many an eyebrow went up, and voice went down, and pang

[221]

went deep, at the spectacle we made, and the living reference we were to all that was meant by love, and suffered, and revered, in its name.

※

My own part in this passion explains itself if enough years are allowed to ensue. But for her part—why did she come to take me out driving in the afternoons, after school, in her electric car? The cushions were grey, there were always violets in the little crystal vases flanking the curved plate glass of the front window, and we were alone together as the batteries hummed us along, and the elegant bell rang at street crossings. We rode for the most part in ecstatic silence through the park, watching for swans on the lake, and if we saw one, our excitement made us hold one another. Sometimes she let me steer the electric. To do so, I had to crowd near to her, and lean upon her lap, the better to manage the long black bar which made the wheels point this way or that. I would steer, she would control the speed by a shorter bar above the other, and we would spin on our way with joy.

"Poor dear, she has no children, and he is like a son to her"—this was one explanation I overheard. It meant nothing to me. What did it matter why, so long as she would put her head down to mine, and leave it there in dreaming silence and contentment? Or hold my hand and play with my fingers, one after another, slowly and broodingly, while flooding me with the daytime moonlight of her eyes? I believed that she never looked at anyone else that way. How could she, what could it possibly mean to anyone else, when she was mine entirely?

Sometimes on our drives she would take me to Huyler's for a

chocolate soda, or again to her house in the park for cocoa with whipped cream. If we were early enough, I preferred her house, where we could be so intimate and private about nothing, but if we were late, I was unwilling to go there because we might then encounter her husband, "Uncle" Dylan.

My reluctance to meet him there had nothing to do with guilt over my love for his wife. I simply preferred to meet him at my house because as a visitor there he always brought me some sort of present. For this I despised him even as I greedily reached for his pockets. He was a rich man, much older than Aunt Bunch, and doubtfully he demanded all that his money could get him. His small, pale eyes always looked dry, in his sandy face, behind his pince-nez glasses. I once heard my father remark that it was somehow easy to see how Dylan would look dead. It was a strange and powerful statement, and I saw what he meant. I'd seen dead birds. Their inert plumage and milked-over eyeballs did suggest Uncle Dylan. He was tormented by the very gifts he made, though everyone always said he was generous. Still, what joy was there in giving if he could never be sure that what he gave was lovingly received because it brought him with it? And so,

"Now, Richard," he would say to me, one greedy creature virtuously reproving another, "let us not be so sure we have a present today. Why should we have? What have we done to earn it? Do we think others are made of money? Presents cost something, my boy. Do you ever think of your poor old Uncle Dylan except when he has something for you?"

Such an attitude made me shudder for him, as he looked over to his wife to see if she smiled upon his humor, blinking both his dry scratchy eyes at her, and as he then besought my parents to witness his openness of heart, forcing them to deprecate his latest gift, and to swear that I would not be allowed to accept another single thing after this time. Then, confirmed and strengthened in his poor power

[223]

over us all, he would sigh, and say, "Try the left-hand pocket," and I would plunge my hand in and find nothing. But by then I was impervious to alarm for I knew that he could not afford to fail me, and when with a feeble start of surprise like that of a vaudeville magician, he would say, "Try the right-hand one, then," I knew the sorry game was about to be over to my advantage.

Even as I bled him unmercifully every chance I had, and knew him for a dullard, I never considered him an odd choice as a husband for Aunt Bunch. He simply *was* her husband, and that ended the matter. As such, he belonged to my world, as she belonged, and I could not possibly imagine any disturbance of its order. So long as they remained fixed, any relationships were accepted. If a new one should appear, the quicker it were absorbed and fixed, the better. Only, let it be added to what existed, without changing anything.

※

In that season of so much love, when the heavy winter brought snow that would stay for weeks, and the warmth and light of our house made a twilight joy after the steely cold out of doors during the day, a familiar friend returned to us as somebody new. He was my father's business associate who had come into his office after the treason of Miles O'Connor. Many months ago he had joined the Army, and was now a captain of artillery on leave before receiving new orders, which everybody knew meant going overseas to France to fight the Hun in World War I.

Now he came to see us in his uniform, with its high collar and stiff stock; its Sam Browne belt, pegged breeches and officer's boots and spurs. Captain Jarvis McNeill seemed like an entirely new individual, with no relation to the occasional visitor of the same name

[224]

before the war. He was unmarried and so appeared at parties mostly as a stray, to fill in. Now home on leave, he took to coming to our house late in the day, when the curtains were drawn, a fire was rippling in the fireplace, and other friends dropped in and out without announcement. Sometimes such little gatherings would turn into supper parties, people would stay, and the animation and conviviality of my parents would have happy expression. Almost always, late in such an evening, the piano would sound, and then Captain Jarvis McNeill would sing in a crackling baritone voice distinguished by volume and purity both. Rather like Miles O'Connor before him, he had an Irish instinct for facile sentiment that wanted most of all to be communicated, and when he sang, I was moved in formless sorrow for what people knew, and were, and did, beyond the boundaries of my certain knowledge.

I always knew when Captain Jarvis McNeill arrived. I would know it by the sound of his boots in the entrance hall. They made a tubey sort of noise when he stamped off the snow. He was a big fellow, and his movements and gestures were necessarily large, though not awkward. In his ruddy face there was a comic appeal that he be understood and forgiven for anything he might do—with a broad hint, in his raised brows, his blue eyes, his dark shaved cheeks, his crescent smile, that he might indeed do anything.

When I heard him below, I held my breath the better to overhear messages from life beyond me. His speaking voice had heavy grain and carried through the rooms. I listened to hear if it grew louder in my direction. Then I would hear the heavy trot of his big body coming up the stairs. He was coming to see me in my room—a real captain, a soldier who fired cannons, who had a sword, and wore boots and spurs, and would himself hang the Kaiser, and was a hero.

One of the qualities of heroes may be their instinct for true worship amid all the false. Captain Jarvis McNeill repaid mine with serious and simple appreciation, which took the form of getting down on the floor of my room where my imaginative possessions were marshalled, and playing there, as I played, so long as the company downstairs would let him. He filled the room with his presence in every way, including the way he brought the spicy, sharp aromas of a barbershop with him—the clean, adventurous smell of a man who has been combed, spanked and shined to his most presentable state, for private and urgent purposes. His cheeks got hotter like mine as he bent down to the miniature tasks of imagination with my large relief model of battlefields in France, set with leaden soldiery and wooden artillery. His collar choked him, his big legs were in the way but splendid with boots and spurs, and he made the double magic of seeing with my eyes and making me see with his.

"Do you have a sword?" I asked.

"Yes. Would you like me to bring it?"

"Yes."

He brought it next time, and let me have it for several days. It lay by me in bed, sheathed and shining. My belly hung heavy in me at the glories that leaped out of the scabbard with that blade. Only in secret did I strap the big sword to my belt, for I was now old enough to know that it would look ridiculous to anyone else. I gave it up with a scowl of indifference that fooled nobody when Captain Jarvis McNeill said to me on our floor one evening that he had to pack a lot of stuff to be shipped, and he supposed his officer's sword had better go too.

"But when I come back you can have it again," he said, and put his big hand like a heavy helmet on my head and roughed me once or twice. That promise was enough for me. To whom else was he offering his beautiful acid-etched sword with its gold sabre-knot and its tinkling scabbard? He was a great captain, a hero, and my friend, and he came to my house almost daily to see me, to crawl with much humorous breathing and difficulty of scale among the delicate litter of my parapets and trenches, my tanks and ambulances and field hospitals. To see me. He was mine to love and to own, through whom I could extend myself into a heroic life as a soldier.

He would stay so long in my playroom that almost invariably others would come upstairs to inquire: and standing in the doorway they would smile and chatter at the sight of the handsome young officer and the hot-faced boy both intent upon war games. At such moments I realized that the grown-up world was about to win all over again. Aunt Bunch usually was one of those who came to see. The sight of her, waiting for me to admit to bedtime, changed, dropped, my spirits, I knew not why. Dimly I did not want her and Captain Jarvis McNeill with me together. I wanted them with me each separately. More, I wanted them never to be together at all, lest each might forget me. How complicated that fidelity, and that betrayal.

At last with comfortable sighs of change, the Captain would rise and put himself in order for his return downstairs with the company. Aunt Bunch would let him go, as she lingered to assuage the endless disappointments of day's end. Invisibly the tendrils of scent from Parma violets sought me out and wrapped me round; and when she left me to go below where unimaginably trivial events were gathering purpose for the adults, I was proved again in love, and the terms I imagined for it were unquestioned, and I felt choked with well-being, rich emotion, and a swelling conviction that nothing would ever change that I loved.

For a boy at the shore of boyhood's farewell, those were passionate loves—Aunt Bunch and Captain Jarvis McNeill; and that was a passionate if scornful loyalty—Uncle Dylan. The issue was not

[227]

whether I was a small monster of sensibility, but whether the power of love is ever really contained within conventions, no matter how desperately appearances may be preserved.

※

We take our parents for granted till we have lost them.

"Richard, Richard," they would say, fondly shaking their heads at each other over my infatuations, recognizing how fixed was my view of life, and how innocent it was of any other values but my fierce, joyful, tyrannical ones which seemed to me eternal, and to them dangerous. They saw everything, even to what must be coming, though not in what event it might come. They tried to rob me painfully but healthily of the possessions of my heart.

"You must not make yourself a nuisance when Jarvis comes, Richard, after all, there are others who want to see him."

"He comes to see me."

"Ah, my darling boy."

"Well, he does too, he told me so."

"Yes, of course, of course," in hurried agreement, as though to conceal from me after all a truth best left with my elders. Or again,

"You will be a young man before long, and you will look for a pretty girl your own age to love."

"I love Aunt Bunch."

"Now, yes. But she is already married. And her age!"

"I thought you loved her too."

"We do, we do, my boy."

"And I thought you loved me."

"Ah, Richard, as if you did not know."

And I hated my father and mother for their good sense which then seemed to me so evil and so hard.

[228]

Our household liked to combine music and society. There was a dinner party before a concert to be given by an illustrious American singer who came to Dorchester as part of the excited Liberty Bond campaign. Uncle Dylan had taken a box for the concert at a price which made a happy outrage upon his patriotism and briefly fed his longing for esteem. The party was to consist of my father and mother, Uncle Dylan and Aunt Bunch, Captain Jarvis McNeill and Monsignor Tremaine, who was very musical and had no prejudice against good company outside the rectory. Largely because of his presence extra effort was made before the dinner party. Special glass and silver and wines were brought out. To help Anna, a caterer was engaged who would lighten the kitchen load, especially after dinner, so she would not have to be "up all night with the dishes," which, sometimes, she felt she could throw one after the other down the cellar stairs to hear them break on the cement floor one by one, and if anyone should scold her, she would tell them to go chase theirself.

It was snowing when the guests arrived. I looked out the window and saw their cars—Uncle Dylan's big limousine with its cabin lighted and his chauffeur standing by the door; Monsignor Tremaine's old touring car with its cracked side curtains up. I counted. Someone was missing. Captain Jarvis McNeill had not arrived with the others. By prearrangement I was permitted to stay downstairs until I had toured the party to say good evening and display my dancing school manners—jerked handshake, ducked bow.

"My. How we have grown, all of a sudden. And are we still a very good young fellow?"

"Yes, M'nsígnor."

A pair of shining, hard, old brown eyes like horse-chestnuts polished in spring seemed to knock at my heart, sounding its formless guilt. *What have we here: a boy who is already feeling certain things? Does he know their true and holy purpose? Does he have to think too much about them? Does he have to lose them in troubling dreams? Ah: how hard it is to inherit feeling before there is knowledge. Ah: does knowledge really help? Let us trust in the mercy of God. God bless you, Richard.* Then the beloved old pastor laughed genially over his power to enter into the secrets of man, and let me go on to Uncle Dylan.

"Well, Richard? And why do you look at me like that? As if I had something for you tonight! Well, sir, let me tell you, you have another think coming."

How disgusting, this arch attempt to torture me, and draw the attention of all to the act of material generosity about to appear, as inevitable, hoped-for and boring as the magician's dry silk flag out of the glass of water.

"All right, Uncle Dylan, excuse me, then,"—and I made as if to pass on.

"He what? Look at him. I never knew such a boy, so impatient, can't he take a little joke from an old man?—All right, try the left-hand pocket."

My father revealed the shame and irritation of us all, though he kept smiling and silent above his tall evening collar and wide white bow tie.

"—No?" exclaimed Uncle Dylan blinking his sandy eyes, "not there? Nothing? How peculiar. Then try the other side!"

So I found a small leather case ("Well, go on, go on, Richard, open it, let us all see what it is, I've even forgotten since I bought it for you") containing a shiny brass telescope, so beautiful it shamed me for all my sins of opinion. I wanted so much to own it that I handed it back to Uncle Dylan.

"What? The ungrateful. No, really, it is for you."

Unable to resolve my feelings, I stood looking at the floor with my hands behind my back. Aunt Bunch saved me. She came forward and knelt down to me as if we were quite alone. By doing this she made me taller than herself. She put her white arms around me and drew my face down to hers. We both shut our eyes: audible smiles once again in the room at the spectacle of the "lovers." Her hair shone like waves under sunset light. She wore a heavy shining dress of some pale color that showed much of her bosom and back and all her arms bare. Violets were held to her breast by a great spray of diamonds in a pin. In a moment she gave me a pat, and said, "There!", and made me release her as she lightly took the telescope from Uncle Dylan and gave it back to me. I kept it. Was there anyone else in the world for whom she had so much love, which she would show so proudly? She had put a spell over everyone by her scene with me, and now it broke, and my father said to her that she had never looked so beautiful in her life, and that—he laughed delightedly—he supposed she couldn't help it.

"Oh, Dan," she replied, but with such a buried passion of hopelessness and hope that without understanding her at all, I was startled and stared at her.

"And now," said my mother, also moved by the extraordinary without grasping its meaning, "you may say good night, Richard, and go up to your tray, and to bed."

"But I want to wait and see the Captain."

"He will not be here for quite some time," she said. "He telephoned. He is delayed. If you are not sleeping when he comes, he may run up to see you for a moment. Now good night, darling."

"Delayed?" said Uncle Dylan. "How delayed? I have not been informed about this. I have his ticket for a box seat right here in my pocket. I might have been told."

"But we just learned," said my mother.

"Dylan, it does not matter," said Aunt Bunch. "If he comes, well and good. If not, everybody will have a seat anyway."

"But in a box," he murmured, drilling for appreciation.

"You are most generous," said Monsignor Tremaine kindly.

"Not at all, the Liberty Bond drive, you know," answered Uncle Dylan, but with the tone of one assuaged for the moment.

A look from my father, fierce in the eye, sweet in the mouth, drove me finally from the room. As I left, I heard them discussing the concert that was to come. The singer was Geraldine Farrar, so gifted, so beautiful, so romantic. My mother, who sang prettily, and was a graceful and animated mimic, began laughingly to sing, "Vissi d'arte, vissi d'amore," with enough exaggeration to excuse the impersonation, so that everyone laughed with her, and said, "Farrar!", and (as I learned later) it was Monsignor Tremaine who moved to the piano, and picked up the accompaniment and went with the aria until the charming joke lost its point and ended in general exclamations and the arrival of cocktails.

※

Anna came achingly up the back stairs with my supper tray and watched me eat for a few minutes, and told of Uncle Dylan's chauffeur sitting in the kitchen, having his dinner before anyone else at all. She said he was a self-satisfied piece, but company was company, and who was she to judge? Soon her mind was elsewhere. Her heart was cocked toward the lives and joys of others.

"Listen!" she said, setting her attitude toward the gaiety downstairs, "How they love it, what dear souls they are. . . ." Smash their dishes? Never in your life.

She made me hear, and in her grey, pocked, Anna-like old face, I saw the glowing room, the fire in the grate, the silky colors and the flowers, the rosy lamps and the dressed-up people, the sparkle of highlight and the rubbed gloss of velvet, as though they belonged not in our house, where I had so recently left them myself, but else-where, away, wonderful and desirable. And then, as though having done a duty in transferring her hungry and idle vision to me, she lumbered to her feet and groaning abstractedly, "Oh, well, God have mercy," she went back to the kitchen refreshed and ready for the responsible moments that were coming to her with dinner.

※

I hurried through my supper tray, changed to my pajamas, carried the tray to the head of the back stairs as was the custom, and then on my belly went to the head of the carpeted front stairs to watch and to listen. I saw them all downstairs when they crossed the hall to the dining room to sit down under the many shaded candles above the table. I strained to hear every car out in the street making its grinding song on snow with tire chains, thinking every car would bring Captain Jarvis McNeill. When the company was through dinner and returning to the drawing room for coffee, I picked out one then another with my new telescope from the distance of the flight of stairs. There, glowing in midair, rimmed faintly with pale blue and yellow optical magic, were those familiar faces, brought near and separate in a new kind of ownership.

A brief halt between dining room and drawing room took place for an important question.

"But what shall I do if he does not come?" asked Uncle Dylan, taking out his wallet and carefully spreading his six box seat tickets like a hand of cards. "I have all the tickets."

"I cannot understand," said my mother. "He did not think he would be this late."

"He must have a thousand things to do," said Aunt Bunch, "getting ready for his orders, and of course he cannot talk about them. —There is no reason," she added with persuasive sweetness, "for anybody who does not have to to miss the concert. Here," she said, leaning forward with grace and swiftly taking the tickets from Uncle Dylan, "leave me two, and since we are the hosts at the box party, I will wait for Jarvis here a little while, and bring him if he comes; and if he does not come soon, I will follow alone. There!" she finished, giving four tickets back to Uncle Dylan, and shutting two into her bag of solid gold mesh, as Uncle Dylan always called it.

"Oh, why, no," said Uncle Dylan, "never," then leaving his mouth open as he looked from face to face for strength; but found none. Nobody confessed to what Uncle Dylan dared not carry further in the presence of others. "But how, what car?" he asked Aunt Bunch in a surge of renewal—a last move to assert authority and save what was already lost.

"You can leave me ours," she said easily, "and Dan can take all of you in his."

"Of course," agreed my father.

"I shall go in my own," said the Monsignor, "for I must hurry home right afterward."

The current had swept once again strongly past and beyond Uncle Dylan. They all vanished into the other room for coffee.

Soon my mother came to say goodnight. I was discovered virtuously in bed. She wore what was called an opera cloak and, to protect her against the snow, a pair of opera boots of blue silk and ermine. She kissed me, idly told me to be good and go right to sleep, and then asked me if I did not love my new telescope.

"Yes," I replied.

"Yes, Richard, then love what you have, *and can have,* and not what you do not have. Good night, my darling," she said in a whisper, leaving me baffled and somehow reduced in spirit.

I listened intently until the sounds of departure were all done.

[234]

From the kitchen dimly came the after-dinner work, and unaccustomed rumbles of conversation as Aunt Bunch's chauffeur talked with Anna and the caterer, who would soon be done with his work, and would head for the streetcar tracks two blocks away leading downtown. I listened for sounds from the drawing room where Aunt Bunch must be. I heard nothing. Planning to go down and see, I fell asleep.

❧

How much later I didn't know, but it felt much later, I awoke to the icy sizzle and clank of tire chains slowing down and stopping in the caked snow out in the street. Then I heard boots on the porch, and the door open and shut as someone let Captain Jarvis McNeill in, and then the stamp in the vestibule to loosen the snow from his spur chains.

He was here at last and my pulse began to rip along. I leaped from my bed, turned on my light, and went over my toys rapidly. The regular ones were ready. In a moment he would come up to see me, to settle down on the floor, as usual, to create and enter in the world where he and I, and only we, were heroes. Leaving the light on for encouragement, I went to my door to wait for him.

But he did not come.

I listened.

Where was he? I heard nothing from below, not even the soft but penetrating diapason of his heavy Irish voice that could enter the fabric of our house and make it vibrate in response.

I turned to my toys that waited with me. Was it possible that he had forgotten my old castle with its real drawbridge, and rows of leaden archers on the battlements, and in the great hall a double throne with a king and queen under a canopy? I had outgrown these things, but surely he had not, who had known them for only a few months! And in the corner, the tracks of a train winding in and out of sized muslin mountains and along a painted river? And in my own country of France that battery of wooden cannons, modeled in perfect detail, that could shoot pellets with a spring? And what else? My grandfather's toy theatre from Germany with its red curtain rolled up on a baton, and its woods scenery in place behind its stiff actors who entered upright in grooves? And even my old fire engine, long broken, but never discarded? Not to speak of the new telescope which he had not even seen?

The silence took on so great a strangeness that a hint of panic came with it.

I could not wait any longer. I took my telescope and went swiftly down the carpeted stairs. He was there, somewhere, for I had heard him come in. And then everything became clear to me. I'd been a fool. It was plain that Captain Jarvis McNeill was enjoying a game with me. He was hiding somewhere in the big front room, waiting for me, even as I had waited for him. The happy hunter came alive in me. I went down to my belly and crawled silently from the hall into the drawing room with my telescope ready. Coming around the forest-like obstruction of a green velvet chair with heavy wooden arms and legs (moss and rock), I carefully put my glass to my eye and slowly swept the softly-lighted far end of the room to find him.

Familiar details came into view—a picture on the wall, flowers on a table, books, a lamp—as I ranged from left to right, toward the great sofa that stood across the last corner of the room. Everything was colored softly and as though by a brush, and as still as the dead.

As still as the dead until into my telescope glided life and motion, and I saw the gloss of dark hair turning and turning and ruddy cheeks above pale cheeks and the heavy massed treasure of golden waves of hair, and pure piercing bolts of light from pale violet eyes that opened and closed, gazed away, and again near, away, and near, with such intensity of expression that it could have meant the extreme of suffering or of joy, or of both, and there came the restricted but mortal leverage of arms holding and closing and enclosing, and all in stillness that with such vision was not quite silence, for little sounds of breath, and lips, and thrust weight traveled to me and told the same that the telescope told, and at the same time, and with the same shattering power.

My world fell.

I knew sharply and deeply that what was mine was no longer mine. Aunt Bunch was mine in just my way no more. Captain Jarvis McNeill was lost to me in the arms of love. Even Uncle Dylan suffered breaking change in the discovery, for he was Aunt Bunch's, and thus mine, though with scorn, in the old order of the world which was now broken.

But he came to see me, Captain Jarvis McNeill? And yes—I knew now that every time Aunt Bunch was there too, as it "happened." I was torn with rage and betrayal.

And this evening? When he was late, who arranged everything, to wait for him, in her great beauty so enhanced by hope and hopelessness? What were the warnings of my parents, and how general were they, and how particular?

I understood nothing, really, except that I was overwhelmingly robbed, and of what, even, I was not then very sure. But the two lost people in my round lens were alone and far away. I must make them crash with me, or I must vanish into thin air.

"No!" I cried out, and lurched to my feet, and threw my telescope at the wall where it broke some picture glass. I turned over the big chair where I had played my hunter's game of hide and seek. So I declared myself.

The more-than-kiss broke apart and the real lovers stared at me with vacant faces.

"Oh—dear," said Aunt Bunch softly and slowly, with solemn sweetness and pity that made a thickness come to my throat until I began to fear the emotions I had made between us all.

Captain Jarvis McNeill roughly pulled himself together and then made for me with his hands outstretched as though to choke me.

"—Than a sneak," he whispered loudly, having said in his mind that there was nothing worse.

"Hush, Jarvis," said Aunt Bunch quietly, knowing what I felt. She was settling her hair, her gown.

"Yes, I'm sorry," he said, and knelt down before me to be reasonable and winning, and tried to take me kindly; but I kicked and flailed at him, shocked by the scared look in his face, a look I was mature enough to know since fear of exposure was childhood's one explicit emotion. In a gesture he tried to recover me, but I pushed at him and ran upstairs to my room, turned off the light and, trampling my battlefield in France which had lost its point, forever, went into my bed with my hands over my ears and my mouth open. I was full of chagrin at the fall of man.

※

Presently in the ringing darkness of my misery with my ears covered and my eyes squeezed shut, I inhaled a waft of that cool, moist fragrance that always meant Aunt Bunch. The scent of Parma violets would always seem to me the odor of purity itself, and yet just as intimately and powerfully, and at the very same time, that of profane love.

She knelt by my bed and put her quiet hand on my hot neck. She said nothing but waited for me to speak if I must. Soon I was trying to rebuild my follies.

"You will stay here with me, alone?" I whispered urgently.

But she refused to be false to what we all now knew.

"Nonsense, my dear," she said gently, "you are going to sleep, and we are going to the concert."

"But—but—" but I could not think of what crowded in me to want. I clung to her and like any betrayed lover begged for lies with my touches. She would not tell them, even with caresses, any more. She held me and I began to die into sleep, suffering for the last time from the confusion called childhood.

The last I remember as I fell asleep, bitter with spent woe under her touch, was the sound of her voice. It returns to me a lifetime later whenever I meet the fragrance of her little flowers, saying the only thing to say in pity and certainty that made me ache even as it promised of life all I did not yet know, "Some day . . . some day. . . ."